# STEPHANIE FAZIO

# DUSKER  DARK

## BOOK III OF THE BISECTER SERIES

Syafant Press

New York, New York



Cover designed by Teodora Chinde



Stephanie Fazio

Visit www.StephanieFazio.com

Printed in the United States of America
First Printing: July 2019

Library of Congress Control Number: 2019908536

ISBN 978-1-7335929-5-6

*To my readers, for taking this journey with me*

# PROLOGUE

## FOUR HOURS EARLIER

I count twelve Duskers.

They're moving through the trees without any attempt at stealth. Their boots tramp through the brush. Their conversation, muffled from behind the masks that are part of the Dusker uniform, sends a flock of birds squawking away in protest.

If I knew of any other way to reach my destination, I would try to slip away now before I'm seen. But Liglette, the Banished leader of the West, gave me specific directions for finding the Crystal Caves. I'm not willing to risk getting turned around and losing time, and so I stay pressed against the trunk of a script tree, willing the Duskers not to notice me.

*That's right. Keep going,* I think as the Duskers continue on their way.

Their voices are receding. My iron-tight grip on my sling loosens. I breathe again.

And then, a capy pig rooting around in the dirt nearby decides to raise its snout and make a noise that is somewhere between a snort and a roar. The Duskers stop.

I curse the capy pig under my breath. The animal has gone back to rooting, oblivious to the disaster it has just caused.

*Should I try to run? Or would it be better to fight my way through the Duskers?*

I wish I had my Zeroes with me. I wish I had Dayne, or Wade, or Ekil. But I don't have any of them. I'm alone.

I reach for the gold Solguard pendant Wade gave me, wanting to feel the familiar warm weight of it in my hand. Instead, my fingers find the more delicate chain of my mother's necklace and the small key dangling from it. I wrap my hand around it, letting the memory of my mother infuse me with strength.

I let go of my necklace. I take a stone out of the leather pouch on my belt and place it in my sling.

"Behind that tree!" I hear a voice call.

An arrow bites into the tree trunk just inches from my shoulder.

I dart out from my hiding place—no sense in blocking off my view when they know where I am.

I wind my sling, taking careful aim, and then release the ropes. My stone hits one of the Duskers. He falls without a sound. Before I can release my sling again, another arrow flies past me. This time, there's a tearing sound as it cuts through the sleeve of my cloak. If I don't do something, they'll keep firing. I can't avoid their shots forever.

*Move, Hemera!*

I run forward, avoiding another crossbow bolt that was aimed at my skull. I tackle the closest Dusker, knocking him off balance. His crossbow flies out of his hands.

The next one swings a sword at me. I just manage to avoid the blow. Grabbing his blade with my bare hands, I wrench the weapon from my enemy's grasp. I hurl the sword at another Dusker. The man falls with a loud groan, the sword embedded in his ribcage.

*Eight more to go.*

My fear and hesitation have fallen away. All that's left is a strength greater than any I've never known.

It wasn't long ago when even the idea of this fight would have left me paralyzed with terror. But since I created the army of Zeroes, there's been a bottomless reserve of power inside me…power that's gone mostly unused. I feel the Zeroes' strength in my veins like water boiling in a pot. If left too long, the boiling water overflows. That's how I've been feeling…like a boiling kettle about to spill over.

Now, finally, I have a release.

Two more Duskers fall as the jagged stone flies from my sling, piercing straight through one and embedding in another.

"It's the Bisecter!" a Dusker screams.

I feel their terror like a living thing, and it makes me smile. The Duskers fear nothing and no one. But they're afraid of me.

"Hold your ground," a voice commands. "Converge."

The Duskers who have been stalking toward me do something unexpected. In a perfectly-coordinated move, they throw the entire weight of their bodies on top of me.

I'm pinned to the ground beneath six grown men.

"Get her arms," someone commands, the echo of his voice vibrating beside my ear.

"Got you now, you monster," one of them pants.

*I don't think so.*

I inhale what little air I can manage with so much weight bearing down on me. Then, I explode to my feet.

Duskers go flying in every direction. One of them sails so high he gets tangled in the branches of a tree. He flails like an insect caught in a spider's web. Two more lay unmoving where they've fallen, at least ten paces away. The few others who are still alive get up and run.

In a different time, I would have let them escape. But everything is different now. The Duskers are the reason why I lost first my army at Tanguro, and then my Aunt Jadem. I whip the sling in my hand and release. The remaining Duskers drop.

While my racing pulse settles, I survey the damage. These Duskers weren't new recruits. They were seasoned warriors…and I defeated them all. I'm not even breathing hard.

A year or even months ago, so much blood and death would have had me retching into the nearest bush. My hands would be trembling and tears would be coursing down my cheeks. But I'm not the same person I was then.

I check the angle of the sun and reorient myself, remembering the directions Liglette gave me, and continue running.

# CHAPTER 1

## FOUR HOURS LATER

I haven't stopped running since my fight with the Duskers.

Ever since Ry and Dellin disappeared on Vlaz, I've been tracking them through unfamiliar lands. Wokee had overheard Ry and Dellin say they were going to the Crystal Caves, a place my mother told me stories about when I was a child. I was always led to believe it wasn't a real place. But Liglette, the Banished leader of the West, had seen the Crystal Caves for herself. She's the one who told me how to find them.

I snuck away during high day when neither Wade nor my brother could come after me. They had told me not to go…not when all of us—Solguards, Banished, Halves, and Zeroes—were preparing to march on Malarusk.

But I couldn't shake the feeling that Ry, one of my best friends, was in trouble. Without our trusted hyenair, I was the only one who could reach the Crystal Caves within a reasonable amount of time.

That's how I came to be running through the heat of high day when I should be helping to prepare for an attack on Malarusk…an attack that has never been attempted. Until now.

The strength of the one-hundred Zeroes I created was enough to convince the Banished to join forces with the Solguards and me. Now, for the first time, we have the strength and numbers to break down the impenetrable iron gate barring the entrance to the Duskers' underground citadel.

I still don't know what I'll find when I reach the Crystal Caves. I've never trusted Dellin, and I can't imagine why Ry would have disappeared from the fortress unless she was in some kind of trouble.

I know Ry. She's a loyal Solguard. She would never do anything to betray us, which means that whatever they're up to, it's because of Dellin.

Distrust and searing anger wash over me at the thought of Dellin. I push away the emotions, forcing myself to put all of my energy into getting where I'm going. I won't leave Ry at the mercy of a Dusker spy or whatever Dellin is. I won't abandon my friend.

The sun's heat is so intense I can barely breathe.

I haven't stopped once, haven't even slowed, but I'm not tired. I've covered the same amount of ground in these last few hours that would take any normal person days. I have no way to track my speed, but instinct tells me I'm faster now than I was before my father helped me to change the one-hundred Dusker prisoners into Zeroes.

There's a tightness in my chest that has nothing to do with the physical effort of covering so much distance on foot. Every mile that takes me farther away from the Zeroes—*my* Zeroes—is like a rope pulling tighter and tighter around my heart. It shortens my breathing and weighs down my every step.

*Go back*, my heart says.

A part of me is afraid I'll stretch the bond linking me with the Zeroes too far. I've never tested the length of the invisible cords that bind us together. I can feel their unease at our separation through the threads of energy that connect us, which only doubles my own discomfort. I can sense the Zeroes' thoughts.

*Come back. Come back.*

Before I left the fortress, I commanded the Zeroes to go with Dayne to the Banished lands, since the army will be leaving Solis before I return. I know my brother will be furious with me when he finds out I've left, and even angrier when he realizes I've told the Zeroes to follow him to the Eastern settlement.

Dayne doesn't fear the Zeroes like most people. He hates them.

I understand the reason for my brother's hatred. Dayne was a victim of my father's experiments to create the earliest versions of the Zeroes. He saw my father's cruelty firsthand. I still don't trust my father, nor have I forgotten or forgiven him for his past crimes. But I can't deny that he's done nothing but help since he rescued us from the trap the Dusker Supreme set.

A sick, nauseous feeling washes through me at the memory of Aunt Jadem kneeling at Crowe's feet…the twist of the Supreme's hands…my aunt's body falling to the ground….

Tears prick at my eyes, mixing with the sweat streaming down my brow. I push myself to run faster.

I look around, even though I don't know what I'm supposed to be looking for. Liglette's instructions were to skirt the western edge of the Subterrane territory, cross the Barren forest, and then keep going until I saw the Crystal River. When I asked her how I'd know which river was the right one, she'd laughed and said, "You'll know."

I pick up my pace. The sooner I get Ry away from Dellin and whatever that girl is trying to make her do, the sooner I can put all of my attention into our attack on Malarusk…and destroying Crowe.

I come to a skidding halt at the sight of the sunlight reflecting off something so bright I have to shield my eyes. It looks like a long, uninterrupted sheet of diamonds. Small rainbows dance above its surface.

I take my sling out of my belt and fit a stone in the worn leather pouch as I inch forward. It's quiet, but not in the enemy-waiting-to-ambush-me kind of quiet I've grown so familiar with. It's just a peaceful stillness.

I'm close enough to touch it before I realize it's not diamonds on the ground, but a river. The sunlight sparkles on its glassy-smooth surface. I can see straight down to the bottom, to the green algae bending with the water's movement. It must be twenty feet deep, but I can see every pebble strewn across the bottom as clearly as if it was one of Aunt Jadem's minnow ponds.

Liglette said I would know when I reached the Crystal River. She was right.

I follow the river, noting the bend Liglette told me about, and then veer off in the direction of the Crystal Caves.

Even as I skirt the diamond-clear water, I can hardly believe it's real. My mother used to tell me stories about this place, but I always assumed it was made up, like the crazy talking animals she was always inventing to make me forget about the Dweller children who were mean to me.

One of the last times I talked to Aunt Jadem, I mentioned these stories about the Crystal Caves. Aunt Jadem had laughed, as had I, and shaken her head about my mother's penchant for storytelling.

Now, I wonder how my aunt could have been as ignorant about this place as I. Aunt Jadem was the Solguard leader and head of the Banished council. She had traveled more than anyone I'd ever met. How could a place like this exist without her having known about it?

My surprised laugh breaks the surrounding stillness when I find the enormous, leafy tree that Liglette said marks the entrance to the Caves. I can't believe I've actually found it.

I'm no tracker, but I recognize the two long skid marks as what could only be Vlaz's giant paws carving a path through the soft earth. I look around but see no sign of the hyenair. Two sets of footprints in the soft ground lead to the stone covering over the caves' entrance.

I keep my sling drawn as I descend the earthen steps.

I'm not sure what I expected, but at first glance, this place is no different from the hundreds of other caves I've seen in my life. The construction of this place is more similar to the Subterrane I grew up in than the cavernous stone caves of Solis. Its walls are bare except for the unadorned torches set on the ground. There are small holes where underground creatures have made their own passages through the earth.

Still, I don't feel constricted down here. The desire I would normally have to get out of a place like this is absent. Instead, I find myself being drawn in. It's like I've been here before, even though I know I haven't.

I keep traveling down until I reach the first cave. It's more cavernous than the previous cave, and when I look up, my breath hitches. Dozens of rock crystals of various shapes and sizes are hanging down from the ceiling.

My mother's voice echoes from somewhere deep inside me.

*There's a magical place. It's a cave, but not like one you've ever seen before. Crystals, clear as glass, grow from the ceiling. They feel as smooth as silk but are sharp as any sword. When you run your fingers along their surface, it sounds like the tinkle of bells.*

Almost of their own accord, my fingernails tap out a musical rhythm on one of the crystals. And I understand this feeling that I've been here before.

I *have* been here. Maybe not in the way I am now, but I've seen these caves a thousand times in the stories my mother told me.

I press my hand to one of the smooth crystals and can swear I feel my mother's presence.

All thoughts of Ry and Dellin flee from my mind. I spin in a slow circle, my gaze fixed on the crystals dangling overhead.

*This place is real.*

I wander through the cave to the opening on the other side. It's just the way my mother described it in her stories—from the crystals growing out of the walls along the path that are sharp enough to slice a person's head off, to the tiny silver flowers that grow down here, to the next cave that's filled with blue crystals instead of clear ones. It's all here, just as she described.

I don't remember my mother ever leaving the Subterrane when I was a child, and yet, one thing is clear. My mother has been here before.

# CHAPTER 2

y mother's stories come back to me as readily as if she had told them to me last high day. I even hear her voice in my head as I move out of the blue crystal cave and deeper into the network of tunnels.

*First the clear, and then the blue,* my mother's voice says in my head. *Enter the green, and go straight through.*

I see the smile on her face as she repeated the rhyme from her story, feel her fingers stroking my hair. The memory of her voice and touch shrouds me, making me feel warm and protected in a way I haven't felt since she died.

*Follow the path that snakes down, deep into the ground. Keep going even when you think there is no more. Only then will you find what you're looking for.*

It was just a rhyme, something silly my mother came up with to put me to sleep. I never even asked her what that last line meant. Now, as I follow the path deeper underground, an overwhelming sense of anticipation grips me.

The tunnel ends in a small cave. I bend down to light the single torch at the entrance. Compared to the others, this cave is unnoteworthy. There are no beautiful crystals, nothing strange to make it stand out from any other cave I've been in. It's empty of furniture or any sign it's ever been used by anyone other than the worms and moles scratching at the dirt. It doesn't seem like the kind of place to discover something important.

There was another variation of the story my mother sometimes told. It was about a clever girl who hid her treasures in a secret wall compartment.

Feeling a little foolish, I walk around the small cave, running my hand along the earthen wall. When my fingers find the groove, my breath catches.

No one would ever find this hiding place unless they knew to look for it. The lip of the wooden ledge is disguised by dirt on an otherwise unnoteworthy cave wall. Small bits of earth crumble as my fingers work their way under the wood.

It's obvious whatever is hidden in here has been left undisturbed for years. My hands are shaking and I'm dizzy with anticipation, but I finally manage to tug the box loose. A shower of dirt and pebbles spatters onto the ground.

A small, nervous laugh escapes me and bounces around the cave. *This box belonged to my mother, and she left it for me.*

The box is small enough to be carried in one hand, but there's a heft to it. The wood groans and sends up a puff of dust as I pull off the top. Inside, there's another box. This one is metal and has a lock fixed to its delicate clasp.

I start to muscle the box open, but something wound around the clasp and lock catches my attention. There's a thin, clear tube filled with a dark liquid. I recognize it immediately.

My father used a similar contraption when he was captain of Subterrane Harkibel. He wound a tube filled with blackwood ink around the handle of the drawer where he kept his letters, maps, and the scouts' reports. If anyone opened the drawer without using the right key, the tube would break and the blackwood ink would flood the scrolls, making them unreadable.

The contraption's design had been my father's idea, but my mother was the one who executed the delicate work of rigging the tube and ink.

My heart races as I hold the small metal box. All I can think is *my mother held this box.* It was her hands that dug its hiding place in the wall…her hands that wound the ink-filled tube around the lock. I trace the edge of the metal, trying to feel her in every groove.

I would have guessed finding this part of my mother would make me miss her more. Instead, I long for Aunt Jadem. My aunt told me so many stories about my mother this past year. She missed my mother and wished for a piece of her as much as I did. She would have loved to see this box and open it with me. My heart clenches.

I'm so engrossed in the box that Vlaz's whine makes me jump straight into the air. I hit my head on the cave's low ceiling.

"You scared me!" I tell the hyenair, as I massage the bump on my head.

Vlaz, who somehow managed to squeeze his enormous bulk into the main tunnel, is poking his head into the entrance to the cave. He has a long, gray fish clutched between his fangs.

"Um, thank you?" I say when he drops the fish at my feet.

Vlaz whines again, part in greeting and part because he seems to be completely stuck.

I laugh at his attempts to wriggle himself free. He seems to forget all about being stuck when I'm within arm's reach, though. Vlaz lowers his head so I can scratch his flopped ear. He gives me a deep, rumbling sound of approval.

"Come on," I tell Vlaz after I've convinced him to back his way out into the larger passage. "Can you show me where Ry is?"

Vlaz slinks back down the tunnel, ducking his head to avoid the crystals. I tuck the metal box under my arm and follow.

Vlaz leads me to a large cave right off the main tunnel. I must have walked right past it. Vlaz gives me a quick nudge before squeezing his way back up the tunnel to the Outside, probably to get himself another fish.

I grip my sling, not knowing what I'll find inside. I kick open the wooden door.

Ry and Dellin are sitting on two bedrolls opposite each other, leaning over something on the ground. Dellin's long blonde hair mingles with Ry's frizzy red hair as they bend over the object. A strange mix of emotions—relief and anger—keep me from saying a word.

Dellin yanks up the hood of her cloak and turns away from me, hiding whatever expression is on her face.

"Hemera!" Ry leaps to her feet. "What in the sun are you doing here?"

"I could ask you the same question." I don't try to mask the coldness in my voice.

"You were worried about me?"

This thought seems to please Ry.

I scowl. "Of course, I was worried about you. I thought—" I let my sentence trail off as I give Dellin a suspicious glare.

My black eyes are enough to scare off most people, but Dellin doesn't balk. Her hood hides what I imagine to be a sour expression on her perpetually dirt-streaked face.

"Oh, everything's fine," Ry says with a wave of her hand.

"Everything's *fine?*" I stare at her. "You stole Vlaz and left the fortress without telling anyone where you were going." My anger is starting to edge out any relief I felt at finding her unharmed. "There are Solguards who think you're a traitor."

Ry recoils. "I'm not."

"Did she kidnap you?" I ask, indicating Dellin with a jerk of my head.

"What? No." Ry shakes her head. "Dellin was the only one I could bring with me."

I'm unprepared for the sting I feel at these words and draw back a step.

"That's not what I meant," Ry says, looking flustered.

A tense moment passes.

"Does Wade know you're here?" she asks.

"I left a note saying we'd meet him at Valior's settlement in the Banished lands tomorrow." I cross my arms across my chest. "Because *I* wouldn't just disappear and leave my friends to worry about me."

I think I hear Dellin snort. I ignore her. Dellin might not have kidnapped Ry like I'd thought, but that doesn't mean she isn't still a spy for the Duskers.

Ry sighs. "I guess there's no point in keeping any more secrets now that you're here."

"How charitable of you," I mutter.

Ry exchanges a look with Dellin, which sends a spike of rage through me.

Ry hands me a rolled-up piece of script tree bark.

I snatch the scroll and unfurl it, immediately recognizing my aunt's flowing script.

*Rylin,*

*If I don't return to the fortress, I need you to do something for me. I have hidden something in the Crystal Caves. Find it, and guard it with your life. It could be the difference between life and death for the Solguards. When the time comes, you'll know what to do with it.*

*I only hope this might be enough to save you from an evil I helped bring about.*
*Jadem*

*P.S. Don't, under any circumstances, tell Hemera or Dayne where you are going.*

Beneath the brief note is a map outlining the way to the Crystal Caves. There is also a drawing of the network of caves itself, although I notice it only shows the first tunnel and adjoining caves. The ones deeper inside where I had just been exploring are absent from the image. The big cave, the one we're in now, is marked on Jadem's map with an X.

Before I can say anything, Ry places a small box on my palm.

I open the lid. Resting on a bed of satiny gray fabric is what must be a seed, although it doesn't resemble any seed I've ever seen. It's golden and radiates a kind of glow. It almost looks like it's pulsing, like a beating heart, but that could just be the golden light playing across its surface. When I pass my hand over the seed, I feel heat emanating from it.

"What is this?" I ask.

Ry shrugs. "The difference between life and death for the Solguards, apparently," she says, reading the words from Jadem's note.

"She said you'd know what it was for when the time came," Dellin adds.

"I don't understand." I shake my head. "When did she give you this note?"

*Why did she give it to you and not to me?* is what I really want to ask.

"She gave it to me at the feast before she went with you and Dayne to capture Hendrix," Ry says.

I remember the feast. I remember seeing Aunt Jadem give something to Ry.

*Right before we left for Malarusk. Right before she was killed.*

"She must have known she might not be coming back," I say around the lump that has formed in my throat.

Before we left Solis, Aunt Jadem had seemed so certain everything would work out. She was so anxious to leave for Malarusk. How could she have been wrong about everything?

Ry and Dellin exchange a glance.

"You know," I say, not bothering to hide my irritation. "You could have brought Wade with you. This really isn't any of *her* business." I stab my thumb in Dellin's direction.

Dellin ignores me, which only makes me angrier.

"Wade had his hands full leading the Solguards," Ry says, planting her hands on her hips. "And I couldn't tell him where I was going because he would have told you." Emotion flashes across her face.

I feel my own cheeks redden at both at the memory of Ry walking in on Wade and me during the feast, and also the kiss she and I shared in the Lair. An awkward silence hangs between us.

"But," I swallow. "Aunt Jadem died months ago. Why did you wait so long to come here?"

Ry gives me an exasperated look. "In case you've forgotten, quite a lot happened after Jadem was killed. There wasn't time right after."

I haven't forgotten.

"Besides," Ry continues. "Not everyone can cross hundreds of miles in a few hours by foot." She gives me a pointed stare. "Taking Vlaz was the only way for me to get here. I needed an opportunity to get Vlaz when Wokee wasn't around, since I couldn't tell him, either."

"Why wouldn't Aunt Jadem have wanted Dayne and me to come with you?" I ask, trying to ignore the hurt those words bring me.

Logic tells me there must be a good reason why my aunt would want to keep us away. Still, I can't help the feeling that all of this is just…wrong.

"I have no idea." Ry huffs out a breath, making an errant curl dangling over her forehead fly up. "But there better be a really good reason why she made me go to all the trouble of coming here." She glares at the golden seed.

"What's that?" Dellin points at the metal box sitting beside me.

I clutch it to my chest, as if the other girl might try to steal it from me. Ry scoots closer and takes the box from my hands to study it better. She gives me a questioning look.

Reluctantly, I explain about how my mother's rhymes led me to the box, and how the ink contraption keeps me from opening it without the key.

When I've finished, Dellin gives me a thoughtful look. "Maybe Jadem knew your mother hid this box here and didn't want you to find it."

"That's ridiculous." I give her a scathing look.

"Maybe not," Ry says, frowning. "That would explain why she sent me instead of you."

Part of me wants to hit her for taking Dellin's side.

"If my aunt knew my mother had left something for me, she would've told me about it. She wouldn't have tried to keep that secret from me."

"Maybe she thought it'd be better for you if you didn't know," Ry offers.

"Then why didn't Jadem just destroy it?" Dellin asked.

Ry thought for a moment. "Maybe she knew the box was somewhere in here, but not exactly where. This place is huge, after all."

I feel a stab of irritation at the way they're carrying on this conversation as though I'm not even here.

"Aunt Jadem never would have done that to me."

Even as the words leave my lips, a nagging uncertainty nestles inside me.

"I guess we won't know for sure until you find the right key," Dellin says.

My hand goes to the silver chain dangling from my throat before I've even processed her words.

*The right key.*

# CHAPTER 3

I practically run back to the cave where I found the box. Something just seems right about opening it in a place where I know my mother has been.

Ry wanted to see what was in the box, but as selfish as it sounded to tell her so, I don't want to share this moment with anyone.

I lean against the wall of the cave, the box resting on my lap, and unhook the necklace clasped around my neck.

*The key to my mother's heart.*

Part of me fears it's too simple. I've worn this necklace since my mother gave it to me on my twelfth birthday. Could it really be possible my mother hid this box at least a decade ago, and then gave me the key and told me the stories, in the hopes that I would someday figure it all out?

There's only one way to know for sure.

My hands are trembling so badly it takes several tries for me to fit the key into the lock. When I finally manage it, the key slides in and turns. There's a small click as the latch pops free from the ink tube.

I manage to re-clasp the key around my neck before I lose it, and then I turn my attention on the box. My heart stops beating. Everything else around me fades away.

Carefully, I open the box.

My hands are shaking so much I almost tear the brittle sheet of script tree bark. My eyes scan the page, packed tight with words. With a pang, I realize I don't recognize my mother's handwriting.

There's so much about her I never got to know.

*My Darling Mer,*

Even those words make my heart ache. I can hear my mother's voice saying them. My scalp tingles at the memory of her hands smoothing back my hair. I can see the crinkle at the corner of her eyes as she smiled down at me. I force in a breath and keep reading.

*There are things about me you never knew. You are too young to understand any of them as I write this letter, but my hope is that when you are older, you will come to know what I have done and understand why I did it. You are as clever as you are strong, and I know you will be able to find this letter. I am so proud of you, my daughter.*

My eyes are too blurred for me to read any more. I wrap my arms around myself, pretending they're hers. The ache I feel for her is almost too much to bear. I blink away the tears and keep reading.

*I am guessing that by now you've learned about my relationship with Clarion. He was brilliant, like your father. We were young when we met and fell in love. He was a Solguard and filled me with ideas about how to overthrow the Duskers.*

*When Clarion witnessed the Halves raiding one of the outer settlements, he saw their power for himself. He said if we could only harness that power for ourselves, we'd have what we needed to defeat the Duskers. His dream became mine.*

*We were both so young.*

*After Clarion died, I married Zeidan. Your father was a true leader, and I believed I could convince him to carry on the work Clarion began. I never gave up searching for a way to bring Clarion's dream to life.*

*Your father helped me to see the world upside down, inside out, and backwards. When I became pregnant with you, I wondered if you might somehow be the answer to all our problems. I wondered…what if I could infuse my own child with the strength of the Halves?*

I stop reading. My heart pounds against my ribcage. She couldn't possibly mean what I think she meant….

*I don't need to tell you my experiment worked. You were everything I hoped you would be and more. But it was only as you began to grow up that I realized there was a part to all of this I hadn't accounted for.*

*Mer, please understand that every hateful glance the Dwellers gave you cut me more deeply than a dagger in my chest. The price for my foolishness became yours to pay. I know the loneliness you have suffered, and I am truly sorry for it. I only wish I knew then what I have since learned…that some outcomes are not worth what is needed to achieve them. I should never have done what I did to you, no matter my motives.*

*You will forever be the key to my heart, my brave, beautiful daughter.*

The words become almost unreadable as my tears fall onto the bark and mix with the ink. I shove the scroll away like it's something poisonous and bury my face in my hands.

I never would have believed even a single word if I hadn't heard my mother's voice coming straight off the page. There is no doubt this letter really came from her. There is no possibility it's some trick, something written to deceive and torture me. It's all true; I know it in my bones.

I turn over the bark and stare at the writing covering its backside. At the top, my mother wrote, *The knowledge of how you were made belongs to you.*

Beneath those words is…a recipe. The kind of thing one would expect to find in a cook's possession. But instead of flour and salt, my mother has listed all the steps she took to turn me into a Bisecter.

*1 month before conception: Began drinking 2 liters of water daily from the Crystal River to enhance immunity to Halve blood….*

I roll it back up without reading the rest.

I squeeze my palms into my eyelids, as if that could be enough to make me forget the words burned into my brain.

How could she do this to me, her own daughter?

Emotions flash through me faster than I can process them. Betrayal, anger, incomprehension….

I settle on anger.

What good does an explanation and apology do me now, after everything I've been through? All the years I spent alone and wishing for nothing more than to be normal. The years I spent sick with guilt for not being able to save my mother from the Halve that murdered her.

A harsh laugh grates out of my throat. What are the chances of having not one, but two psychotic, experimenting-on-people parents?

My mother. My perfect, loving, good mother…experimented on her own daughter. And she waited to tell me through a note I might never have found. Everything I always thought about her, all my memories, now feel like a lie.

I'm shaking from my fury and sense of betrayal.

I pick up the letter, my fingers aching to shred it into bits. But some stupid, sentimental part of me refuses. This letter is a part of my mother. No matter how angry I am with her, I can't bring myself to destroy it. It's the same reason why I don't rip the delicate chain from around my neck and hurl it across the cave.

A thought gives me pause. Is it possible Aunt Jadem knew all of this, about what my mother did, and about the letter my mother left here? If my mother was so involved with the Solguards, my aunt would have had to know about what she did to me.

Is that why Jadem didn't want me to come here—why she told me the Crystal Caves were just a legend and told Ry to come here without me—to keep me from finding this letter and getting hurt?

I don't know what to think anymore. My head aches. The tug of my bond with the Zeroes is nagging and persistent. If I stay here for another second, I'll go mad. I need a distraction.

My feet bring me to the cave where Ry announced she would be sleeping. It's set apart from the main cave, so I'm hoping Dellin stayed put for the high day, and I'll find Ry alone.

I think about the way Ry kissed me so many weeks ago. She made me feel like I could have anything, do anything. Like nothing was beyond my grasp. I need to feel that way right now.

I don't let myself think about Wade. I push the thoughts of my mother's letter from my mind. All I want right now is to escape from all of it.

I inch open the door to Ry's cave and step inside. The hesitant smile on my lips dies.

Ry and Dellin are asleep, tangled in each other's arms underneath one blanket. I start to back out of the cave, but before I even reach the door, Ry startles awake.

"What is it, love?" Dellin's sleepy voice murmurs.

When Ry doesn't say anything, Dellin sits up.

I feel my jaw drop.

Dellin's face, which in all the weeks I've known her has always been filthy and shaded by the brim of her hood, is spotless. And it takes less than a second for me to understand why she's gone through such pains to keep her skin covered.

Her skin is white as bone. Only someone of direct Dusker descent could have skin that pure.

"I knew it," I breathed. "I knew you were one of them!"

"Mer, just calm down." Ry makes a gesture with one hand as she uses the other to keep the blanket up to her chin.

"Calm down? She—you—"

"It's not what you think." Dellin's calm is the opposite of my stuttering, stumbling fury. "Oh really? Then what is it, exactly?"

"Well, maybe part of it is what you think." Dellin looks at Ry in a way that leaves me breathless. Pure, unmasked adoration brightens her gray eyes.

I finally understand Dellin's sneers and the way she always tries to keep me away, like she's protecting Ry. I had assumed Dellin hated me because I was a Bisecter, but it wasn't that at all. It was jealousy…for the way Ry acted toward me.

I turn to them, only to see Ry looking back at Dellin. There's an expression on my friend's face I've never seen her wear before. It's not like the way she looked at me right before she kissed me. It's the look of someone who shares a secret that only the two of you understand. It makes me want to punch through the nearest wall.

But all of that is unimportant compared to Dellin's bone-white skin.

"I knew you were a spy," I fume, because it's easier to yell at Dellin than look at Ry.

"I'm not a spy," Dellin replies.

"Dell's been hiding from the Duskers her whole life," Ry explains. "She hates them as much as we do."

"Like I'm supposed to believe that," I shoot back. "There's no such thing as a Dusker who leaves Malarusk."

There's only one way to escape Malarusk, as I know only too well. It would be lunacy for a Dusker to try and escape through the wormkill tunnel. Whatever else I might think about Dellin, she's never struck me as crazy.

"It's true," Dellin says. "They killed my father. My mother took me away to the Banished Lands before the Duskers could kill us, too. I've been running from them my entire life."

With those words, a dozen small oddities click into place. Dellin always covering her pale skin, her refusal to talk about her background, her absolute terror whenever she gets anywhere near Malarusk, how she always seems to know things about the Duskers the rest of us don't....

"Maybe," I allow. "But even if that's true, you still can't be trusted. You can stay here, but you can't come back with us to the Banished lands. Not when there's so much at stake."

"Since when do you get to tell me what to do?" Dellin's sneer is back in place. "Why don't you go—"

Ry puts a hand on Dellin's arm. "Give us a minute," she murmurs.

Dellin looks like she's going to argue, but at a look from Ry, she pulls on her cloak and stomps out of the cave.

"She's not coming with us," I tell Ry the moment the door has slammed shut. "I don't care what you say. Once a Dusker, always a Dusker."

"I would expect you of all people to understand a person doesn't need to live up to the reputation of who—or what—they came from."

I flush. "This isn't about me."

"Isn't it?" Ry raises an eyebrow.

"It's about the Solguards. It's about needing to trust the people fighting beside us. Dellin might be telling the truth about her parents, but who knows where her loyalties really lie."

I'm breathing hard with barely-contained rage and a feeling of betrayal I'm not sure is justified.

"I'll be responsible for her. I'll vouch for her." Ry crosses her arms. "But we're not leaving here without her."

"You've let your feelings for her cloud your judgment," I accuse.

"She's trustworthy. I swear it." Ry fists her right hand, the one with the Solguard tattoo, and puts it over her heart. "She's proved it—"

"I'm sure she has." I let my eyes drag over the rumpled bedroll and then give Ry a pointed stare.

"That's not what I meant." Ry's cheeks are almost as red as her hair. "What I meant was that if she was a Dusker, she wouldn't have helped me figure out…." Her words trail off, and her expression turns troubled.

"Figure out what?" I press.

Ry shakes her head. "I just know she's on our side, okay?" Her voice softens. "Please trust me, Mer." She reaches out to touch my hand, but I snatch it away.

"If she becomes another Gorgoran," I tell Ry, "don't say I didn't warn you."

# CHAPTER 4

I think I'm really getting the hang of riding this guy," Ry shouts over the wind rushing in our ears. She gives Vlaz's side an affectionate rub. When Vlaz turns his head to look at her with his orblike yellow eyes, Ry loses her grip on the rope tied around his neck and lurches to the side. She grins sheepishly back at me as she regains her balance. She puts a hand to her belt, making sure the box holding the strange seed Jadem said was so important is still tucked safely away.

*How could something so small be the difference between life and death for the Solguards? And why would Jadem have brought it here instead of leaving it in Solis?*

My mind is filled with everything I learned in the Crystal Caves, and all the questions I still have…questions that may never be answered since both my mother and my aunt are gone. I reach for the silver key still hanging around my neck, but touching it doesn't bring the same comfort it once did. A longing for my brother and Wokee comes over me. It feels like homesickness.

It's low day, and we're speeding toward the Eastern settlement where the Solguards and Banished are gathering. My mind is a jumble of emotions, and I'm grateful for the rushing wind that helps drown out some of my thoughts.

"Do you think everyone else is already at the Eastern settlement?" Ry asks.

I'm still angry with her, but right now, there are more important things to worry about. Still, my gaze keeps shifting to Dellin's hands looped around Ry's waist.

"I know they are," I say.

I can feel the pull of the Zeroes, the tautness in the bond easing the closer we get. My eagerness to be reunited with them helps me block out thoughts of my mother's letter and all it contains.

I slip my free hand, the one that isn't wound into Vlaz's fur, into my pocket. My fingers close around my mother's letter. I tell myself I only brought it so I can show it to Dayne. We share the same mother, after all. Besides, I'm not sure he would believe me if I told him about what it contained without having any proof. I know I wouldn't believe any of it if I hadn't read the letter myself.

We stop only once to let Vlaz rest. As he dips his entire head into a stream, the rest of us pass around a waterskin. Ry kneels down on the bank and splashes water on her face. Dellin, her face streaked with dirt once again, watches her.

"Don't you mind your face always being filthy?" I ask.

"I hate it," Dellin replies.

*That's the price you pay for deceiving everyone,* I think without sympathy. It's only because I'm not in the mood to fight with Ry right now that I don't say it out loud. Instead, I ask, "So, what did you father do to make the Duskers kill him?"

Dellin's posture goes rigid. *Hiding something,* a voice in my head warns.

Dellin seems to be struggling with something. Finally, she says, "The Supreme doesn't take well to people who disagree with her."

*Crowe is the one who killed her father?*

Interesting. I store that bit of information away for later. If Crowe cared enough about Dellin's father to kill him herself, he must have been someone important.

*Maybe he was a Solguard sympathizer,* I think, before immediately dismissing the idea. If he had been, Dellin's mother would have gone to Solis instead of one of the outer settlements.

The closer we get to the Eastern settlement, the quieter Ry becomes. Her brow is furrowed as she fusses with the seed at her belt for the thousandth time. When I ask her what's wrong, she just shakes her head and mutters something about needing to figure it all out first. Whatever that means....

* * *

We reach the Eastern settlement, Valior's territory, at lowest day. After Solis, it's the largest network of caves in the Banished Lands and is the closest to Malarusk, which makes it a convenient meeting point for all of the armies before we attack the citadel.

I hadn't thought much about what we would find when we arrived…perhaps Solguards and Banished gathering weapons and packing supplies, maybe the Halves practicing their fighting with Brogut, or maybe even my brother and Wade waiting for us on the Outside.

I didn't expect to hear screaming.

When Vlaz's paws hit the ground, sending up a cloud of dust that blocks my vision, the screaming only intensifies. Ry and I exchange a look, and then we're sliding off Vlaz and running toward the chaos.

The hairs on the back of my neck prickle. The voices have an inhuman quality to them, like an animal right before it's pierced by a hunter's spear. The sound is torturous. It makes me want to run as far away as I can get.

I'm so focused on the sounds of agony I don't notice the way my nose is burning and my eyes watering. By the time we reach the source of the tumult, both are impossible to ignore. My eyes are streaming and my head aches. The smell, which makes it feel like my nostrils are on fire every time I inhale, is one I recognize.

It's the scent of the black smoke I saw hanging over Malarusk. It's the smell of the black substance coating the Solguard scout who Wade said was burned from the outside in. And now, that black stuff is everywhere.

I remember Wade's warning from weeks ago. *Once it touches your skin, it doesn't come off.*

"Watch your step!" I call back to Ry and Dellin.

The substance is covering the ground in crisscrossing, sticky black footprints. The trail leads us to a mass of people. They're running around, in no particular direction, it seems. And they're covered from head to foot in the black stuff.

I shield my mouth and nose with the collar of my shirt, but it does little good. The skin on my face stings. I can't shake the feeling that when I reach up to touch my cheeks, I'll find my skin has been burned away.

"What's happened?" I hear Ry's frantic voice from somewhere behind me.

"Who are these people, and where did they come from?" I call to a passing Solguard.

The Solguard doesn't seem to hear me as he races past.

At the same moment, a man covered in the black substance turns toward me.

My screams mingle with those of the man standing before me. His skin and clothes are literally melting off him before my eyes. His agony and horror are written all over his face as he reaches one hand out to me. I can't help but flinch back as the man's drooping cloak sleeve separates from his body and flops to the ground with a splat.

"Help me," he rasps.

No sooner have the words left his lips, the rest of him begins to decompose.

Horror-stricken and utterly helpless, I watch as the man's head melts into his neck. The mass of flesh disappears into his shoulders. For several moments, he moves forward on still-solid legs as a headless creature covered in the oozing black muck.

His legs crumple. At first, I think he's collapsed. But when I look closer, I see his legs have actually melted in on themselves. I only have time to cry out once before the man has become a shapeless black blob twitching and oozing onto the ground.

The black puddle, for that is all that's left of the man, remains on top of the ground. Normally, the water-starved earth would swallow up anything liquid on its surface. But it's like whatever this man has become is too intolerable for even the ground to accept it.

I'm filled with equal parts disgust and shock.

*What in the sun did I just witness?*

I pull my gaze from the puddle-that-used-to-be-a-man at my feet. All around me, the same scene plays out over and over again. There are dozens and dozens of these goo-covered people. Some of them are making wheezing, gasping sounds, like they're trying to call for help but their insides are already too melted. It's all so foreign, so inhuman, my senses can't register the grief I know I should be feeling.

There are Solguards in blue interspersed among the dying. I hear orders being shouted, warnings of *be careful* and *stand back*.

The cries of the dying surround me.

"Barely got away," I hear a person who is only partially charred saying to a Solguard. "The Duskers were containing the fire, so we ran."

"…was all a trick. They were never going to protect us…."

"…made us their slaves…."

I look up to see a familiar figure running between the victims. Camike is like a beacon in a storm, the colorful feathers in her thin hair flying as she darts between the screaming, wailing people. She carries bundles of dried herbs, and two Halves are trailing her with pails of water in each hand.

"Camike," I gasp. "What's going on? What do we do?"

"Make humans comfortable," she gives me a distracted shake of her head as she indicates to the Halves where they should bring the water. "All will die."

"But we have to do something," I argue.

"Nothing to do." Camike gives me a sympathetic look as she continues on. "They are beyond help."

"Water."

I leap back to see one of them coming up behind me. He—or she, it's impossible to tell at this point in their disintegration—reaches out a slimy hand to me.

"Water," the person rasps again.

"I'm sorry, I don't—" I look around.

It's then that I see that many of the Solguards are racing back and forth with buckets of water.

I find the nearest Solguard and take her pail.

"Hey," the woman protests.

"I need this," I call as I race back.

I hesitate for only a moment before tossing the pail's contents all over the person. A terrible hissing sound is accompanied by a puff of steam that comes from every place where the water touched the black stuff.

A raspy voice begins to speak. It's barely audible from whatever has already been done to the person's insides.

"The darkness is coming."

The look in the person's eyes, or maybe the rasp of the voice, makes my blood run cold. It's the Duskers' prophecy, the blessing every Dweller in the Subterrane territory prays for. Except now, coming from this person, it sounds like a curse. Or a promise.

I remember months ago, when the Duskers were holding me prisoner in Tanguro, one of them talked about the darkness like it was more than some idle hope for the future. She talked about it like it was coming, and soon.

It's a stupid thought; the Duskers are always talking about the darkness. Still, I can't help but think there's a connection.

"More water," the person begs, pulling me out of my reverie.

The person's skin continues to smoke and sizzle as I overturn the pail, letting the remaining water drip onto the person standing before me.

The water has slowed the decomposing process, and for a moment, the person's senses seem to sharpen. His voice deepens and becomes more masculine as he coughs phlegm from his lungs. The whites of his eyes have filled with the black goo until they look almost like mine. He turns to me.

"There was a fire, and we escaped while the Duskers fought the blaze," he wheezes. Black bubbles form at the corners of his mouth.

"What is this stuff?" I ask. "Why is it doing this to you?"

"Killing us slowly for two days," he says, his voice weaker. "Duskers' secret weapon…."

"What is this weapon?" I demand. "Tell me!"

Almost without realizing what I'm doing, I lean closer, like it will help me understand the dying man better. A rattling cough makes him gasp and splutter. He gestures me closer. Faster than I would have thought possible for someone in his condition, the man reaches up a blackened hand. It tightens around the Solguard pendant around my neck, which has come loose from the collar of my shirt.

"Help…me…."

He clutches at my necklace like it will anchor him. I pull back, revulsion coursing through me.

I don't hear the snap, but I feel the cord come away from my neck. The pendant flies into the air, the sunlight flickering off the smooth metal surface of the carved flames, before it lands on the ground just out of reach. The cord, now dripping with the black stuff, is still clutched in the man's sticky, decomposing hand.

I lunge for the pendant. All I can think about is that it's all Wade has left of Sal. Wade trusted me to keep it. I can't lose it.

Using the empty water pail, I scoop up oily black dirt until the barest glint of metal emerges. I'm so relieved I almost cry.

I shake out as much of the dirt from the pail as I can without touching any of the black substance. Except for one of the swirling rays, the entire pendant is black. The gelatinous stuff clings in stubborn, sticky globs to the metal's surface.

I tear off a piece of my shirt and try to scrub at the metal without getting any of the black stuff on my hands. The cloth disintegrates almost as quickly as I can use it, and still, the black residue clings to the metal. The golden sheen of the pendant has been replaced by black.

I carry the pendant in the empty bucket for now, promising myself I'll clean it properly and find a new cord to string it on later. Still, the sight of it fills me with a dread I can't explain.

As I turn back to the charred man, something clicks in my mind.

"You're one of the Banished who went to Malarusk for protection, aren't you?"

The man gives me a jerky nod.

I remember the group of Banished, starving and half-crazed from their battles with the Halves, who were desperately trying to reach Malarusk. I remember Dellin, their prisoner at the time, saying the Duskers promised them protection from the Halves' raids. I remember Aunt Jadem telling them that the Duskers don't offer something for nothing.

The man reaches his hand out to me once more. "The darkness," he rasps. "It's coming."

# CHAPTER 5

Wade, what in the sun happened?"

Ry jogs over to where Wade and the other Solguards are congregating.

Everyone is coughing. One archer sneezes, and then gasps at the sight of her blue cloak, which is now specked with blood.

"Ry, get the archers to make a ring around the compound," Wade tells her, his voice all business. "If any Duskers are coming after those slaves, I want them dead before they get near the caves."

She nods and disappears into the crowd, rounding up Dellin and the rest of the archers. The Solguards disperse to carry out Wade's other orders.

Wade's distracted gaze finds mine for a fraction of a second. His normally golden eyes are red and bloodshot.

"Council meeting," Wade says. "Now."

Just like that, he's gone again, swallowed up into the crowd of guards and scouts waiting for orders. I don't have time or energy to think about what we might have said to each other if we'd had a moment of time alone.

"Come on, Bisecter." Tut, the Banished leader of the North, shoves his way through the crowd and gestures for me to follow.

"What happened to those people?" I ask, my eyes lingering on the lumpy puddles of black goo.

It's almost impossible to think about the fact that the gelatinous puddles were once living, breathing people.

"It's obvious, isn't it?" Tut turns to face me, and I'm almost blinded by the reflection of the sun on the gold threads stitched into his cloak.

Beneath his cloak and hood, I know Tut's wrists are covered in gold bangles, his teeth are plated in gold, and gold thread is even wound into his goatee. I think it's absurd, but Aunt Jadem said it was the Northerner's way of remembering better times.

"Spell it out for me, Tut," I say. My exhaustion is catching up to me, and I don't have the energy for games.

"The Duskers' weapon. The one we *told* you they were preparing. It's ready."

"Their weapon is…black goo?" I ask, raising an eyebrow.

"That there is no normal substance." Tut points a gloved finger in the direction of the blackened, disintegrated corpses.

I know he's right.

"That's the devil's work," Tut continues. "A plague sent down from the Dark God Himself."

"I never took you to be the believing type," I tell him as we skirt the edges of a black pile of decomposed cloak and flesh.

"There's no man alive who could conjure such a weapon," is his only reply as he picks his way around the dead.

I follow more slowly, trying to absorb everything I've just witnessed.

"The dead were all formerly Valior's people who surrendered to the Duskers about a month ago," Tut is saying. "They got here at low day and it's been all we could do to keep them from going down into the caves."

Tut leads me past the dried-up remains of what must have once been a garden. He kicks aside some broken shards of pottery strewn across the ground.

I had expected the Eastern settlement to look like a bigger version of Subterrane Harkibel, with some kind of wall bordering it from the surrounding land and orderly crop fields dotting the ground above the caves. But there's nothing of the sort. Instead, the path leading up to the compound is littered with broken farm tools and other refuse. The only markers of the tunnel's entrance are the sticks in the ground.

If it weren't for all the people and Halves milling around, this place would look abandoned. It's nothing like what I pictured from Jadem's description.

"What happened to this place?" I ask.

"The Halves happened," Tut snaps. "The brutes pillaged our lands and devoured our crops until nothing was left." The small group of his soldiers following us nod in agreement. They direct their accusing stares at the Halves, all of whom are standing around the marked entrance to the caves, seeming unsure of whether to enter.

"It's not their fault," I say. "The Duskers took away their river. There are no more animals for them to feed on, and nothing will grow in their territory."

"So, that gives them the right to steal? To kill?" There is venom in Tut's voice as he kicks aside what looks to be the skeleton of a long-dead animal.

"Of course not," I say. "But it's the Duskers who are to blame. They're the ones you should be angry at."

It's not the first time I've had this conversation with a Banished leader, and I try not to let my frustration show. If we're all going to face the Duskers together, if we're going to have any chance against their soldiers, then the Halves and Banished need to tolerate each other.

Vlaz is heading toward me. He's snuffing the ground, growling and wrinkling his nose every time he gets near the black substance. Both humans and Halves rush to get out of his way. Most of the Solguards are used to Vlaz by now, but the Banished and Halves are still wary of his fangs and claws.

I give Vlaz a distracted pat as I watch Tut's people continue to glare at the Halves.

When Ekil sees me, he gestures the other Halves forward. Tut rests a hand on the pommel of his sword, but at a warning look from me, releases his grip.

"Are the Halves alright?" I ask Ekil, scanning them for any sign of the black substance. They all appear unscathed.

"Halves all alive," Ekil replies.

"Why haven't you all gone down into the caves?" I ask, not wanting to think about the Banished slaves anymore.

Ekil gives a meaningful look at Tut. "Humans don't want Halves."

"They'll have to get over it," I tell him. "We all want the same thing in this fight. The Banished just need to know they can trust you."

Brogut, Ekil's second, lets out an animal-like growl as he raises his tree trunk spear.

I scowl at the brute. "Put that down," I order him.

I still haven't forgiven Brogut for injuring my Zero during the demonstration fight a few days ago. I can still feel the phantom pain in my own stomach, in the same place where my Zero was stabbed.

"Won't attack them if they don't attack us," Brogut informs me.

"You coming in?" Tut huffs, tired of listening to what must just sound like gibberish to him and the rest of the humans. "You heard your boyfriend—council's waiting."

"Come on," I turn back to Ekil and the rest of the Halves. "You have as much right to be here as anyone else. I'll make sure no one bothers you."

We leave Vlaz, who can't fit into the hole in the ground, on the Outside. I would have been worried about him touching the black stuff, but he seems to hate it as much as the rest of us. I give his flopped ear a quick scratch before descending underground into the tunnel.

Unlike Solis or even Subterrane Harkibel, with their labyrinthine tunnels and hidden caves, there is only one roughly hewn tunnel in this entire settlement. Caves are hollowed out on each side, with nothing except for a ragged cloth hanging over the entrances to the sleeping caves. Bedrolls are tucked into every available cranny, out of the way of the endless movement of people and supplies up and down the tunnel. It looks like a place that's suddenly absorbed far more people than it can comfortably accommodate, which, to be fair, it has.

The compound is swarming with activity. We pass a group of Banished pushing rickety wooden wheelbarrows full of swords and other weapons up the tunnel. I know they're Northerners from their gold bracelets and the gold hoops dangling from their ears.

Everyone tries to clear a path as a group of Westerners herding capy pigs come into the tunnel. Their long hair is braided with beads in a similar fashion to Liglette's. They're more somber than the Northerners, skillfully maneuvering the stubborn animals without all the yelling and cursing Tut's people seem to require.

I look for my brother and Wade, but I don't see them in the crush of soldiers gathering weapons and organizing supplies.

When Valior emerges from one of the caves, a cry of "our leader" erupts from his people, the Easterners.

Valior's eyes, which are usually red and swimming from the liquor in his flask, are the clearest I've ever seen them. His back is less bowed, and even though he leans on his cane, there's an air of excitement surrounding him as he gives orders and discusses battle strategy with the people surrounding him.

When Valior raises a hand to me in greeting, I notice he isn't carrying his flask. It's the first time I've ever seen him without it.

"Welcome to our humble dwelling," Valior calls as he makes his way to me.

The old man's voice carries across the tunnel and doesn't waver as much as I remember. He doesn't seem like the weak and dejected leader of the Eastern settlement I first met in Solis months ago.

"You don't seem overly concerned about all of the dead people who just disintegrated right above your settlement," I tell him.

Valior shrugs. "They stopped being Banished when they gave themselves up to the Duskers."

I bite my tongue to keep from reminding him that, before the Zeroes' demonstration, he and the other Banished leaders had every intention of surrendering to the Duskers, too.

"I don't know what those things were," Valior continues. "But they weren't my people. At least, not anymore."

# CHAPTER 6

The other council leaders are already assembled when Valior, Tut, and I enter the cramped cave. It's nothing like Jadem's meeting chamber. Everyone sits on old cushions on the ground instead of around a table. Valior needs three cushions to put him at eye level with the rest of us. Reams of script tree bark are scattered everywhere.

Luckily, Dayne and I have time for only a quick hello before Valior calls the meeting to order. If we'd been alone or there'd been more time, I'm sure he would have told me off for going after Ry when he'd specifically told me to stay put. Not to mention the part where I ordered my Zeroes to follow him from Solis to the settlement….

Sadness sweeps through me at the sight of the empty cushion at the head of our small group. That position of honor belonged to my aunt. A crushing weight sinks onto my chest. For a moment, it's difficult to breathe.

"Let us dispatch with the usual ceremonies," Valior says. "Present circumstances demand speed rather than finesse."

I see Wade raise his eyebrows. He's never been fond of the debates and arguing of the council. Wade describes the Banished leaders behind their backs as a bunch of old, bleating goats.

"Works for me," Wade says.

"Let me begin by addressing the most pressing of issues," Valior says. "We must delay our attack on the citadel."

"What?" Wade and I demand at the same time.

"You are very young and eager," Valior tells us, putting up a hand to stop either of us from arguing. "But as the leader of my people, I cannot even consider sending them into a fight until we're ready to properly oppose our enemy."

"Meaning…?" Wade demands.

"Meaning that iron and wood will be of no use against their demon weapon." Valior shudders. "We must change our tactics."

"You mean the black goo?" I ask. "We're changing everything around based on that stuff?"

"That black goo, as you call it, is the deadliest substance I've ever encountered," Valior retorts.

Everyone goes quiet as we think about the Banished people melting into gelatinous puddles before our eyes.

"Has anyone ever seen anything like it before?" Dayne asks.

We all shake our heads.

"I told you there was a good reason the Duskers hadn't attacked Solis yet." Tut points an accusing finger at Wade. "They needed to prepare their weapon, and it seems they've done just that."

"It's not like there was anything we could have done about it, regardless." Wade crosses his arms.

"No, there wasn't," Valior agrees.

"So, what do we do?" Liglette asks, leaning forward on her cushion.

"We must find out more about this weapon," Valior replies.

"Send more Solguard scouts to find out what they're up to," Tut suggests.

"I'm not sending any more of my people into Malarusk to die," Wade shoots back. "Send your own damn scouts."

"We can't send in scouts," Dayne cuts in. "The Duskers have posted guards all along the Darkness River. They know the Banished and Halves are desperate enough that you might try take water from their territory. They'll see any scouts coming a mile away."

"Well then, what do you suggest?" Tut taps the pommel of his sword in agitation.

"I can do it," I say. "I'll go during high day when there aren't any guards and figure out what the Duskers are doing."

"No," Wade and Dayne say at the same time.

"It'll be fine," I tell them, barely containing my irritation. "There will be no one on the Outside. I won't be in any danger."

I can see Wade relenting, but my brother still looks furious.

"Alright then," Valior agrees. "Find out what it's made from, how we defend ourselves against it, and if it can be destroyed." He ticks each point off on his arthritic fingers. "We need to know everything about the substance before we can revise our battle strategy."

"I'll go this high day," I say, my frustration mounting. "We don't have to delay any of our plans."

"Young people are always in such a rush." Valior chuckles.

I feel my face heating with anger. "I'm not sure you realize how important it is that we move quickly," I say through clenched teeth. "It won't be long before the Duskers realize why we're all gathering here. Crowe's smart…she'll figure out what we're planning."

"No one's smart enough to predict something that's never been done before," Tut argues. "Hell, their scouts will probably see everyone gathering and assume the Halves are here to make war on us." He glares at Ekil, who returns his hostile stare.

"I agree," Liglette says. "We must proceed with the utmost caution."

A part of me knows Valior is right. We can't simply march into Malarusk with swords and wooden clubs and expect to win when the Duskers have that black substance. And yet, every day that passes is one more for the Duskers to gather their strength…to attack us here before we're fully prepared. If they discover what we're planning, then we might as well give up now.

But that isn't all that's bothering me. I don't quite know how to give words to the misgivings that have been growing in me since I got here. I can't help but feel like we're missing something…something important.

"Then it's settled," Valior says. "Hemera will investigate this weapon during the high day, and then we'll proceed based on her report."

Hours later, when Valior finally calls the meeting to a close, my backside is sore from sitting on the ground for so long. My head aches from all the changes in our original plans, and my nerves are frayed from so much time apart from the Zeroes. I have to stop myself from running straight to them.

When we get back to what appears to be the settlement's main cave, we're greeted by a strange sight. A line of Halves and humans has formed in the center of the space. Camike sits on the ground, tending to all of the injured, both human and Halve.

"I don't want a Halve touching my people," Tut says, striding forward to pull his men out of line.

"Our best healer died from the Burn months ago." Valior puts a hand on Tut's arm to stop him. "Her presence is more than welcome."

While Camike stitches small wounds on the Banished and tends burns on the Halves who spent too long on the Outside, Jarosh tells jokes. He says the first part of the joke in the human language and then does his best to translate it into Halve-speak. The humans roar with approval at his witty punchlines and bawdy commentary. The Halves are laughing for a different reason. Jarosh has gotten the basic phrases of their language, but nothing more complex. Thus, *What happens when two Halves walk into a cave* becomes *When two Halves ate me, I sang sweetly.*

Camike shakes her head, smiling up at Jarosh as she works. It only encourages him.

There's something so simple and beautiful about the way they interact with each other. I don't even realize I'm looking for Wade until I find his golden eyes already on me. In the amount of time it takes for our stares to connect, black eyes and gold, my heart has begun to race. I feel a pull toward him, as real as the one I have with the Zeroes.

Wade closes the distance between us, and I know he's sharing my thoughts.

When he's beside me, he reaches down and our fingers interlace. I turn to face him, not knowing quite what to say, just knowing I want to be near to him.

The spell is broken when Dellin, her arms laden down with several quivers' worth of arrows, passes by.

"Where's Ry?" Wade asks her.

*She doesn't know* everything *about Ry*, I want to say, but I keep my mouth shut.

Dellin pauses. It's difficult to tell her expression with the dirt covering her face, but her eyes dart to our interlocking hands. I step away from Wade.

"She'll be back before high day," is all she says.

"What's that supposed to mean?" I demand.

"There's something she had to figure out," Dellin replies.

Wade frowns. "You mean she needed to figure out something with the other archers?"

Dellin shrugs. "I don't think it has anything to do with the battle."

Wade and I exchange a look.

"It couldn't wait?" Wade presses. "What in the sun could be so urgent she would need to take off? *Again?*"

Dellin's dirty, chapped lips quirk. She seems to be enjoying knowing something about Ry we don't.

There's a commotion behind us when one of the Banished holds up a bottle that makes the others cheer.

"I'm not interested in your riddles," I tell Dellin as I turn back to face her.

But she's already vanished.

"Strange girl," Wade comments.

# CHAPTER 7

Well, look who decided to show up!"

Jarosh, who has managed to extricate himself from the crowd of Halves and humans surrounding him, greets me.

I shake my head. Only Jarosh could maintain his perpetual grin even after everything that's happened. When I look closer, though, I see the sleeve of his cloak is torn and he's sagging with exhaustion.

It doesn't stop him from slinging an arm over my shoulder and giving me a playful wink. "I was beginning to think you and Ry got cold feet about the battle and were hiding out somewhere."

"Hardly." Ry, her hair looking even more frazzled than usual, appears out of nowhere and scowls at Jarosh. She peels his hand off me.

"Where in the sun have you been?" I ask her.

She gives me a shake of her head as if to say *not now.*

Fury lances through me. "How dare you disappear…again…without telling anyone," I hiss.

"I did tell someone," she whispers back, her gaze immediately finding Dellin in the crowd of people and Halves.

I tell myself my anger at Ry has nothing to do with the fact that, once again, she confided in Dellin about where she was going instead of me.

Camike joins our group, giving me an excuse to turn my back on Ry. She's carrying a basket filled with bandages. Her black eyes go straight to Jarosh, and she smiles at him.

"Hello, Halve Saver," Camike says when she notices me. She speaks with a slight lilt but uses the humans' language almost flawlessly. "Apologize I could not save humans."

I can't even think of those disintegrating masses as humans. Even though my brain knows they were once Valior's people, all I can see are those charred, melting things.

A tug on my arm makes me turn back to Ry.

In a whisper only I can hear, she says, "We need to find Wade and Dayne. I'm afraid I'm going to lose this stupid seed. Maybe one of them will know something about it, or at least what we should do with it."

*Jadem's seed.* With everything that's happened, I almost forgot about it.

"Fine," I say. "But later, you're going to tell me where you keep disappearing to."

Ry swallows, but she nods. Dellin, probably sensing how much I don't want her around right now, tags along.

We find Dayne first. I don't know why seeing him fills me with so much emotion. Maybe it's because of everything I witnessed on the Outside, my frustration at the council, my irritation at Ry, or all of them together. Or maybe it's because seeing my brother here, with mere days before the greatest battle of our lives, is like finding water after wandering the Wild Lands at highest day. I throw my arms around him.

"Mer," he pats my arm, "Mer, you're crushing me."

"Sorry!" I let go and step back.

It's then that I notice my brother's haggard look. Even in the dim light of the tunnel, I can see the dark, purplish shadows rimming his eyes. Deep lines crease his forehead, and his cheeks are hollow with a thinness that is almost skeletal.

"Don't you worry about me, little sis," Dayne says, reading the concern on my face. "Although," his expression sours, "you could have told me you ordered your army of beasts to follow me all the way here."

"That must have been a sight," Ry snorts.

"And you," my brother rounds on her. "What were you thinking, disappearing like that?"

Ry's grin falters under my brother's glare, and I feel more satisfaction than I should. Her fingers fumble for the pouch tied to her belt. "I come bearing a gift. Or, I think, maybe…."

"There you are." Wade's baritone seems to fill the entire tunnel.

"Oh good, you're here." Ry smiles at him like nothing's amiss.

Wade gives her a glare of his own. "What was so important you had to steal Wokee's hyenair and make us all worry about you?"

"You were worried? About me?" Ry bats her eyes. "Aww, that's so sweet."

Wade rolls his beautiful eyes at her.

As if the mention of his name has summoned him, Wokee comes skipping into the tunnel.

"You're back!" he squeals. He stops mid-stride, clears his throat, and says in a much lower, more forced tone, "I mean, you're back."

I make myself keep a straight face. Dayne's lip twitches, and I know he's struggling to do the same.

"Well, before you disappear again," Wade narrows his eyes at Ry and Dellin, "I may as well tell you that the council is going to need your help during the battle."

"'Course," Ry says. "You going to have us ride Vlaz while we pick off the Dusker archers?"

She and Wade exchange a knowing grin. All of their earlier tension disappears.

"Wait," Dellin holds up a slender hand. "I don't go inside the iron gate."

Wade frowns. "Technically, you'll be above it, not inside."

"I don't think it's such a good idea to have Dellin be part of this, either," I say.

Dellin gives me a look that says she doesn't appreciate my opinion.

"Why not?" Wade looks perplexed. "It makes sense to have our best archers protecting you and the Zeroes."

"Because," I say, "Dellin's a—"

Ry slaps her hand over my mouth, stopping me from saying more. She gives me a pleading look before dropping her hand.

Ry turns back to Wade. "We'll do it. Not a problem."

Dellin is shaking her head back and forth. "I can't get that close."

Ry turns to Dellin. "Can't, or won't?" She fists her hands on her hips.

"Ry, you don't understand," Dellin pleads.

"I think I understand perfectly." Ry frowns. "You know, I thought you were brave for staying away from them. But now, I'm starting to think you're just scared."

Dellin doesn't back down. "You have no idea what they'd do if they found me."

Ry scoffs as she thrusts her tattooed hand in front of Dellin. "I've got a pretty good idea, and guess what? It's the same risk we all take by going in there. The only difference is the rest of us aren't whining about it."

"It would be different for me," Dellin says, her voice meek in a way I've never heard it before.

If I didn't dislike Dellin so much, I'd feel sorry for her.

Ry shoves her curls off her face. "For sun's sake, Dellin. Pick a side! I'd even forgive you if you didn't choose mine. But you have to pick something. You have to care."

"I don't want to remember!" Dellin yells.

An awkward silence follows. Her outburst makes no sense in the context of their argument, but I remember months ago when Dellin awoke from a dream shouting those same words. I wonder what she means by them, but from one look at Ry's face, I can tell she's as confused as the rest of us.

Dellin leans closer to Ry. "You'd think, after everything I've told you, after everything I've helped you figure out, my loyalties shouldn't need to be questioned."

A long silence follows. The two of them glare at each other as the rest of us shift awkwardly on our feet.

"I guess I'll just go, then," Dellin says, her perfect postured drooping.

"I think that would be a good idea," Ry replies without looking at her.

Dellin has only made it a couple of steps when she turns back. "I'm not a coward," she says, and this time, she addresses all of us. "I'll do it. I'll help take out their archers."

"Um, thanks," Wade says, when it's clear Ry isn't going to say anything else. "I think."

Ry keeps her back turned until Dellin has gone.

"Well, that was weird," Wade says. He scratches his head. "What a crazy."

"You stay out of it!" Ry snaps.

It's only then that I see her eyes are watering.

"Sorry?" Wade looks at Ry, and then at me, confusion furrowing his brow.

"Don't worry, Ry." Wokee takes her hand. "Girls are always getting emotional about something."

"Are you some kind of expert on girls now?" I ask him.

Wokee wrinkles his nose and sticks his tongue out at me.

"Rylin," Dayne says. "What was it you needed to tell us?"

My brother snaps us all back to the reason Ry gathered us in the first place.

"Oh, right." Ry sniffs, straightens her shoulders, and takes the small wooden box out of her pocket and opens it.

Golden light spills from the seed. I don't know if it's my imagination, but the cave we're in feels warmer than it had been a second ago.

Wade, Dayne, and Wokee lean in as Ry tells them about Jadem's note. They each take their turn holding the box and examining the seed. Wokee holds it the longest. We all wait while he pinches the seed between his fingers, rolls it around on his palm, sniffs it, and even touches the edge of it with his tongue. After all the time he spent with Aunt Jadem in the orchards of Solis, he has a better chance at recognizing this seed than the rest of us.

"I've never seen anything like this before," Wokee finally declares, putting the seed back into its box. "Or felt a seedling that radiated its own heat." He continues to stare at it in awe.

My hopes sink. Whatever answers this little seed might hold about my aunt and what she had planned for the Solguards, I'm not going to learn them today.

"I can't believe a little seed could be as important as Jadem says." Wade narrows his gaze as he stares at it. "The difference between life and death? She must not have had much confidence in my ability to lead her army."

"I'm more curious about the last parts," Dayne says, scanning the note again. "An evil she helped bring about? And what is all that about not telling me or Hemera?"

"Because she knew if we went to the Crystal Caves, we'd find the letter our mother left for me," I say.

Dayne gives me a sharp look. "What does our mother have to do with any of this?"

I realize I don't want to talk about this in front of the others. It feels…private…a family matter. "Tell you later," I mumble.

"Well, we can't do anything with the seed now," Wade says in the uncomfortable silence that follows. "We better find somewhere to put it where it won't get lost or destroyed."

"I can hold onto it," Wokee offers.

The rest of us exchange a look. I can tell we're all having the same misgivings. Wokee means well, but he's still just a kid. He has a short attention span and he's messy, always leaving his belongings strewn about. And yet, the way he tended the plants at Tanguro was anything but careless.

"Alright," I say, speaking for all of us. "Keep it safe until we can figure out what to do with it."

Wokee takes the box from Ry, handling it as carefully as he would a baby bird. His chest is puffed out with pride at this responsibility. "If anyone can figure out what this does, it'll be me," Wokee says, pocketing the small box.

"Humble as always," Dayne notes, ruffling Wokee's hair. His smile fades as he says, "Jadem would be proud of you."

Wokee ducks his head. To him, there could be no greater compliment.

Ry and Wade make their excuses and follow Wokee out of the cave, leaving Dayne and me alone.

"What's happened, Hemera?" my brother asks as soon as the others are out of earshot.

Instead of answering, I fish out our mother's letter and hand it to him. I watch the expressions on my brother's face as he reads. His emotions go from shock, to disbelief, to anger in the same way mine did. When he's finished, his hands drop to his sides. The script tree bark flutters to the ground. I bend to pick it up.

"Hemera, I didn't know," Dayne says, his voice rough. "I swear I would have told you if I did."

"I know." My throat burns. I clench my fists to keep from breaking down again.

"I knew my father was a Solguard and that our mother helped him, but I thought—I assumed—when she married the Captain she was done with all of that." Dayne shakes his head. "I would have expected something like this from the Captain, but never from our mother."

"That's what I thought, too." I reach for my mother's necklace the way I always do when I need comfort, and then release it just as quickly. She lied to me. She betrayed me.

I stare at the recipe—ingredients for making me.

"I'm sorry, Mer," Dayne says. "I'm so sorry."

"She was hoping to convince the Captain to give up his allegiance to the Duskers and help the Solguards." My voice is dull, and I feel as defeated as I sound.

"This is why I didn't want to be a Solguard anymore." Dayne's voice is almost a growl. "They're willing to sacrifice anything…anyone. For all they value freedom, they don't give a damn about whose lives they ruin along the way."

At whatever look is on my face, Dayne quickly clarifies, "Not that I would have you any other way, little sis."

I give him a small smile.

"So, what do we do, now that we know?" Dayne asks.

I shrug. "What can we do? This doesn't change anything, really," I say.

*Liar*, my heart screams. Learning what my mother did changes everything.

"Dayne," I say, my voice hesitant. "Do you think Aunt Jadem knew about this…about our mother turning me into a Bisecter on purpose?"

Dayne's lips are pursed, and I can tell he's already considered this question.

"Yes, I would imagine she did."

He meets my gaze, and I know we're having the same thought. More betrayal from the ones who were supposed to love us the most.

"If I had to guess," Dayne continues, "I'd say Jadem knew our mother wrote the letter, but didn't know exactly where in the Crystal Caves she'd hidden it. That would explain why Jadem didn't want to risk either of us going there and finding the letter for ourselves."

I nod as my brother confirms what I suspected.

"Why wouldn't Aunt Jadem have just told me?" The question I've been asking myself over and over again spills from my lips.

Dayne looks helpless, like he's searching for the right words to make this better for me, even though he knows there's nothing to say.

My shoulders slump. "Maybe Jadem just didn't want me to get hurt." Even as I say the words, a voice in my head tells me there must be more to it than that.

"I'll never lie to you," Dayne promises. "You'll never have to worry about me keeping secrets from you. I won't do it."

I'm not prepared for the flood of emotions his words cause me. My eyes smart, and then the tears start to fall.

"Come here, little sis." Dayne wraps his arms around me as my body shakes with silent sobs.

He holds me without speaking until I'm exhausted and my tears are spent.

"Thank you," I whisper, hugging him back.

# CHAPTER 8

I don't need to ask Valior where the Zeroes are being kept. I simply have to follow the incessant tug on my heart. It takes me deep into the settlement, until I can no longer hear the clank of weapons or the shouts of men.

Relief hits me like a tidal wave when I push aside the burlap curtain draped over the door and step into the Zeroes' quarters.

It's obvious from their bloodstained lips and the chunks of meat still in their bare hands that the Zeroes were in the middle of their meal before I arrived. But every one of them abandons their food when I walk through the doorway.

The Zeroes scent the air, their slitted nostrils opening and closing as their heads swivel toward me. They know me, their creator. Their master.

I know I should feel fear at the sight of them. Even the smallest among them is taller even than Brogut. Their black eyes are emotionless and unblinking, somehow more pitiless than mine or the Halves'. A scythe rests against the wall behind each Zero within arm's reach. The long, curved metal blades are polished to gleaming perfection.

Their clothes, made out of linked metal chains, jingle with their every movement and give them an otherworldly appearance. My father was right to have them wear these. Even the hardened Dusker soldiers will be afraid when my Zeroes march up to the iron gate.

This is not a ragtag bunch like the Banished and Halves scurrying around in the settlement's other caves. This is an army.

Just looking at them makes me feel powerful. A smile curves my lips at the thought of marching up to Malarusk's iron gate with the Zeroes at my back.

*Crowe won't know what's coming for her.*

Still, something feels strange as I walk all the way into the cave. It's like my expectations were too high, which is making our reunion somewhat of a letdown. The flood of power I usually feel in the Zeroes' presence seems less strong than I remember.

*I must just be getting used to the bond.*

"You're back."

I jump. My attention had been so wholly on the Zeroes that I hadn't even known my father was in the cave.

"Thanks for feeding them." I nod at the Zeroes, who are now back to devouring the bloody meat.

I expect my father to criticize me for not attending to my duties, for being so irresponsible that I would disappear without caring for the creatures who share my blood. But he doesn't.

"It was my pleasure," is all he says.

My father is fiddling with something on the other side of the cave. I hear clinking as he bundles up what must be the knives he used to cut the Zeroes' meat. When he comes into view, he's winding a bandage around the wound on his arm, the one that's been there for weeks. Fresh blood leaks out from beneath the bandage.

"Do you want Camike to take a look at that?" I ask him.

"It isn't deep." My father waves his hand, dismissing my concern.

"I would have thought as a healer you'd be able to stitch it up yourself," I tell him.

My father's lip quirks. "That was many years ago. It seems I have lost my touch."

I stare at my father in open disbelief. "Did you just admit a weakness?"

In response, my father just smiles.

I clear my throat. For a moment, I had forgotten my father is my enemy. I almost forgot what he did to Dayne and to our mother.

*Our mother.* A complicated array of emotions passes through me.

"When did you start experimenting on people and Halves?" I ask, trying to sound nonchalant.

My father gives me a *what relevance does this question have* look, but he says, "I began my experiments after I discovered what you were. I began to wonder whether I could replicate the process."

"But did you think about it before I was born?" I press. "Did you discuss it with anyone? Like my mother?"

"No, and no." My father is still giving me that quizzical look. "I loved your mother, but we both had our secrets. I didn't trust her. Why are you asking?"

I search my father's face but see no lie. The last shred of hope I had, that my father had somehow influenced my mother—forced her even—to experiment on her own body to make me, wisps away. My father has done monstrous things, but he didn't give my mother the idea to make me. That came from her alone.

My disappointment flares again. Betrayal at the woman I thought I knew. Anger at the way that, even now, I'm doubting her own words and searching for a way to exonerate her.

"No reason," I mumble.

My father gives me a hard, appraising stare.

"Hemera, did something happen?"

I try one more time. "Are you sure you never wrote down your ideas about how to make…me…before I was born?"

*Please let all this have been his idea. Please let my mother have been the person who told me stories and protected me from the other Dwellers. Please let my mother have been only that person.*

"Had it crossed my mind, I might have." My father seems to be choosing his words carefully, his keen eyes never leaving my face. "But it did not."

I turn away so he can't see the disappointment on my face. "I should probably take the Zeroes out to train now."

I turn all of my attention on the Zeroes. Their black eyes never stray far from me as they await my order. My hand gestures have become second-nature with them. I've learned to anticipate the commands the Zeroes will understand and how to reframe the ones they won't. We've developed our own language. So when I flick my index finger, there is hardly a second's lapse before the Zeroes are picking up their scythes and congregating around me.

I lead them out into the main tunnel, wondering whether I should try to find a more secluded path to bring them to the Outside so they won't terrify everyone else in the compound. I decide that if the others are going to fight alongside my army, they may as well get used to seeing the Zeroes.

I look up and see Dayne striding down the tunnel toward me. He's carrying a lute—a replacement for the one he had to abandon outside Malarusk. His expression is stormy.

"You shouldn't spend time with the Captain alone," he tells me. "He's no less slippery now than he was when we were in his Lair."

"I'm fine," I try to reassure my brother. "He doesn't want to hurt me, and he couldn't even if he wanted to."

Dayne's hard, disapproving stare rakes over the Zeroes before settling on me. "Are you sure you're alright?" he asks. "Did the Captain do anything? Say anything?"

The look on my brother's face promises death to my father if he's hurt me. I feel a flood of gratitude for his protectiveness, even if I don't need it.

I meet Dayne's gaze. "I thought maybe he forced our mother to do what she did to me." I shake my head. "But he didn't. It was all her."

Dayne's anger fades, and his gaze softens.

"I know how much she loved you. I believe what she said in her letter, about regretting what she'd done," Dayne says. "But she was wrong. She was so wrong." My brother's expression darkens as he stares in the direction of the Zeroes' cave.

"I think he might be starting to change," I say, referring to my father. I know the words are those of a naïve child, but I don't try to take them back.

My father has seemed different since he rescued us from Malarusk. He's still the same person, but he's less intense, somehow. It's like he's trying to help me with the Zeroes to make up for everything else he's done.

"Don't forget who he is, Hemera," Dayne says as though he's reading my thoughts. "He'll use your trust to manipulate and control you." His hands clench around his lute like he's trying to strangle it. "We should kill him now, before we leave for Malarusk."

I know it's what we talked about, why we searched for him for months, but the idea of murdering my father doesn't hold the appeal it once did.

"I don't think that's such a good idea," I say.

Dayne's eyes narrow.

"I just think it's possible he's changed. Or maybe things were never that simple. We thought our mother was some kind of hero who was accidentally sprayed by Halve blood when she was trying to rescue children…."

Dayne's grip on my arm is like iron. "People don't change." He bites out each word. "Our mother might not be all we thought she was, but that doesn't mean the Captain is trustworthy."

"All I'm saying is that things are more complicated now," I persist.

Dayne makes a frustrated sound. "Look around you, little sis. These *creatures* aren't your pets. Don't for one second think the Captain will so easily relinquish control of them."

"He isn't your father. Maybe you don't know him as well as you think you do."

Dayne's jaw goes slack. I know I should be sorry for what I just said, but I'm not.

My brother hates the Zeroes, and he despises my father even more. He isn't thinking clearly. Instead of apologizing to Dayne, I step away from him and closer to my Zeroes.

"These Zeroes were designed by the Captain, made by him, for his own purposes," Dayne hisses.

"They weren't made by him at all," I argue, my voice rising. "*I* made them. *I* control them."

I'm breathing faster now. The Zeroes feel my anger and their own muscles contract, readying to spring. I force myself to calm down.

"People can change," I say again.

Dayne looks at me for a long moment. "I guess they can."

He turns and walks away.

* * *

There's a hollow feeling in my chest as I march the Zeroes up the tunnel to the Outside. The Banished who haven't yet seen my army gasp. Those who have stare with wide eyes. Their reactions make me stand a little straighter.

This is the army that's going to bring down Malarusk. And they answer to me.

Out in the blistering sunlight, I force all thoughts out of my head except for the task at hand. The Zeroes know when I'm distracted, and it confuses their own thoughts. I can't afford to have their understanding muddled during the battle, and I can't be unfocused now.

I need to know I can deliver on my promise to the council. *One or two minutes to take down the iron gate*, I'd told them. I can't wait to see Tut's face when the Zeroes demolish it in half the time.

The Zeroes shift on their feet as they sense my rising adrenaline.

Our entire attack on Malarusk hinges on one assumption: the Zeroes will be able to break down the iron gate. I don't doubt their strength, but I'm not willing to bring the Solguards, Banished, and Halves to the Duskers' doorstep until I'm satisfied the Zeroes can do what I've promised.

I look around, searching for something that will give the Zeroes a challenge. I point at the scraggy hills in the distance that mark the border between the Banished Lands and the Dusker Territory. They're the closest thing we have to Malarusk's impenetrable iron gate.

"Make a hole through the hills." I point in their direction, miming a chopping motion.

This used to make me feel stupid, like a child playing a game. But I've seen what the Zeroes can do. I've felt the surge of our bond every time they carry out one of my commands…felt the spike in my own strength. It doesn't feel stupid anymore.

53

The ground rumbles as the Zeroes cross the stretch of land in a blur. Their scythes are nothing more than blinding flecks of metal as they streak over the dry land.

I see the explosion of dust and rock fragments as the Zeroes barrel through the stone. They use their scythes and bare hands to carve a path straight through the hills. I would be worried about jagged stones tearing at their skin, but I can feel through the bond that none of them are hurt.

When Brogut attacked one of my Zeroes, I felt its pain like it was my own. I now know that if any of the Zeroes are injured, I'll feel it, too. All I sense from my army is their single-minded need to do what their master has commanded.

And I feel their rage. It's always simmering just beneath the surface, waiting to be unleashed.

*You won't have to wait much longer*, I think.

As I watch the Zeroes get farther away, as I feel the distance pull at our connection, my satisfaction sours. What if they keep running? What if they don't come back?

From here, I can see the new path cutting through the rocky hills that hadn't existed mere minutes ago. I turn my attention on the bond, tugging on the invisible line between us.

I don't breathe again until the Zeroes are back. They make a ring around me with barely any space between them. Their sniffing, which used to send shivers of dread down my spine, is a comforting reminder that they know me, can sense me. It reminds us both I'm their master. They belong to me.

"They're not even winded," a voice observes.

I hadn't heard or seen my father, hadn't even known he was standing right behind me. I was so intent on the Zeroes I didn't notice a small crowd of Solguards and Banished had formed. They're applauding now, their awe apparent on their faces.

*Good*, I think with satisfaction. They'll tell the others what they've seen. It might even help wipe away the frightened expressions I've seen on so many of the Banished people's faces. After seeing what the Zeroes can do, there's no one who can say our army doesn't stand a chance against the Duskers.

It's our enemy who should be afraid of us.

"They destroyed those hills like they were nothing," Wokee says. He stands on the edge of the group of Solguards, but he isn't applauding with the rest of them. His eyes have a faraway look. "It's like when the Duskers destroyed the Tanguro orchards."

I crouch down in front of him.

"I'm so sorry about your orchards," I say, remembering how lovingly he had tended to every one of the trees.

Wokee nods slowly. "They were just trees," he says. "I'll grow new ones."

He lets me draw him into a hug. "Yes, you will," I tell him.

"Probably best to let the Zeroes rest up before the battle," my father says after I've released Wokee and stood back up. "They've been tested enough."

As I turn to lead the Zeroes back into the settlement, Vlaz, shaggy coat dripping with water from a recent swim, bounds up to us. At first, I assume he's coming to greet Wokee and me. But as he gets closer, I realize his hackles are raised and his fangs are bared. He's coming at us too fast.

My only thought is to protect Wokee. I use my body to shield his as the enormous hyenair comes to a skidding stop. It's not us he's paying attention to, though; it's the Zeroes. He lowers his head and hunches his massive shoulders, snarling. He's never looked more fearsome.

"Vlaz!" Wokee speaks in a sharp voice as he claps his gloved hands together.

I try to stop him, but Wokee has already ducked out from behind me and is approaching Vlaz.

The sound of Wokee's voice distracts Vlaz enough for me to order the Zeroes back into the tunnel. As soon as the last one has disappeared, Vlaz relaxes. His fur settles back into place and his jagged fangs fold back into his lips. Vlaz gives Wokee and me each a slobbery lick.

"Silly boy," Wokee says, ruffling the fur on the hyenair's leg.

"What's gotten into him?" I ask.

Wokee shrugs. "He doesn't like the Zeroes. Maybe their metal clothes scare him."

I look back at Vlaz once before following after the Zeroes. Before my foot reaches the first step down into the compound, my father stops me.

"If you'd like," he says, "I can give the Zeroes their high day feeding. That way you can get some rest, too. You won't be any good to them if you're exhausted."

I try to remember the last time I had a decent high day's sleep. I can't.

I've been too afraid to sleep. Every time I close my eyes, I see that little Dusker girl my Zeroes slaughtered. The girl had been at the back of a company of Duskers climbing up to Darkness Peak. I hadn't known there was a child in their company until it was too late. Now, whenever I try to rest, I see her twisted neck and glassy gray eyes.

I don't have time to sleep now, anyway. As soon as it's high day, I have another task. I need to go to Malarusk and find some answers for the council about the deadly black sap.

"That'd be great," I tell my father.

"Don't worry," he says. "I'll make sure they're looked after."

# CHAPTER 9

When it's high day and the caves are filled with sleeping people, I leave the compound. The usual sense of peace I feel at being alone on the Outside during high day has been replaced by anxiety at being separated from the Zeroes. I would have brought them with me, but they can only stand the high day sun for a few minutes at most. I don't want to take the chance of any of them getting the Burn.

I run along the path the Zeroes blazed through the hills and through the open stretch of land that separates the Banished lands from the Dusker territory.

Without the Dusker archers positioned in the lookouts, I can walk right up to the iron gate. A wave of sadness hits me with so much force I can't breathe. This is the place where I watched the gate close with Aunt Jadem on the wrong side. This is where I peered through the space between the gate's hinges and watched Aunt Jadem and Crowe fight. This is where I saw my aunt fall.

I remind myself of why I'm here to keep my anger and heartache at bay. *Figure out the black substance. Report back to the council. Make a plan to kill them all.*

The cranks that push the gate outward are on the other side, and the metal is too tall and smooth to climb. The gate is positioned between two tall, unscalable and impenetrable mountains that stretch around the Duskers' territory on either side.

The empty lookouts cut into the mountain are a constant reminder of the crossbows that will be pointed straight at our army when we attack during low day.

I pick up my pace, following the length of the mountains that ring the compound. It would take any normal person days of traveling to cover this distance, and if there are any travel caves in this barren land, only the Duskers know about them. For everyone except me, the only way into Malarusk is through the front gate.

Hours later, when I make it to the other side of the mountain, the landscape changes. Where there had been only arid, desert land before, my boots now sink into mud and splash through puddles. There are new streams and rivulets leading to Malarusk, the result of the Duskers re-coursing the Banished River.

I take care to disguise my footprints. If the Duskers get even a hint of suspicion that an outsider has been in their territory, they'll have more reason to send out scouts to investigate. If they discover what we're up to, we'll be defeated before the battle even begins.

There is a thick stone wall, easily a dozen feet tall and as many wide, bordering this side of the citadel that closes the gap left by the two mountain ranges. Seeing the way the mountains frame Malarusk, it really is possible to believe this place was created by the Dark God. I know the more logical explanation is that the Duskers used the natural barrier of the mountains to build their underground citadel, but it doesn't stop the feeling of awe and foreboding that grips me in its presence.

Even though it's high day, a creepiness surrounds this place. I take care to quiet my steps. I feel like there are enemy eyes on me, even though I know there aren't.

As I slosh through the mud, a thought bothers me. The over-saturated ground must be seeping down into the citadel's caves below. This much water flowing into their living space is dangerous. It could weaken walls and support beams, and even make the dirt-packed floors of the tunnels collapse.

If all the Duskers wanted was to redirect the Banished River, they could have made it flow to somewhere else in their territory. But they didn't. They directed the water right to the citadel, which means they must want all of this water here for some reason.

The smaller rivulets converge in a deep stream that is moving with a swift current. I follow the stream to the place where it dips under the stone wall.

I pull off my silk cloak and boots, even as every part of me screams a warning to run in the opposite direction.

The last time I was in Malarusk, the wormkill almost devoured me. The last time I was here, I saw Crowe break my aunt's neck.

*Breathe, Hemera.*

I step into the stream before I can think better of it and am immediately in water up to my chest. Taking a deep breath, I sink under the water and let the current carry me under the stone wall and into the compound.

I bob back to the surface in darkness. I'm inside Malarusk.

There are no torches, and it's impossible to see. I strain my ears for any sign of Duskers, but I hear nothing except for the gurgling of the water.

I'm starting to wonder if this stream is leading me nowhere when I smell the now-familiar acrid scent of the black residue. My eyes begin to water.

*So close.* I'm so close to seeing the secret of the Duskers' new weapon.

The stream gets shallow enough for me to stand. It narrows until it ends altogether, and I'm left with no other choice than to slosh forward barefoot through the mud.

A dozen more steps bring me to a tunnel lit with torches spaced along the wall. Dayne and Wade would tell me to get out of here, but I can sense how close I am to the Duskers' weapon. I can't turn back now.

I reach the final torch and suck in my breath. Whatever I had been expecting—a cave full of armed guards, a prison full of slaves, Crowe's sword—it wasn't this.

I'm looking into a cave bigger and loftier than even the dining cave in Solis. At first glance, it appears empty. When I look closer, though, I realize it isn't empty at all.

I didn't see them at first because their dark color blends in with the earthen walls of the cave. But that smell, the acrid, stinging smell of the black substance, is everywhere. When my eyes finally adjust to the dim light, I see the cave is filled…with trees. Their top branches brush the cave's ceiling, more than a dozen feet overhead. And they're black.

I've never seen anything like it.

My father, even with all of his experiments back in the Subterrane, only managed to grow plants on the Outside. Jadem was the most talented botanist I'd ever met, but she still needed to build her caves in a way that allowed sunlight to reach the plants growing within. She also grew flowers and vines; nothing so big as trees.

And not just any trees. *Black* trees...as black as my eyes.

They're tall and thin, with gnarled branches spidering out in every direction. There are no leaves or buds. If it weren't for the roots popping out of the ground, I would think these trees were dead.

As I stare at the rows of trees, I realize there's a complicated irrigation system down here. All the water dripping down from the walls and flowing through the tunnels meets in this one cave.

Troughs are cut into the earth down each row of trees, directing the flow of water. A steady stream is deposited at each clump of tangled, black roots.

This observation stops me cold. *This* is why the Duskers stole the Banished River...to feed this underground orchard of black trees.

I walk down one of the rows. The trees go even farther back than I'd thought. I count more than one-hundred rows of the orderly black trees before I reach the far end of the cave. There, I stop and stare up at one of them.

Gnarled branches snake out in every direction. Sticky-looking, black sap oozes from between the bark's grooves. It looks like the tree is bleeding.

"What in the sun is going on down here?" I wonder out loud.

"Oh, you'll find nothing of the sun down here," a voice replies.

My blood goes cold.

"I figured you'd make an appearance one of these high days," the voice continues.

"Who are you?" I demand, forcing down my panic. "Show yourself!"

Even though I've never seen him before, I know the man coming down the path toward me. The cloak of his hood is thrown back, and with it, the mask that usually covers all Duskers' faces.

The man's perfect, unscarred face is on full display. His skin is a flawless white, like he's carved from marble rather than made of flesh and bones. His emerald eyes, too bright in the lantern light, are fixed on me.

All my fear vanishes. I stare at the man before me with loathing.

"Hendrix."

Crowe's second-in-command raises an eyebrow. "I didn't realize we were on a first-name basis." His lips quirk in a smile that doesn't meet his eyes. "Although I do believe you were acquainted with someone who you *thought* was me."

The first time we infiltrated Malarusk, it was to capture Hendrix and use him as leverage over Crowe. Our failure was the reason Aunt Jadem had nothing to bargain with, and why Crowe was able to kill her. I curl my fists and step toward him.

"Oh, I wouldn't do that."

There's a rustle of cloaks, and then at least twenty Duskers holding crossbows converge on us from between different rows of trees. Even amid my growing panic, it doesn't escape me that the Duskers all move carefully to avoid touching any part of the trees.

"What do you want from me?" I demand through clenched teeth.

"All in good time," Hendrix replies, his voice almost lazy.

He stares up at the tree I had been examining.

"We call them Darkness trees," Hendrix says. He looks completely at ease, while every muscle in my body is poised to run. Or fight.

"They need so much water." He sloshes his boot through the muck at his feet.

"What is the purpose of all of this?" I ask.

Hendrix tilts his head up at the trees. "Seeing one of them burn is a sight to behold."

I remember the Banished man who was covered in the black substance, and how he had been screaming something about a fire.

"Are you going to chop down these trees and try to use them to burn up Solis?" I ask.

As soon as the words leave my lips, facts that hadn't made sense before click into place…why the Duskers waited after attacking Tanguro instead of going straight to Solis…why they allowed Banished into their citadel….

They must have needed extra labor to care for all these trees. And later, they'll need their slaves to help transport all the wood to Solis.

"I won't spoil it for you. Better for you to be surprised," Hendrix says. "But I will say this: the darkness is coming."

The way he says it reminds me of the Banished slave's words as he disintegrated before my eyes. It wasn't the words themselves—the Dusker prophecy I've heard all my life—but the way they were said. The words leave Hendrix's lips in the same way now, like a promise that will soon be fulfilled.

I suppress a shudder.

"I'm not in the mood for riddles," I tell him, forcing my voice to come out stronger than I feel. My eyes dart to the Duskers surrounding us. "There must be something else you want from me aside from choking me with the stench of these trees."

"Strong *and* clever." Hendrix smirks.

I don't say anything. I refuse to give him the satisfaction of knowing how unnerved I am.

"Crowe has this brilliant way about her," he continues, staring up at the gnarled branches of the black tree. "She always manages to accomplish her goals in half as many actions as it would take the rest of us."

I don't say anything, unsure of where he's going with this.

"Take our problem with watering the trees, for instance. They needed more water than the Darkness River could provide. I suggested using our own soldiers to cart in buckets from other water sources. What other choice did we have, after all?"

Hendrix doesn't wait for my answer before continuing. "Crowe came up with the idea of re-coursing the Banished River. It took more time and labor, so the rest of us were skeptical. But look at what she accomplished in the end." He fixes his green eyes on me. "The Darkness trees grew, and the Banished and Halves will destroy themselves without us ever needing to set foot inside their filthy settlements.

"The Banished willingly came to us for our protection. Their labor, along with our new water source, was all we needed to grow the trees."

I had guessed as much about the river.

"How are you going to use these trees against us?" I ask.

Hendrix seems in the mood to talk, and I need answers.

"Two birds, one stone," Hendrix says. "Just like what she's doing with you."

I start. "Me?"

"Yes." Hendrix's voice is a calm that makes goosebumps race up my arms. "If it had been up to me, I would have killed you months ago. Oh, it wouldn't have been quick." His gaze narrows, all traces of mirth gone. "I might have thrown you to the wormkill and let you try your luck against it a second time. Or, I might have flogged you until every drop of brown blood drained out of your body." He laughs a little. "Or, I might have cut out your still-beating heart while you screamed for mercy."

Hendrix's voice is soft, almost serene, as he lists the ways he's thought about murdering me.

I look at Hendrix, and for the first time, I realize why his eyes make me so uncomfortable. It's not because of their almost luminescent color, or even the fact that he's the second-most-powerful Dusker. It's the raw hatred in them. He looks at me the way I know I'll look at Crowe when I face her. It's a hatred that goes beyond the fact that I'm a Bisecter. It even goes deeper than the black swirls on my hand that announce to the world I'm a Solguard. It's something more visceral, something darker, than any of that.

Sweat slithers down my spine.

He continues, "There were a thousand ways I could have done it. I would have made sure you suffered for every moment of the rest of your miserable life. And yet, it never would have been even half of what we've suffered."

He says this last part quietly, like he's talking to himself. When he looks at me, the pure loathing in his eyes is like a promise of things to come.

"You've suffered?" a short bark of laughter escapes from me. "Please, tell me all about how *you've* suffered, when the Duskers are the ones who set the Halves and Banished at war with each other."

*Tell me how you've suffered when you're the reason my aunt is dead.*

"The Dark God has given the Duskers dominion over all," Hendrix hisses. "You are the one who spat in his face by taking away his child."

I scoff. "If you think all Duskers are children of the Dark God, then I've killed *many* of his children. I could kill you right now, if I wanted."

Hendrix smirks. "If you kill me," he says, his face the hard mask of a Dusker once again, "you'll never see the outside of this cave."

He flicks his hand, and I hear the telltale click of arrows being fitted into crossbows.

I go still.

"Well, what are you waiting for?" Hendrix asks, his voice a deadly quiet. "You may leave, for now."

"You're going to let me go, just like that?"

I don't believe him for a second.

"When she's ready for you, you'll come to her. You'll come like a fish on a line…with no other choice or path."

My heart takes an involuntary leap. There's no question who he means by *she*.

*Crowe.*

With the Dusker archers still pointing their crossbows at me, I retreat down the row of trees. I hunch my shoulders as I go, prepared for the feeling of a crossbow bolt entering my back.

I keep going until I reach the stream. When I turn, I can see the gleam of the archers' arrows as they follow my every move. Hendrix's green eyes are pinpricks in the dark.

"I wonder how long it will take before you're begging for death," Hendrix calls, his voice carrying down the row of trees.

I can still hear his quiet laughter as I plunge into the water and swim for the safety of the Outside.

It's only when I'm on the other side of the stone wall and can no longer feel the Dusker archers' eyes trained on me that I process what just happened.

Hendrix, the Dusker Supreme's second-in-command, let me go.

As I make my way back to the settlement, I can't help but think that whatever the reason Hendrix let me go, I would have been better off if he had just dragged me back to the wormkill.

# CHAPTER 10

The first thing I do when I get back to the settlement is wake up the Banished leaders and assemble the council.

Tut yawns and grumbles all the way to the meeting cave, but as soon as I start to speak, his sits forward on his cushion and stares at me.

No one interrupts as I tell them about the underground orchard of black trees. I recount everything except for the part about Hendrix.

Dayne might actually erupt from so much pent-up fury if he knew how close to danger I'd come. Besides, I still don't know what Hendrix meant by most of what he said. But I have a pretty good idea about what they're planning to do with these trees.

"You think they're going to chop down the trees and use their wood to burn all our settlements?" Liglette asks when I've finished speaking.

"What else could they be planning?" I counter. "We've all see how deadly the trees' sap is. Just imagine how much poison will be released when the wood itself is burned."

"If what Hemera is saying is true," Wade says, "then the Duskers would never have to set foot inside Solis or any of the settlements. They could just set a fire at the tunnel's entrance and sit back while the fumes do their work for them."

I nod in agreement. "I think they've waited this long because they wanted the trees to finish growing."

Everyone is quiet while they digest this news.

Dayne says, "So long as we take the battle to Malarusk before they can attack us, the Duskers won't be able to use the fire or sap from the trees against us. That substance is volatile, and they wouldn't be able to keep it from killing their soldiers right along with ours."

"Right, so we need to attack before they can cut down the trees and come to us," I say. The sense of urgency I feel whenever we discuss the battle is growing stronger by the minute.

Dayne holds up a finger. "But we need to consider the very real possibility that we won't be victorious. And if that happens, all our people who survive will be vulnerable to the Duskers' attack."

No one speaks.

"We need to destroy those trees no matter what else happens," Dayne continues. "That is our highest priority, no matter how the battle goes."

A somber mood descends on the council.

"If the Duskers overpower our army, how are we going to destroy their greatest weapon?" Tut asks.

"I may have a solution to that particular problem," Valior says, "provided one of you can get inside that underground forest."

"I can do it," I say immediately.

"We can come back to that," Wade says, giving me a meaningful look. "Let's discuss how we're getting into the citadel itself."

Valior turns his gaze on me. "Are you certain those creatures of yours will be able to take down the iron gate?"

At the mention of the Zeroes, I reach inside myself for the bond that connects me with each of the hundred. I can feel them, close by, waiting for my return.

"Absolutely," I say without hesitation.

"Tut, how are the weapons coming along?" Valior asks.

From their days of mining gold and other precious metals, the Northern settlers are the only ones equipped to make enough weapons to arm all of the Banished.

"The spears are ready but we'll need at least a week to finish the swords," Tut is saying.

"A week?" I gasp. "We can't—"

"Any benefit you might have from surprising the enemy will be worthless if your soldiers don't have weapons to fight with when you get there," Tut shoots back.

"Young lady," Valior says, making a soothing gesture with his hand.

"Stop calling me that," I grate out.

"You must remember we are not soldiers like the Solguards," he continues. "Our people do not come prepared to fight."

"My people made cutlery and ornaments," Tut grumbles. "Weapons aren't exactly our strong point."

I bite back my retort.

"If the Solguards help your bladesmiths, can you be ready sooner?" Dayne asks.

Tut thinks for a moment and then nods.

"Good," Valior says. "Liglette, what's the report on the pack animals?"

"We have capy pigs and stags for carrying everything we'll need," she replies in her soft, musical voice. "My people can disguise our supplies so the Duskers won't see us coming until we pass over the hills."

"Well, that all sounds good to me." Tut rubs his hands together and stands.

"Where are you going?" I demand. "We still need to talk about coordinating our attack on the tunnels."

"That's not really my business." Tut smiles, his gold teeth on full display. "I'll leave that to those of you who will be fighting to hash out."

I look around at the others, but from their expressions, I can tell they know something I don't.

"You make it sound like you won't be fighting with us," I say.

"Sorry to disappoint you, girl." Tut shrugs like he isn't at all sorry. "I said we'd help the cause, not that we'd be sacrificial lambs."

I can't believe what I'm hearing.

"You said you'd help." My voice is rising. No one else in the room seems surprised, though.

"Tut's skills are not in battle," Valior says. "And I am too old to fight. We will both be staying behind." Unlike Tut, Valior seems aggrieved that he won't be fighting with us.

A choked sound of disgust comes from my throat. Tut is a pathetic coward. He's made no secret of the fact he is only helping us because he thinks we have a real chance at defeating the Duskers, not because he supports our cause.

A tense moment passes.

"I'll be leading the Eastern settlers, and Jarosh will take the Northerners," Dayne says. "It'll be fine."

"Let's discuss the specifics of our attack," Wade says. "Once we get through the iron gate, there are seven entrances that lead down into the citadel itself…."

After what feels like hours of mapping travel routes, assigning tasks, and arguing, it's low day.

My anxiety continues to rise with each passing hour. I know the importance of planning and preparation, but more than a small part of me wants to storm the citadel now and figure out the rest as we go along. My instincts tell me the longer we wait, the worse our chances of success will be.

I'm jittery from going so long without seeing my Zeroes, which is making me more short-tempered. Even though I can sense they're nearby, I know my heart won't ease until I see them standing before me.

I go to check on them as soon as the meeting is over. Th Zeroes are eating again, and my father is watching over them like some kind of sentry. I lose my footing and stumble as I come into the cave.

"You look exhausted, Daughter," my father says. "Get some sleep, or you'll be tripping on the battlefield."

Knowing he's right, I set off in search of somewhere to rest for a few hours.

By some miracle, I discover a cave holding nothing except sacks of flour. The bags are piled high enough to give me some semblance of privacy—a scarce commodity in the Eastern settlement.

It's here that I lay out my bedroll. Exhaustion makes my eyelids heavy and my movements slow. Before sleep can claim me, I take my mother's letter out of my pocket. Every time I move my leg or slip a hand into my pocket, I'm reminded of her confession.

I take my dagger out of my belt and cut a slit in the side of my bedroll. I slide the letter inside, making sure it's secure. On a whim, I go to my pack and fish out the map I've carried around ever since I left Subterrane Harkibel. Even after I discovered my father—and not Brice, as I'd originally thought—had left the map for me, I kept it. I told myself it was only because the marked travel caves might come in handy. I slide the map into my bedroll beside my mother's letter. Then, I lie down.

* * *

The battlefield is covered with dead Solguards, Duskers, and Zeroes. Blood coats the ground. Except the blood isn't like normal human or Halve blood…this blood is pure black.

There's so much of it the ground can't hold it anymore. It starts to gather in pools and continues to rise as more are killed. It laps around my ankles. I can hear the squish of my boots in the blood-soaked earth.

Wokee and the other children are screaming, running. I try to ask them what's happening, but they're too afraid to answer. Wokee points behind me. It's only then that I see the tidal wave of black blood heading straight for us.

"Run!" I tell the children.

They are, as fast as they can, but the blood is outpacing them. It's going to swallow them. I have to fight it—have to stop it—

"Hemera."

The tidal wave is upon us. My eyes fill with blood. I try to scream, but the blood fills my throat, choking me.

"Hemera!"

That voice. *His* voice.

I stop trying to reach the surface. The blood starts to drain away.

"Wade?"

My eyes open.

Instead of the blood-drenched battlefield I expect to see, I'm in a cave. There are no dead bodies, no scattered weapons. There are only bags of flour piled against the wall. And then I remember where I am.

My gaze searches for Wade. I find him kneeling beside me, his golden eyes on fire.

I cover my face with my hands as I start to shake. Wade gathers me in his arms.

"Shh, I'm here, love."

Wade rubs soothing circles onto my back with one hand while he holds me tight with the other.

"I'm here," he says again.

Wade's presence helps, but I can't banish the sick feeling growing deep inside me. My dream felt so real.

"I'm sorry," I whisper. "I know you have more important things to deal with than my bad dream."

Except, it hadn't felt like a dream at all. It still doesn't.

"I don't mind." Wade wraps his arms tighter around me and kisses the top of my head. "It gives me an excuse to do this."

When I look up at him, he's grinning at me.

"You're too good to me," I tell him.

Wade pretends to ponder my words. "I know something that might even things out a bit."

"Oh?" My lips curve into a smile as Wade's warmth banishes my memory of the dream.

"A kiss."

"Just one?" I ask, playing along.

"I guess it'll need to be a good one." Wade sighs in resignation.

I tilt my head up, and our lips meet.

Wade's scent, the press of his body against mine…it's dizzying. Intoxicating. His lips move from my mouth to my neck and track a path across my collarbone.

He pulls back to look at me. The serious look in his golden eyes has been replaced by the mischievous gleam I haven't seen since he took over command of the Solguards.

"We still have a few hours before low day." His hands roam up and down my sides, leaving a line of fire in their wake. "And I intend to make the most of them."

Wade presses me back onto the bedroll, his body covering mine. A shudder runs through me as a lock of his hair brushes against my cheek.

*I love you, Wade.* I almost say the words, feel them on the tip of my tongue. I swallow. My throat is too dry.

Wade and I haven't made each other any promises, but I know he wants us to be together. He had said he was waiting for me. Unbidden, the thought of the kiss I shared with Ry comes into my mind. Wade has no idea about that, and it feels like I'm betraying him by not telling him about it.

"There's something I have to tell you." I give Wade a gentle push, needing some separation so I can think.

"Ry—" I break off, not knowing how to continue. "Me and Ry," I try again. But I never get to finish.

Jarosh stalks inside the cave, cursing. His face appears over the top of the flour sacks. Camike and Ekil are close on his heels.

Wade groans in frustration as he sits up. "Did living with the Halves make you forget how to knock?"

Jarosh's grin stretches the width of his face.

"Well, well, well." He puts his hand to his mouth in mock horror. "What have we here?"

"They are mating," Ekil grunts matter-of-factly in the Halve language.

"We are not!" I push myself away from Wade as heat rushes to my face.

"We heard you were down here resting." Jarosh cocks his head at Wade who is still stretched out across my bedroll. "But who am I to judge?"

Wade scowls. Camike giggles.

"As much as I hate to break this up, we need to talk." Jarosh plops down onto the bedroll beside Wade and stretches out his long legs. Camike sits next to him. Wade gives me an exasperated look as they settle themselves into our private space.

I nudge Jarosh over so I can at least sit next to Wade. Wade puts his arm around me, and I snuggle against his side. Who knows when we'll be alone again? This might be the best we'll get.

"Halves need to know the battle formation," Ekil says without preamble.

Jarosh nods before switching to the human language. "We're thinking of coordinating the Halves and Northerners. We can take two different entrances to the citadel. If all goes well, we'll fight our way through the tunnels and meet in the middle."

Wade nods, his expression serious once again. "We'll have to talk to Dayne about the layout of the tunnels and caves down there."

"Halves will need extra protection," Ekil tells me. "Or gray cloak archers will kill us at the gate."

"The Solguard archers will help you," I tell him. "And so will the Zeroes."

Ekil hesitates at the mention of Zeroes.

"They're the best protection you could hope for." I hear the defensiveness in my voice. "You can't be enemies with everyone."

The expression in Ekil's black eyes seems wounded at my harsh words.

"I'm sorry," I begin. "I didn't mean it like that."

"We are happy for any help the Halve Saver will give," Camike says. "We thank you."

Her diplomatic words make me feel worse, but there's nothing to be done about it now.

"It's going to be fine," I tell them. "You'll have your river and land back before you know it."

I don't think anyone is fooled by my too-bright voice.

"Hello? Wade, are you in here?"

Dellin steps around the flour sacks and comes to stand before us. Her eyes go directly to Wade and me, with his arm over my shoulders and my hand resting on his leg.

Her gray eyes narrow.

"Do you feel no shame?" Dellin turns on me with the speed and ferocity of a predator. "Selfish bitch."

Wade's arm tightens on my shoulder.

"Hey now," Jarosh gives her a puzzled look. "That's a rebel leader you're talking to."

"And my girlfriend." Wade's eyes flash. "So watch your mouth."

"It's fine," I mumble, wanting nothing more than for this conversation to end.

"You needed something?" Wade asks, his voice flat, his stare cool.

Anyone else would be intimidated by the strength of his presence. But Dellin isn't cowed.

"Liglette sent me to find you. She wants to know which of her archers will be riding Vlaz with Ry and me."

When she says those last few words, *Ry and me*, Dellin gives me a meaningful look.

"Well then," Jarosh scratches his chin as an uncomfortable silence falls over us. "We'll get going and let you get back to…." he waggles his eyebrows at Wade and me.

"Mating," Ekil supplies.

Camike gives them both a disapproving glare.

Jarosh, Camike, and Ekil file out. Dellin stays where she is. As though we're one person, Wade and I stand. The air is thick with tension.

"Interesting," Dellin says when it's just the three of us. She flicks a bit of dust off her cloak. The gesture would be laughable, given her face and neck are covered in dirt, if I didn't have a sick feel about what she was going to say next.

"What's interesting?" Wade asks, his jaw tight.

And then, as if things couldn't get any worse, Ry's frizzy red hair bobs over the sacks of flour.

# CHAPTER 11

Dellin stares at Wade.

"What's interesting?" he asks again. His voice is calm, but I can feel his body tense beside mine.

Dellin shrugs a delicate shoulder. "You just must be a very nice person if you're so willing to share."

Wade's brows knit in confusion.

"There you all are." Ry steps around the sacks of flour. When she sees the three of us facing off, her eyes widen and her smile fades. "What's going on…?"

"Share what?" Wade asks Dellin, ignoring Ry. "What in the sun are you talking about?"

"Just that you don't seem like the type who'd be fine with your *girlfriend* kissing other people."

Ry gasps. "Dell, that's not your secret to tell."

But it's too late. The words are out, and there's no taking them back.

I expect Wade to get angry, to turn on me and demand an explanation, but he doesn't do either. He laughs.

"I don't know what your problem with Hemera is," he says, lacing his fingers through mine, "but you might want to get over it if you want to stick around." All the mirth leaves his face. "And you'll want to do it fast."

"Dellin is here by my invitation." Ry stands shoulder-to-shoulder with the other girl. "Even if you don't know it yet, she's proved her loyalty to the Solguards. And she's important to me." Ry glares at Wade. "I won't have you or anyone else threaten her."

Wade turns to me. I will my voice to work, to make the words come.

"Wade." It comes out as a pathetic whisper. "We have to talk."

✱ ✱ ✱

I can't get the image of Wade's hurt expression out of my mind. He listened as I told him about the kiss with Ry. I watched as his trust turned to betrayal. And then, I saw the light in his gold eyes dim.

He said he could forgive me for the kiss. He said it was the secret part—the part where I kept something like that from him—that was the worst part.

Wade listened to my apologies without really hearing them. He was already far away, hidden behind the mask he seems to wear more and more these days.

I've broken his trust. It feels like a stab in my heart. I would give anything to go back in time and fix this.

I didn't get a chance to say anything else. I didn't get to tell him I love him, that I should have realized it sooner…should have told him sooner. A flurry of guards came to collect Wade for a meeting with the Northerners. And then he was gone.

I don't know how many hours I sit behind the flour sacks with my head in my hands. A thousand *what ifs* circle through my mind until I think I might actually go insane.

When Valior finds me and says he wants to introduce me to someone, I follow him, half in a daze. Dayne, Wade, and the rest of the leaders are already waiting for us. Wade doesn't look at me as we follow Valior down the tunnel. My heart is like a stone in my chest.

Valior brings us to a cave that has a door—the only one I've seen in the entire settlement.

"Watch your step," he warns as we follow him inside.

The floor is littered with shards of metal, clear flasks filled with strange-colored liquid, and chunks of minerals.

"What in the sun is all this?" Dayne asks.

Valior gives him a crooked smile. "The solution to your problem with the black trees."

The old man peers into the gloom. "Everlyn?" he calls. "I've brought some people to meet you."

There are soft footsteps, and then a young girl appears out of the gloom. Something blue is smudged across her face. One of her sleeves looks singed, but not from the black sap, just a regular old fire. She looks about the same age as Wokee.

"Everlyn, meet the rebel leaders. Leaders, meet Everlyn."

Everlyn's round face is dusted with freckles. She's tinkering with a box that has metal wires sticking out of it, her fingers dancing in an intricate pattern as they separate and twist the wires together. Her wavy hair is braided down to her waist, but most of the strands around her face have come loose. She looks up at us, her fingers still working at the wires, and smiles.

"I know you," I say, making the connection to where I've seen her before.

"I come to visit my brother in Solis once a year," Everlyn says in a breathy, high-pitched voice. "You probably saw me there."

I nod. "You're the one who gave Wokee that ribbon at the feast."

I realize as soon as the words are out of my mouth it was the wrong thing to say. But Everlyn isn't embarrassed. Her smile widens, and her cheeks turn a pretty pink.

"He told you about it?" she asks, her voice sounding hopeful.

"No, but I always see him carrying it with him."

"Always?" she squeaks.

"Mhm. He tries to hide it, but I've seen him pull it out whenever he thinks no one is looking."

Everlyn rewards me with a smile so big I can't help but return it. Her obvious crush on Wokee has me turning to catch Wade's eye before I'm even aware of what I'm doing.

Wade is looking at one of the flasks on the ground. He's always sensed when my attention was on him before, but if he feels my gaze, he chooses not to meet it now.

"What does she have to do with the black trees?" Wade asks, finally taking his eyes off the ground. He gives a pointed look at the doorway as if to say he has more important things to do than be here. My heart gives a painful squeeze.

"If you wish to destroy the wood before the Duskers can cut it down and bring it to Solis," Valior says, "young Everlyn has the skills and brains to help." He turns his attention on the young girl. "Show them what you can do, my girl."

Everlyn beams at Valior before scuttling back into the gloom. She returns with three beakers and a satchel tucked under her arm. She kneels on the ground and lines the beakers up in front of her.

All of our gazes are fixed on her.

Her face pinched in concentration, Everlyn begins reaching into the satchel and taking out boxes filled with colored powders. She uses different-sized wooden spoons to measure the powders into the beakers. Tut starts to ask something, but Valior shushes him.

When Everlyn is finished, she gives Valior a nod. She marches out of the cave with her beakers cradled in her skinny arms. We all follow her out of the cave and into the tunnel. Valior waves away our questions, promising, "You'll see soon enough."

Once we're on the Outside, Everlyn leads us to a place where the ground is pocketed with holes. Some are only a foot or two deep, while others are easily more than ten. She draws a circle in the dirt with her toe over an unmarred part of the ground. Then, she overturns the contents of the first beaker into the circle's center. She repeats the process with the second beaker. A white smoke begins to waft from the place where the two sets of powders have mixed. With the third beaker in her hand, she pauses.

"Take cover." She points a small finger at a stone wall reinforced by bags of sand twenty paces away.

Valior hobbles toward the wall. After exchanging puzzled looks, the rest of us follow.

"Ready?" Everlyn yells after we've ducked behind the wall.

"Whenever you are," Valior calls back.

Valior motions for us to peek around the wall while keeping our bodies shielded. Everlyn dumps the third beaker and then sprints toward us. She throws herself onto her belly and slides behind the shelter at the same moment a boom rocks the ground.

A plume of blue smoke puffs up from the new hole in the ground where Everlyn's powders used to be.

"Well done, my girl!"

Valior and Everlyn caper around each other, chuckling and gripping each other's hands.

Valior turns to the rest of us. "Well, go have a look."

The circle Everlyn drew in the dirt is gone. In its place is a round hole, at least ten feet deep.

"Well, I'll be," Tut mutters.

"Her concoction will blow those black trees to smithereens," Valior says, out of breath from his walk over. He winks at Everlyn.

"Impressive feat," Tut mutters as he stands at the edge and peers into the hole in the ground.

Dayne focuses on Everlyn. "Can you make enough of that stuff to blow up an entire cave?"

"A really big cave," I add.

"No problem." Everlyn thinks for a minute. "Unless the trees are already on fire. My powders combined with the fumes from the fire would kill you before you could get away."

"Destroy the trees before they're on fire," I say. "Got it."

"You see now, don't you?" Valior asks. "Everlyn will give you explosives to destroy the underground orchard. This way, even if the battle goes sour, the Duskers won't be able to use the black trees against what's left of our people."

"I'll have to mix everything up for you beforehand," Everlyn tells me. "And it will take me *hours* to explain how to make sure you don't blow yourself up."

Dayne grins. Even Wade seems to be fighting a smile.

"I think I can find a few hours to spare," I assure Everlyn.

She smiles at me and then gestures me closer. When I lean down to her, she whispers in my ear, "Will you tell Wokee about what I did?"

"Do you want me to?" I ask.

Everlyn crosses her arms. "He's always bragging about how his orchards are so important to the Solguards." She scowls.

I smile. "I'll tell him you blew a ten-foot hole in the ground like it was the easiest thing in the world."

Everlyn beams. She gives me a quick wave and then skips back to the compound.

"Are we insane for putting such an important task into the hands of one little girl?" Tut asks Valior.

Valior watches Everlyn disappear into the tunnel. "Possibly. And yet, this whole endeavor is insane. That's what makes me think we might just stand a chance."

# CHAPTER 12

Later, I seek out Wade. There were things we both left unsaid, and I'm determined to say them before we go off to fight the Duskers. But that isn't the only reason I want to talk to him. Hendrix's words have been replaying in my head and bothering me more with every passing hour. I can't tell Dayne because he would go berserk that I put myself in that much danger. And I can't tell Ry because she's missing again.

I find Wade in a corner of the main cave with Jarosh. They're surrounded by a group of Solguards and Halves, and they're pouring over drawings of the citadel's entrances. There's a great deal of noise, because every time a human or Halve says anything, it needs to be translated for the others to understand.

"Wade."

He looks up at the sound of my voice. A dozen different emotions pass across his face before his expression becomes impassive.

"Not now, Hemera. We're busy." He turns away from me and returns to the drawings.

The formal emptiness of his words makes me go as still as a statue. There's a stinging in my eyes that I don't think has anything to do with the puddles of black goo still outside the settlement.

I force down my own hurt, telling myself he has every right to be angry with me.

"It's important," I say. "It's about—"

"You can tell one of my guards, and he'll make sure to relay anything of importance."

Jarosh looks up from a map he's been studying. He gives Wade a quizzical look, and then turns to study me.

"Jarosh, if you're ready." Wade makes an impatient gesture.

Jarosh gives me an apologetic look before turning his attention back to the drawings.

I turn around and walk back in the opposite direction. I have no destination. I just need to get away from here before I break down and humiliate myself.

I've seen Wade angry before, hurt even. I've made him feel both those emotions. But he's never been so cold and distant. He's never dismissed me.

*I pushed him too far.*

Why didn't I tell him about my feelings when I had the chance? Why did I throw it all away, and for what?

Kissing Ry was fun, beautiful even. But it isn't her face I see before I fall asleep. It's not her I'm always searching for in a crowd.

And now that I know, it's too late. Wade won't forgive me. He can't…not after everything I've done to push him away.

I have so many regrets, and I've lost so much. I don't know how to bear losing him, too. There's a tightness in my chest that's making it difficult to breathe.

"Aw, why the long face, young lady?"

Valior, hobbling up the tunnel with the help of his cane, reaches into his pocket and offers up his flask to me. "I had love troubles back in my day, too." He gives me a wink.

As if things couldn't get any worse, now I'm picturing Valior's love life. Before my imagination can go any farther, I reach out my hand to accept the flask.

Before I can feel the cool metal in my palm, the flask is whisked away. Dayne returns it to Valior.

"Liquid sun might do the girl some good," Valior tells my brother. He gives the flask a hard look and then, his eyes full of regret, puts it back into his pocket without taking a sip.

"If you drink that," my brother tells me, "you'll regret it. I've spent enough high days hurling my guts up to know."

Valior grins at Dayne. "I remember you at your first Banished feast, although I'm guessing you don't."

Dayne's expression sours. "I remember enough."

Valior looks at me, clearly enjoying himself. "Your brother passed out, and when he woke up—"

"That's quite enough reminiscing," Dayne cuts in, scowling at Valior.

The old man doesn't seem to notice.

"That's what we need." His arthritic fingers manage a weak snap.

"Drunk people?" I ask.

"Everyone unconscious?" Dayne asks at the same time.

"A celebration!" Valior announces. "Everyone's all wound up with pre-battle jitters. Best to give you all something good to refocus on before you start getting yourselves into trouble."

Neither Dayne nor I say anything, but Valior doesn't seem to need any encouragement. He gives my arm a distracted pat. Muttering to himself—something about a batch still distilling—he shuffles up the tunnel.

"Do you good," he calls back to us. "Give Dayne a chance to break out that lute of his."

"So, what happened at your first Banished feast?" I ask my brother.

"Don't ask." Dayne's skin goes a little green at the memory. "But if there's any advice I can give you as a survivor of the experience, it's to avoid Valior's liquid sun."

* * *

I wander the settlement's empty tunnels during high day while everyone else is asleep. As tired as I am, I'm not willing to risk falling back into one of my bad dreams and needing Wade to come rescue me.

I don't even know if he would.

Ry is still missing, but I don't have the energy to wonder where she is or bring myself to care. A part of me is angry with her for what happened between Wade and me, even though I know that's ridiculous. What happened is my fault, and mine alone.

I go to the only place where I think I'll find any comfort: the Zeroes' chamber.

I open the door and step into their cave. I wait for the sense of rightness and belonging to wash over me.

I don't know if it's because I'm still thinking about my fight with Wade, but being near the Zeroes doesn't give me the sense of peace it usually does. The bond between us doesn't feel as strong. I'm not getting the same sense of euphoric power that being with them always used to spark.

For a panicked moment, I wonder if my continually being away from the Zeroes has weakened our connection.

"You seem troubled, Daughter."

I jump at the sound of my father's voice. I hadn't seen him when I came in, but of course he's here. I wouldn't have expected him to be anywhere else. A flare of irritation goes through me.

"Don't you have anywhere else to be?" I snap at my father.

"As a matter of fact, I don't," my father replies. "You did bring me here, if you recall. And the only task I've been given is feeding your army."

"It's not like you to be content with idleness," I prod.

I'm itching for a fight, and his perpetual calm is maddening.

My father regards me. "What's really bothering you, Daughter?"

"Nothing," I say. "Nothing's wrong. I just feel—"

*Empty. Wrong.*

"You're worried about the battle, I presume?"

*Yes, that must be it.* What was it Valior had said?

"Pre-battle jitters," I say, repeating the old man's words.

My father laces his hands behind his back in the way he always used to when he was giving a speech as Captain Harkibel.

"It's natural to have doubts," he says, "but be comforted by the knowledge that you're doing what you must."

"I don't even know what I'm supposed to be doing anymore," I admit.

"Self-pity is unproductive, Daughter. You are too strong for that."

His words make my anger flare again. How dare he lecture me, when he's the one….

"You're doing what you must to make sure Jadem's death wasn't in vain," the Captain continues. "You're doing what you believe is right."

My anger melts away, replaced by something much worse…doubt.

"But what if I'm wrong?" My voice comes out as a whisper. "About everything?"

"That's always the risk with big ideas, isn't it?" My father shrugs. "But if there wasn't risk involved, there wouldn't be the possibility of great rewards."

I take an unsteady breath.

"Thanks," I tell my father, and I'm surprised to find I mean it.

I never would have guessed that, as the rest of my life crumbled around me, my father would be the one who made me feel like myself again.

"Hold your head up high, Daughter."

I stop. Those words…they were ones my mother always used to say to me.

I look at my father, wondering if he's just trying to torture me after all, but he's gone back to chopping up raw meat for the Zeroes' next feeding.

# CHAPTER 13

I've been looking for you."

My heart leaps at the sound of Wade's voice.

When I turn around to face him, though, he doesn't meet my gaze.

"Well, here I am," I say, trying for levity and failing.

He still won't look at me.

"Jarosh wants to know if you can spare a few of the Zeroes to help his team."

"Of course, whatever he needs."

Wade nods. "I'll let him know." He turns to walk away.

I almost let him go, but I can't stand to have it be like this between us. Not after all we've been through together.

"Wade, please." My voice breaks.

He stops walking, his back to me. I hurry to catch up. I walk around to face him.

"I'm so sorry," I say, feeling the inadequacy of those simple words. "I was so messed up after Brice…."

Even now, it takes me a few seconds to swallow the hurt that comes with even saying his name.

Wade searches my face, and for a moment, his mask slides away. The pain in his golden eyes, pain I caused, is enough to break my heart.

"I know," he says, his voice low. "I gave you time. I would have given you more, but Hemera—" he rubs his neck, and I can tell I'm not going to like whatever he says next. "That, I could handle. Hell, I'd even forgive you for kissing Ry and taking so damn long to tell me about it."

I shake my head, confused. "Then, what—"

"You've changed. I know you don't see it, but you have. And it's like even when you're with me, you're not with me. I feel like you're always looking over your shoulder for those Zeroes."

I shrink away from him. "That isn't true."

"It is." Wade takes my hands, and his warmth is both a comfort and torture. "Hemera, I know you…and ever since you made the Zeroes, you haven't been you."

I pull my hands out of his grip. "If you don't feel the same way about me anymore, you could have just said so," I tell him, my voice hard as stone. "Just admit this has nothing to do with the Zeroes."

"It has everything to do with the Zeroes."

"You don't want me," I say, my voice rising. "I get it. There's no shame in saying what you really mean."

"Why won't you listen to me?" Wade's voice rises to match my own. "Why do you refuse to see it? Ever since you started to trust your father and do what he says—"

I put up a hand to stop him. "All I can see," I return, fighting back tears, "is that you don't have a clue what you're talking about."

"I don't like what he's done to you!" Wade's chest heaves as we glare at each other. "Look at you. You aren't sleeping, you've lost weight, and," he grabs my hand and lifts it to eye level. We both stare at my nailbeds, which are bitten down to the quick. "You never used to do this."

I yank my hand away while a shame I don't want to feel flushes my cheeks. "I'm the same freak I always was." There's acid in my voice.

"You're not yourself." Wade's voice is softer now, which is somehow worse. "I'm not saying what happened with that little Dusker girl was your fault.…"

He trails off at whatever look crosses my face.

*What happened with the girl* was *my fault. I don't need Wade to remind me.*

"Look." Wade closes the distance between us. "I know how hard it can be to see your parents for what they really are. Hell, no one knows that better than me."

A fleeting look of bitterness crosses his face, and I know he's thinking about how his own father chose loyalty to the Duskers over his own family.

"I'm not some little kid who can easily be fooled. And I'm not you, Wade."

Wade steps back from me, a stunned look on his face as though I had just struck him.

"That's for damn sure," he says.

When he walks away, I don't try to stop him.

* * *

"Hemera! We're celebrating!"

Jarosh shoves a clay cup in my hand, sloshing some of its liquid in the process. Just the smell of it makes my stomach curdle, and I have no doubt it's Valior's infamous liquid sun. I dump it onto the ground when Jarosh isn't looking.

"What are we celebrating?" I ask, supporting his weight as he drapes an arm over my shoulders.

"The end of the world, of course. And—hey!"

He turns as Camike plucks the cup out of his hands. "No sick," she informs him as she kisses his forehead.

Jarosh stretches up on his toes, takes Camike's face in both his hands, and kisses her on the mouth. There is some hooting and boos from the others milling around them. Neither of them seems to care.

I excuse myself, knowing they're past hearing me, anyway, and make my way into the main cave.

I've been to Jadem's feasts before, so I thought I knew what to expect. It turns out the Banished have a different idea of celebrating than the Solguards. There's a meager sideboard with sad-looking roasted birds and scant berries and nuts. The liquid sun, however, is limitless. Overflowing clay cups are crammed onto every available space. Some of the Banished are drinking it straight from dusty glass bottles.

I see Dayne in a corner with the other musicians. Their fingers are moving on the strings of their instruments, but there's too much shouting and drunken singing to hear their music.

The Halves, with the exception of Camike, are clustered on one side of the cave. They are weaponless and seem not to know what to do with their hands. They look awkward and uncomfortable, too big for the low-ceilinged cave. They surround Ekil, who is making soothing gestures with his hand.

It isn't hard for me to make my way through the crowd to them. No one else is trying to get near the Halves.

"You don't have to be afraid," I tell them. "We're all allies now. You have nothing to fear from these people."

The Halves give me a look that says they very much doubt my assurances.

"This will all be over soon," I say with as much confidence as I can muster.

"And then humans give us peace?"

"I swear by the sun." I close my right fist, with the rebel sun swirls inked into my skin, and place it over my heart.

The Halves bob their heads, seeming satisfied with my promise.

Incessant, rude sounds keep coming from the back of the group. I skirt around them to see what's going on.

Wokee and Brogut are facing off. Wokee doesn't even reach the Halve's waist, but Brogut is doing his best to bend down to Wokee's level, making it clear who's in charge.

"No, no, no," Wokee is saying. "Like this."

He opens his mouth wide, releasing an enormous belch. He grins. "It's all in the throat." He points to the appropriate place on himself.

Brogut grunts and scratches his head, trying without much success to mimic the sound.

"Wokee, what in the sun are you doing?" I ask.

"Teaching Brogut how to burp. Obviously." He rolls his eyes. "You'd think someone so big would be better at it."

"*Why* are you teaching him how to burp?" I rephrase.

"Because…it's awesome…." Wokee gives me a look as if to say *I thought you were smarter than this.*

"Boys do really gross things," a voice says from behind me. "It's better not to ask why."

I turn to see Everlyn. Her hair is in two braids with blue ribbons tied on the ends. She's also wearing a blue dress. It's threadbare, but I can tell from the way she keeps twirling around it's her favorite. Her lips are shiny like she put oil on them, and there's a glimmer of sparkly powder across her cheeks. She holds a flask in her hand, which she's mixing with a spoon.

"Who asked you, anyway?" Wokee demands, his face scrunched in petulant annoyance.

"What do you have there?" I ask before Everlyn can retort.

"Just another solution for the explosions," she says, tossing her braids. "You know, in case their soil composition is more acidic than it is here."

"Soil compo-what?" Wokee asks.

He holds up a finger before Everlyn can reply and releases another belch.

"Did you know," I raise my voice over the sound of Brogut's attempt, "Everlyn is really good at making things. It's kind of like," I pause, pretending to think, and then snap my fingers. "It's kind of like you, Wokee, with your plants!"

"Psh, no it's not," Wokee says, but I see him slip his hand in his pocket, and I know he's holding the ribbon Everlyn gave him months ago.

I wink at Everlyn when Wokee isn't looking, and she gives me a thumbs-up.

I look up to see Ry coming down the tunnel. Her cloak is dirty and her boots are covered in mud. A pulse of anger goes through me.

*Where has she been?*

"I'll see you later," I tell Wokee and Everlyn.

I stop just a few paces from Ry, an accusation already on my lips, when Wade crosses her path. I don't think he sees me, and after everything we said to each other, I don't want him to. I wait, hoping whatever Wade has to say to Ry will be over quickly so I can take my turn yelling at her.

"…can't keep disappearing," Wade is saying. "You look…."

I can only make out part of their conversation with all the other noise. I move closer, telling myself it's only because I want to know what Ry's been up to.

"I look better than you," Ry says. She reaches up to push aside a lock of Wade's hair that has fallen across his face. "Just because a war is coming, it doesn't mean you can't cut your hair."

I stand off to the side, feeling, for the first time, like I'm not one of them. When Ry looks past Wade and sees me, I drop my gaze to the floor, uncomfortable in a way I've never been with the two of them before.

Wade follows her gaze, and his expression hardens. "Ry, I want to know what's going on with you by low day. That's an order."

He strides away without giving me another glance.

"What's eating you?" Ry calls after him, but he's already disappeared into the crowd.

I want to talk to Ry, to see if I can have any better luck than Wade in figuring out where she keeps disappearing to. But all I can see is that image of her reaching up to brush away Wade's hair. My fingers tingle at the memory of its softness—softness I might never touch again.

I shake my head, trying to jolt myself out of such idiotic thoughts.

*There's a war coming, and* this *is what I'm worrying about?*

My head is starting to ache.

It's too loud in here. I push my way back through the crowd toward the tunnel. No one will notice my absence. I'll go check on the Zeroes….

"Captain Harkibel!" Valior's voice somehow carries through the mayhem.

I turn, expecting my father to appear. I don't see him. Instead, I see Valior gesturing at me. The people between us separate, leaving me with a clear path to the center of the cave.

*Oh.*

It's too late for me to tell Valior that my father is the only one who goes by that name. Shouts of *Captain Harkibel*, followed by ridiculous titles like "greatest weapon" and "savior of humanity" ring in my ears. I think I also catch a few calls of "devil maker" and "abomination," but those voices are quickly hushed.

When I reach Valior, he uses my arm for support as he climbs onto a small platform. He waves at me until I join him. He motions for someone to bring me a cup. When I try to refuse, the crowd surrounding Valior's pedestal boos.

The same process is repeated with each of the other council members. Valior calls them up to cheers, they're given a cup of liquid sun, and then they crowd onto the dais with us. When Wade makes his way to the stage, a woman in the crowd calls, "I love you!"

I have to stop myself from jumping down and strangling her.

Liglette, curse her, steps to the side so the only place for Wade is next to me. He shows no emotion as he moves to stand beside me. When I steal a glance at him, he's looking at the crowd, but I can tell he isn't really seeing any of them. Whatever he's thinking about, his mind is far away from here.

Tut is standing on my other side. It's obvious he's already sampled the liquid sun because as he takes a step, he lurches into me. I almost fall off the dais, but Wade wraps his arm around my waist to keep me on my feet.

Before I've even opened my mouth to thank him, he's dropped his hand back to his side.

Valior clears his throat. After a few hoots and cheers from the Easterners, the cave goes relatively quiet.

"I won't bore you all by reminding you what we're soon to face. After all, this high day is for celebrating."

A whoop goes up from the Easterners. Liglette's people clap politely. The Halves shift on their feet as Camike quietly translates for them.

A man passes by the dais and hands us each a fresh cup of liquid sun. Even though I haven't touched my first one, it's whisked away and replaced with one that's so full the liquid sloshes over the rim.

"True Banished hospitality," Valior says with a grin as he points to the cups.

The Easterners roar with approval and raise their own drinks.

Valior lifts his flask to Liglette. "We thank the Westerners for the meat we have all enjoyed this high day."

"To Liglette and the Westerners!"

Everyone around and below me takes a sip from their cup. I raise mine to my lips, but, heedful of Dayne's warning, only pretend to drink.

Out of the corner of my eye, I catch the Halves muttering angrily. They no doubt see the food, spare as it is, and are reminded of how the Banished stripped the land of all it had to offer and left them with nothing.

"To our leader from the North," Valior continues. "For providing our weapons. May every one of the Duskers die by one of your blades. And to Jarosh, for leading the Northern force!"

Another round of cheers and drinking follows. Personally, I can't figure out why anyone would be cheering for Tut, coward that he is. But the liquid sun seems to have put them all in a good mood.

"To Dayne Clarion. Without his knowledge of Malarusk, we'd be attacking blind."

The Banished hoot and stomp their feet in appreciation.

Valior raises his flask again. "And to the memory of my brother, who sacrificed himself to the wormkill so that Dayne could live."

This time there isn't any shouting or whistling. Everyone raises their cups and sips. The Easterners put their hands over their hearts and bow their heads.

My brother grips the neck of his lute in one hand and his filled cup in the other.

Valior turns to Dayne. He speaks quietly enough that only those of us on the dais can hear his words. "Do his memory proud. Make the Duskers pay for what they stole from us."

My brother nods. He closes his eyes like he's remembering the man who sacrificed his life so he and Jadem could escape all those years ago. Then, he lifts his cup and clinks it against Valior's flask. They both drink.

"Now." Valior shakes himself, and with it, the mood in the cave is festive again. "Where were we?"

People laugh. A voice calls out, "Hemera! You were up to her!"

I look down to see Wokee beaming up at me.

"Quite right, young man," Valior agrees.

I wish I was wearing a cloak so I could hide under the hood's shadow.

"To Captain Harkibel, the mastermind of this bold and wonderfully insane plan."

I have to remind myself he's talking about me, and not my father.

"To insanity!" someone yells, and everyone laughs.

"And not just the mastermind." Valior raises a finger before everyone drinks. "She is the leader of the New Army."

Just then, I look into the crowd, and my gaze lands on my father.

"To the New Army!" the crowd choruses.

There is an amused look on his face as my father raises his cup to me.

"Lastly," Valior says, "Now that the head of the council is lost to us, we must appoint a new leader to take her place."

The mood sobers as the Banished and Solguards toast my aunt. I stare down into my full cup, but all I see is her body stretched out on the enemy's land.

"And so, it is my duty and honor to name the new Solguard leader."

I start. I hadn't thought…hadn't realized….

First confusion, and then anger, fills me. *They can't just replace Aunt Jadem.*

Valior turns his attention on Wade. Wade looks like he expected this but wants no part of it. I don't think anyone else can tell what he's thinking, though, because he holds Valior's gaze without blinking.

Valior talks about honor and responsibility, and then officially pronounces Wade the new Solguard leader.

I place my right hand, the one covered with the sun tattoo, over my heart with the other Solguards. My motions are mechanical. I look out at the other Solguards acknowledging Wade as their leader. It's nonsensical, but I can't help but think of us all as traitors to Jadem.

Wade accepts his accolades stone-faced. His golden eyes dim as he takes the script tree scroll from Valior that decrees him the Banished leader of the South. He doesn't want this, that much is clear, but he's doing it anyway because someone needs to…because it's expected of him…because he's the best person for it.

I understand how he must feel.

Then, Wade is speaking. His rich baritone stretches across the cave and warms me to my soul. It takes every shred of restraint I have not to reach down and clasp his hand.

I don't listen to his words. Instead, I read his face.

The boy I met in Solis, the one who laughed and joked and always said more than he should, is gone. In his place is a man, all muscle and hard edges, with a seriousness I don't recognize.

It makes me swell with admiration and ache for him at the same time.

"…and in the words of Sal," Wade says, "it's not about numbers, but about heart. And we," he raises his cup, "have heart."

There is shouting and toasting. Wade raises his own cup to his lips. Before he takes a sip, he catches my eyes for a fraction of a second. Then, his gaze moves down to the hollow of my throat.

Abruptly, he steps off the pedestal and is swallowed into the crowd.

I reach up to the place where his gaze lingered, wondering what he was looking at. My fingers wrap around the delicate chain of my mother's necklace.

My heart sinks like a stone.

Sal's pendant, the one that always hangs next to it, is gone. I washed off the black sap, but it's still stained. I left it with my other belongings until I could find a new cord to string it on. But Wade doesn't know what happened. All he knows is that it's no longer around my neck.

"Give him some space." Jarosh, one arm on my elbow to steady himself, leads me down from the platform and steers me away from Wade.

"But—"

"Don't worry," Jarosh elbows me in the side, "Wade's not one to hold a grudge."

"This is different," I manage to say.

"Ah." Jarosh gives me a one-armed hug, stumbling a little as he does so. "Love makes that other stuff," he hiccups, "not matter."

He isn't looking at me. His half-lidded gaze is fixed on Camike, who is smiling at him from across the cave.

Jarosh gives me a wink as he goes to her. I try to speak, but my throat won't work.

I watch the other leaders smiling and talking with the people surrounding them. No one surrounds me, though.

How could so much have changed, and yet so much remain the same? For the first time in a long time, I feel a heavy loneliness creep over me.

I think about my own responsibility in all of this. If anything goes wrong with our attack, if the Zeroes don't do what I've promised they will, every death will rest on my shoulders.

Not for the first time, I wonder if my aunt, and everyone else, misplaced their faith in me.

*You will save us all.*

I raise my cup to my lips and drain it in a single draught.

# CHAPTER 14

I know now why it's called liquid sun. The stuff burns as it goes down my throat. I feel its fiery path all the way down to my stomach. I hold back a cough but can do nothing about the tears streaming from my eyes.

How could Valior—how could anyone—like this stuff?

"Captain Harkibel, savior of us all!"

Two burly Solguards, clearly well into their own mugs of liquid sun, lift me off my feet and onto their shoulders. There's shouting and laughter, and as the guards carrying me make their way through the crowd, Solguards and Banished shout my name. Some of them even brush against my dangling legs like I'm some kind of lucky charm.

I should be humiliated by their attention, but I'm not. In fact, I'm actually starting to enjoy this party. All of my fear, all my worries, have melted away.

I feel good.

When I catch sight of red hair in the crowd, I leap from the guard's shoulders, landing in a less-than-graceful tangle of limbs.

"Where been?" I try to ask Ry, but my tongue feels strange in my mouth.

Her face is slightly out of focus, like I'm looking at her reflection in a pool of rippling water. I stare at her like I'm just noticing her for the first time. Her cloak is dirty and she smells like the Outside. An unruly curl hangs down across her forehead. Dark smudges give her eyes a more dramatic look, like she's rimmed them with kohl.

"Mer?" Ry taps a foot. "Mer, you're staring at me."

How have I never realized it before? Ry's—

"Beautiful," I say.

"Huh?" Ry cocks her head at me.

"You're beautiful." I grin at Ry.

"Um, thanks?" Her slightly puzzled look at my greeting changes to something like recognition when I waver on my feet.

"Hemera," she gives me an amused look as she reaches out an arm to steady me, "you didn't by any chance drink the liquid sun, did you?"

I lean toward her, wrapping my arms around her neck. "You feel nice," I tell her. A hiccup escapes from my lips.

"Whatever." Ry shakes her head. "Mer, we need to talk. It's important. Where's Wade?"

"I don't want to talk to Wade." I cross my arms and make a pouting face. "I thought you—"

"Shhh." Ry covers my mouth with her hand. "You don't know what you're saying."

"I know what I'm saying. You're amazing, and I think we should—"

I lean toward her, closing my eyes. When the expected kiss doesn't come, I open them.

Ry is leaning back, only a few inches from me, but she isn't looking at me. She's staring across the cave. I have to grab her arm to keep myself from falling over as I follow the direction of her gaze. When I see Wade, his mouth slightly ajar as he stares, I want to dissolve into the floor.

His mouth shuts, and I can imagine the sound of his teeth grinding together. He turns and walks away without a second glance. The liquid sun turns to acid in my stomach.

"Damnit, Mer," Ry says. She prods a finger in my chest. "Stay here." Then, she pushes past me. "Wade!" she calls, hurrying after him.

I don't remember the time between Ry leaving and returning. All I remember is that when she does, she's with Dellin, and the two of them are dragging me out of the party and into an empty cave. Dayne and Wade are there.

"What are we doing here?" Wade asks. "I have other things to do."

"I need to tell you all something."

Ry yanks on a curl, tugs on her sleeves, and shifts her eyes around the cave. I don't think I've ever seen Ry nervous before, but that must be what this is. Too late, I cover my mouth with my hand as a hiccup escapes me.

Dellin gives me a bored look. I try to glare at her, but it makes me dizzy, and I have to lean back against the wall.

My brother raises an eyebrow at me, and then he shakes his head in understanding.

"Whatever it is, Rylin, let's hear it," Dayne says.

"Well, the thing is," Ry's eyes dart to each of us. "You're not going to believe me when I tell you."

Her gaze comes to rest on Dellin. The other girl gives her a nod of encouragement. I feel my hackles rise. It's clear that whatever Ry has to tell us, Dellin already knows.

"Does this have something to do with where you keep disappearing to?" I ask, even though I already know the answer.

Ry nods. "I needed to know for sure before I told you."

"Told us what?" Wade grinds out.

"It's about Jadem."

It's the last thing I expected her to say. Just hearing my aunt's name is enough to jolt me out of my drunken stupor.

*Did Ry figure out what the seed is for? Did she find another note my aunt left behind?* My heartbeat quickens.

"Just tell them," Dellin says.

For once, I'm in agreement with her.

"Well, as it turns out, Jadem didn't die the way we thought she did."

I shake my head. I thought the liquid sun was wearing off, but it must be clouding my mind more than I thought.

"I saw her," I say. "We all did."

"I know," Ry says. "It seems crazy. That's why I didn't tell you sooner. I knew you wouldn't believe me. I didn't even believe it myself at first."

"So then, how did she die?" Wade asks. He crosses his arms in a way that makes it obvious he's just humoring her.

"That's the thing," Ry says. "She didn't die at all."

"What are you saying?" I ask in little more than a whisper.

"Mer." Ry stares straight at me. "Jadem's alive."

# CHAPTER 15

Either I'm drunker than I thought, or you are," I say, but Ry's shaking her head.

"Listen," she says. "It seemed crazy to me at first, too, but then I got to thinking…."

"Why don't you start from the beginning," my brother says. "Tell us everything, and we'll do our best not to interrupt."

"Okay." Ry takes a deep breath. "It all started when Jadem gave me that note before we left for Malarusk. The way she was talking, it just seemed like she knew she wasn't coming back. It made me wonder why she would have suggested that mission, pushed so hard for it, even, if she thought it would fail."

I remember my aunt's strange behavior, her sad, faraway looks, and the way it kept feeling like she was saying goodbye. I had known the mission was risky, but it had also felt like Aunt Jadem knew more than she was saying.

"Yeah, but—" I start, but Dayne gives me a look.

"When we found the seed and saw it was wrapped in that gray fabric, Dellin said she thought the material was part of a Dusker robe." Ry's look of discomfort deepens. "I started to wonder why Jadem might have a piece of a Dusker robe, and Dellin said the only ones who have robes made out of such a high-quality satin are the Captains."

"She could have kept it from when she pretended to be a Dusker to spy on them," I argue, too stubborn to stay quiet.

"After all those years?" Wade replies. "That doesn't make sense."

"You're right, it doesn't," Ry agrees. "Unless you consider the possibility that Jadem never stopped working with the Duskers."

"You lying, conniving—" I move toward Dellin. I'm so angry I can't form a sentence. "What kind of nonsense have you been stuffing in my friend's head?"

"Mer, stop." Ry puts up a hand.

"I got this," Dellin says coolly, like she hasn't just accused the Solguard leader, my aunt, of being a traitor to her own people.

"Just wait," Dayne tells me. "We promised to hear them out."

"When Ry and I found the seed and were trying to figure out what it could all mean," Dellin says, "Ry mentioned she wished Jadem was alive so she could ask her."

Her calm voice seems like it's mocking me. I clench my fists at my sides.

"It got me thinking," Dellin continues. "I happen to know the Dusker Supreme usually holds public trials and interrogations before executing her prisoners."

A dark look crosses her face, and I wonder if she's thinking about her father's murder at Crowe's hand.

"Anyway." Dellin shakes herself. "I couldn't figure out why Crowe would just kill the Solguard leader without torturing her for information."

I don't know where this is all going, but a sickness that has nothing to do with the liquid sun is settling in my gut.

"That's when I remembered," Dellin says, "the last time Crowe staged a fast, public murder."

"And when was that?" I ask, my jaw clenched so tightly it aches.

"When she faked her own death," Dellin replies. "It's how she was able to plan her coup. Everyone thought she was dead, and so no one expected her to be a threat."

"How do you know so much about Crowe?" I demand.

Dellin falters for the space of a moment, but she recovers quickly. "Common Dusker knowledge."

"Jadem helped her set that up during her time in Malarusk," Dayne says. "I remember her saying something about it once. She helped Crowe overthrow the rightful Dusker Supreme. Crowe became the only Supreme who hadn't inherited the title by birth."

"And then I started to wonder," Ry jumps in, "what if they had done the same thing again?"

"Aunt Jadem would never have done anything like that," I argue. "She'd have no reason to."

Ry gives me a pitying look, and I want to slap it off her.

"I couldn't get it out of my mind." Ry scratches her head. "I mean, we were too far away to see what she and Crowe were saying. We saw Jadem's body fall, but there wasn't any blood or really anything to prove she was dead."

"I saw her." My voice wavers. "I saw Crowe break her neck. And you dare to—"

"But that's the thing," Ry insists. "We *thought* we saw Crowe break her neck. But it's possible she just pretended to, and Jadem just pretended to die."

The idea is so preposterous I can't even think of anything to say in response.

"But the more I thought about it," Ry continues, "The more it started making sense. If Jadem knew she was going to 'die'," she puts air quotes around the word, "it would make sense why she stayed behind while the rest of you ran through the gate."

I remember Dayne and I running from the wormkill tunnel. I remember dragging Fake Hendrix's limp body with us. I remember turning around on the other side of the gate and seeing no sign of my aunt.

But there could be a dozen explanations for that…the least likely of which is that Jadem stayed behind to fake her own death.

"And it would explain why she left Ry with the note," Dellin adds.

"Or," I say, "Maybe, she just knew there was a *possibility* of something going wrong, which would make sense given that we were going to *Malarusk*." My voice drips with sarcasm.

"Right," Ry says, "which is why I went back to search for her body."

"You did what?!" Wade and Dayne demand in unison.

"I was careful," Ry says. "I stole a cloak from an idiot recruit and started poking around."

"Do you have any idea how dangerous that was?" Wade's lips are white.

"Yes, Wade, I do." Ry rolls her eyes. "But anyway, like I was saying, I couldn't find the body."

"And Crowe always displays the bodies of her victims," Dellin adds.

"Alright." Dayne puts up a hand. "I'll grant you this is all possible. But so is any one of a thousand other conjectures. What makes you so sure about this?"

"I saw her." Ry's voice is so quiet I'm not sure I heard her right.

"The Duskers all look the same in their cloaks," Dayne says, his voice uncertain.

"It was her."

"Maybe you just thought it was her," Wade says.

Ry gives him a hard stare. "I fought by Jadem's side for years. It was her."

"I don't believe it," I say.

If my aunt was alive, she would have come back to us. She wouldn't have stayed in Malarusk. She wouldn't have betrayed us.

No one else speaks.

"She would have come back," I insist. "I know she would have."

"She's working with them." Ry says the words gently, like it will soften their impact.

Before I can process what I'm doing, Ry is pinned against the wall with my hand at her throat.

"Mer, let her go," Dayne commands.

I don't take my eyes off Ry.

"Why?" My voice breaks. "Why would you destroy her reputation? She's dead!"

"I saw her," Ry chokes out. She doesn't try to struggle. "She was giving orders."

I let Ry go and slump against the wall. This can't be true. Ry must be confused. Maybe Crowe dressed someone else up to look like my aunt. Maybe….

"Fake Hendrix!" I say. "It's like that. She made you think you saw Jadem, but it's really just some random Dusker they disguised to look like her."

I know I sound crazed, but I don't care.

"Look, I knew you wouldn't believe me," Ry says. Her hurt expression says I've let her down—that, in spite of what she's saying, she'd wanted us to believe her.

But how could I? I've just learned about my mother's betrayal. How could I even begin to process my aunt deceiving me, too?

I can't believe Aunt Jadem would do something like that to me. I won't.

Ry takes a breath and hardens herself. "Let's go."

"Go where?" Wade asks.

"To Malarusk. I'm going to prove to you that Jadem's still alive."

# CHAPTER 16

We leave Dellin behind. No surprise—she'll spout all sorts of facts about the Duskers, but when it comes down to it, she won't go anywhere near Malarusk.

Dayne makes some vague excuses to Valior about where we're going, and as soon as it's low day, we ride Vlaz to the Dusker territory.

I spent most of the high day hurling up my guts. Now, I just feel empty. My head aches, which is only made worse by the pumping of Vlaz's wings. Dayne said the only reason I'm even able to stand up today is because of how quickly my body heals.

Wade still won't look at or talk to me, but my mind is so full of thoughts of Aunt Jadem I hardly notice.

Ry sits in front, directing Vlaz. From the ease with which she communicates our direction to the hyenair, it's obvious they've travelled this route before. As we fly, my mind turns over all the possible explanations for what Ry thinks she saw.

It has to be Crowe disguising someone to look like Jadem, just like she did with Hendrix. It's the only possibility that makes sense. Crowe would plant the imposter in hopes that one of our people would see her. It would make the Banished doubt the Solguards and sow the seeds of distrust. After that, we would be so embroiled in conflict with our own people the Duskers could attack without us posing a cohesive defense.

*That must be it*, I tell myself.

Except, I can't ignore the thought that keeps niggling at the back of my mind…the one that says my explanation doesn't make sense, either. If Crowe wanted to stir up conflict, she would have sent the fake Jadem into our territory. Crowe had no reason to suspect one of our own would be scouting so close to Malarusk. No one would have ever seen this Jadem imposter if Ry hadn't gotten suspicious and went looking for her….

Vlaz sails over the mountains and lands on the far side of Malarusk where I had come on my own during the high day. As soon as we're on the ground, Ry unhooks the pack she tied around Vlaz's neck and sends him back before any Duskers notice a hyenair outside their walls.

"What did you bring?" Wade asks Ry.

Instead of answering, Ry reaches her hand into the pack and pulls something out. There's a flicker of light and the earthy scent of cammamoss as she hands what looks to be an armful of air to Dayne. She does the same for each of us, and when it's my turn, I feel the delicately-woven blanket of cammamoss drape over my arms.

Cammamoss is one of the plants that came from Tanguro. After we returned to Solis, Wokee managed to make it grow there. I guess he brought enough of it to the Banished territory to make these cloaks. I'll have to remember to thank him later.

Ry leads us through the mud, along more or less the same path I took when I swam under the stone wall and into the citadel. The cammamoss covers about a third of each of our bodies, so we look like a group of disconnected limbs.

It's low day now, so there are archers in the lookouts cut into the mountainside and on top of the iron gate on the far side of the compound. We move slowly. No one speaks.

When Ry stops, we're at the place where the streambed deepens. She motions us up to the stone wall. We pull the cammamoss over our heads and peer over the wall. Warm, muddy water squishes beneath my feet. There's the unpleasant sensation of liquid absorbing into the soles of my boots.

Ry draws her hand from the sleeve of her cammamoss cloak to indicate the direction she wants us to look.

When I came here the last time, the ground above the citadel was empty. Now that it's low day, the place hums with activity.

People dressed in ragged, filthy cloaks are pushing carts stacked high with something I can't make out from the tunnel and onto the Outside. They're not Duskers, or even new recruits.

*Banished*, Ry whispers, and I immediately understand.

These are the Banished people who accepted Crowe's offer of trading their labor for protection. Even from this distance, I can tell there's only one word to describe these people: slaves.

I don't feel pity for them. Aunt Jadem told them not to trust the Duskers. She said the Duskers wouldn't welcome outsiders into their citadel unless it benefitted them. But then I remember the reason the Banished people were running to Darkness Peak was because they were desperate to escape the Halves and starvation. I feel guilty for judging them so harshly.

Duskers carrying whips follow the slaves as they push and pull the laden carts through the mud. They overturn the carts somewhere out of sight and return for more. There's a steady stream of the carts going and coming. I wish we could get closer so I could see what it is they're emptying just past our view, but there are too many Duskers.

I'm not really paying attention to any of that, though. My focus is intent on every single Dusker who comes within view. My eyes scan the gray-clad figures as I try to spot Aunt Jadem among them.

I'm not sure if I'm relieved or devastated when I don't catch a glimpse of anyone who even remotely looks to have her build.

I signal to Ry. *Time to go.*

The cammamoss doesn't hide us nearly enough, and it's a miracle we haven't been spotted yet.

Ry pulls off her cammamoss to stare at her shadow, measuring the angle. Then, she holds up five fingers. *Five more minutes*, she mouths.

I shrug. I can humor her.

It's fewer than five minutes when two Duskers appear from the tunnel. I can tell they're important from the way the slaves shrink away and the Dusker slave masters grovel at their feet. As they step out of the shadows, all of the air leaves my lungs in a whoosh.

There's no mistaking her, even at this distance and with her Dusker cloak and hood. My aunt's thick features, the stalking way she moves, even the way she turns her head slightly to the right whenever she's talking to someone to keep them in view of her good eye.

I don't even realize I'm gripping the stone wall and bracing myself to swing onto it until rough hands yank me back.

"Don't be stupid," Wade hisses.

He's right. There are at least fifty Duskers who would see me the moment I crossed onto the other side of the wall. Still, it's little better than torture to stay hidden when she's there, no more than twenty yards away.

I can't breathe. I don't know what to think.

I saw Aunt Jadem die. And yet, here she is, very much alive and giving orders.

I can hear the harsh bark of her voice from here, although I can't decipher the individual words. The Dusker beside her is a man. He turns his face toward me for a fraction of a second, and I think I see the sunlight reflecting off green irises beneath his hood.

*Hendrix.* The name has a bitter taste as I whisper it.

I catch a single word, barked out from my aunt's lips: *more.*

The slaves scurry back into the tunnel with their carts. Other slaves are on their hands and knees, speaking to my aunt in frantic, fearful tones.

My aunt, dressed in full Dusker uniform, is pointing at something out of sight and back at the tunnel. Hendrix is nodding. The slaves are hurrying to do whatever she's ordered. I stare, desperate for some sign of shackles, a guard following her around with a dagger at her back, anything to prove she's here because they've forced her and not because she's chosen it. But it's clear my aunt is the one giving the orders, and not the other way around.

I feel sick.

A Banished slave scuttles up to my aunt, his skeletal frame bowed. He stretches up to say something to her. Jadem looks in the direction the man is pointing. She makes a motion with her hand, and two more slaves approach.

They're carrying something bulky between them, and they seem to be struggling under its weight. My aunt bends to stare at whatever they're holding, and then she points a finger in our direction.

I duck down, my heart hammering in my chest. I'm terrified my aunt will see our poorly-camouflaged group. At the same time, I wish with all my might that she would. But when I peek back over the stone wall, she's turned away and is speaking with Hendrix again.

"Look," Ry whispers, pointing straight ahead.

The Supreme, immediately recognizable by her tiny form and the guards swarming around her, comes out of the tunnel. She, Hendrix, and Jadem huddle together as they discuss something. Jadem waves a gloved hand as she explains something to Crowe. More words are exchanged, and then the three return into the tunnel together.

Ry's cammamoss cloak has slipped down, and I see the resignation on her face. She isn't surprised by anything we've just witnessed.

The two slaves who had been speaking with Aunt Jadem shuffle through the mud, stopping to adjust their heavy burden several times along the way. I exchange a panicked look with Ry when I realize the slaves are heading straight toward us. There's the grating sound of metal on metal as Wade eases his sword from its sheath.

The slaves stop only a few yards from us on the other side of the stone wall. We all duck down, and I wonder whether the others can hear the pounding of my heart.

"One, two, three!" the slaves grunt in unison.

A shadow passes right over Dayne's head, and then there's a dull splash as whatever the slaves threw hits the water behind us. The slaves' boots squelch through the mud as they make their way back to the citadel.

We inch toward whatever they tossed in the water, keeping low enough that no one will be able to see us from the other side of the wall even if our cammamoss slips.

The water makes a strange sucking noise around the object they threw, and for a moment, I'm reminded of the wormkill slithering through the bowels of the dungeons. The memory makes my stomach turn.

It takes me several moments to make sense of the long, black lump lying in the mud. It's only the boots, which are still intact, that tell me what we're looking at.

It's a corpse.

The water has slowed the decomposing process, but I know this person died the same way as the other Banished who made it back to Valior's settlement.

The body is charred black…black as the darkness in the Duskers' prayers. His cloak, boots, and what's left of his skin and hair are all black. But the most disturbing part is the man's mouth. It's open in a scream. All the teeth are blackened and the lips have disintegrated. Even so, there's no mistaking the agony that is permanently etched onto the slave's face.

As the shallow water trickles over the corpse, the mud turns from brown to black. That familiar, acrid smell rises from the corpse and makes my eyes and nose sting.

"The trees," I whisper.

I don't see any signs of a fire, but maybe the slave just touched one of the black trees by mistake.

I turn away from the corpse, which is now little more than a blackened lump. If I spend a second more in this place, I'll go insane.

"Get me out of here," I say to Ry, not even caring if I'm heard. "Get me out."

*Before I fall apart.*

Ry nods. There's no smug satisfaction that she was right; there's only a look of pity on her face. Somehow, it makes everything worse.

# CHAPTER 17

We don't speak as we trek far enough away from Malarusk for Ry to call Vlaz. On the ride back to the settlement, we're all silent. No one says a word until Vlaz has carried us back to the Banished lands.

After we all dismount, Vlaz sniffs us and then slinks a few paces away without offering any of his usual sticky slobbers. He whimpers and shields his nose in the crook of his paw.

"I'm assuming you'll have to call a council meeting, now," Ry says, breaking our silence.

"Wait," I say. "Aunt Jadem…we…." I swallow. "We have to help her."

The words sound fragile—stupid—even to my own ears.

"She doesn't look like she needed our help," Wade says, his words laced with disgust.

"You knew her best," Ry says to Dayne. "What do you think?"

My brother doesn't speak for several moments. Then, he looks at me.

"I always believed she cared about the Solguards more than anything else. More than her own family, even. But," he pauses, searching for the right way to say whatever he's thinking. "But it always seemed strange to me that she wouldn't allow the Solguards to attack the Duskers outright."

"Sal said something like that, too," Wade says. "That's why he organized the mission to Tanguro."

I look at Wade, knowing how many memories the mere mention of Sal's last mission dredges up for him. He doesn't meet my gaze.

Wade continues, "I always just assumed it was because she didn't want any other Solguards to die. You know, after her experience in the dungeons and having her eye stabbed out by Crowe. I didn't think it was because she was loyal to the Duskers."

I can't believe they're all willing to give up on Jadem so easily. I want to scream at them. I want to hate them for betraying my aunt. And yet, what other possible explanation could there be for what we just saw?

I remember her cold expression as she motioned for the slaves to toss away the corpse, like it meant nothing to her. The Aunt Jadem I knew never would have been so heartless.

A small voice in the back of my head asks if I ever knew my aunt at all.

"We know she worked closely with Crowe when you infiltrated Malarusk," Ry says to Dayne. "Did you ever get the sense that she…kept in touch…with Crowe after?"

Dayne shakes his head. "I honestly don't know."

I open my mouth to say something in her defense.

*Aunt Jadem isn't a traitor. She must have her reasons for working with Crowe. It must be part of some plan to help us, but she couldn't tell us what that was because….*

Everything sounds too feeble in my own head for me to speak the words out loud.

"You have to admit," Ry says, "she was acting weird before we went to kidnap Hendrix. And she botched that mission in an un-Jadem-like way."

"That doesn't mean," I begin, but stop. There is nothing else it could mean. Aunt Jadem is working with Crowe.

I keep seeing the Dusker Supreme as she twisted my aunt's neck. I keep seeing Jadem's body collapse in the mud as the Duskers swarmed out of the iron gate.

"I've found that the most likely explanation is generally the correct one," Dayne says, his mouth set in a grimace. "We must assume that if Jadem is in Malarusk, unchained and giving orders, it's because she wants to be."

"Well, whatever her reasons, she's not our concern now," Wade says. There's a bitter edge to his words.

*No!* I want to shout. *We have to find a way to talk to her. We have to get her out. We have to do* something. But the words stick in my throat, and so I say nothing at all.

"Wade is right," Dayne says. "Our responsibility is to the men, women, and Halves back at the settlement. Whatever Jadem is doing, it's in her hands now."

"But we can't just leave her." Tears burn the back of my throat. A horrible feeling has wrapped around my insides.

"Yes, we can." Dayne says the words with finality. "Our duty is to prepare to battle the Duskers. There are many who are depending on us."

"But all these slaves," I argue. "We can't just leave them, either."

But I know we can, and we must.

"They chose to go to Malarusk even though we told them not to," Ry says. "I'm not saying they deserve what they got, but we warned them what to expect."

My brother's face looks pained, but he nods. "Their best chance at surviving all of this is if our army can overthrow the Duskers."

"Speaking of which," Ry says. "What is *all of this*? What are the Duskers doing out there?"

"Getting ready for something, clearly," Dayne says. "I have a bad feeling."

"So do I," Wade says. "The sooner we can mobilize our forces and put an end to Malarusk, the better it will be for all of us."

I couldn't agree more.

I imagine the Duskers swarming out from their tunnels, and the look that will be on their faces when they realize the iron gate is broken and their greatest weapon has been destroyed by a little girl's powders....I imagine their swords crashing against the Zeroes' scythes, as useless as wooden practice swords against the Duskers' crossbows.

Wade rubs his eyes. "We need to talk some sense of urgency into the Banished leaders."

"Good luck with that," I mutter.

"We should talk it over among ourselves before we meet with the other leaders," Dayne says. "It isn't going to be an easy conversation, and we'll need to stand as a united front."

"I agree," Wade says. "But it's almost high day, and there isn't anywhere in the settlement where we'll be able to get any privacy." His gaze flicks to me for a fraction of a moment before his eyes move on again. It's enough to make my heart leap.

"There's a travel cave nearby," Dayne says. "I suggest we spend the high day there, discuss how we want to broach all of this with the council, and then call a meeting in the low day."

Ry makes a sweeping gesture with her hand. "Well, then, lead on."

I can't imagine how we're going to look into the other leaders' eyes and tell them Aunt Jadem betrayed us all. I don't want to tell them she helped enslave their people. Just the thought of it makes me feel dirty.

I keep trying to think of some way to explain it all…some way to convince myself that Aunt Jadem isn't what she appears to be. But no matter how far I stretch my mind, all I can see is her directing the slaves to toss away the corpse and then disappearing back into the citadel with Crowe and Hendrix at her side.

*  *  *

After we strategize about the council meeting, we all go quiet, each of us lost in our own thoughts. After Ry and Dayne have fallen asleep, and it's just Wade and me staring at the fire, I work up the courage to look at him.

I crave Wade's touch, his warmth, the rumble of his voice as he tells me everything will be alright.

"Wade," I say, my voice sounding too loud.

He meets my eyes for the first time in what feels like an eternity. I forgot how startling his golden eyes are. The anger and hurt in his gaze are enough to steal my breath away.

Now that I have his attention, I have no idea what to say. I force myself just to start talking.

"It's you, Wade," I tell him, finally saying the words I should have spoken months ago. "It always has been. I was just too stupid and too much of a coward to see it…."

I stop talking when I realize Wade isn't looking at my face. He's looking at a spot just below my chin.

"Are you even listening?" I ask, my embarrassment turning to irritation.

115

Wade lifts his eyes for a moment, and what I see makes my heart sink. There's nothing…no sadness or anger or forgiveness.

"The necklace."

Even his voice sounds dead.

"What?" I shake my head, not understanding.

"You took it off."

I look down at my chest before remembering Sal's pendant…the pendant I left soaking in a bowl of water behind the flour sacks to try and remove the stain.

"Oh, no," I say quickly. "One of the Banished grabbed it and ripped the cord, and then it got covered in the black sap," I explain in a single, hurried breath.

"You could just say you didn't want it anymore," Wade says, his voice flat. "But I guess that much honesty would be too much to ask for."

His words are like a slap.

"Wade—"

"I'm going to sleep," he announces, his voice as cold as a Dusker's. "Don't bother me anymore."

# CHAPTER 18

We get back to the settlement, hungry, exhausted, and heartsick. We agreed we'd need to tell the council about Jadem, but none of us is eager for the task. It feels like a betrayal to tell anyone else what we've seen. But of course, that thought is ridiculous. Aunt Jadem is the betrayer. She's the one working with Crowe. She's the one helping to create this weapon that is meant to destroy her own people…her fortress.

In the amount of time it took for us to walk from the travel cave to the settlement, I tried every mental exercise I could conjure to exonerate Aunt Jadem. Each time, I came to the same conclusion. Aunt Jadem is alive when she made us believe she was dead. She never tried to contact any of us. And she was talking with Crowe and Hendrix as their equals.

I'd tried to convince myself she might just be pretending to be one of them again to gain some necessary piece of information. But from everything I know about Crowe, the Supreme isn't one to fall for the same trick twice. Besides, if Jadem was only spying on the Duskers, she could have told us what she was planning.

I'm so wrapped up in my anxiety about the council meeting, and my impatience to be back with the Zeroes, that I don't pay attention to what's going on around me as we descend into the settlement.

The sounds of metal on metal and shouting don't register until I'm partway down the tunnel.

"What in the sun?" Ry asks.

We stand before the main cave, mouths agape, as we try to make sense of the scene before us.

When we left, people and Halves were drinking, eating, and talking. The cave looks nothing like the way we left it.

Tables holding food and drink have been knocked to the ground. Broken shards of pottery are scattered across the cave. Embers from the cookfire caught on a cloth that had been draped across one of the tables. The whole cave is filling with smoke. No one is paying attention to the spreading flames, though. All they seem to be focused on is the fighting.

At first, I look around for gray cloaks, thinking the Duskers somehow figured out what we were planning and came to attack the settlement. I have my sling loaded and I'm searching for my first target before I realize there isn't a single enemy in sight. I blink.

There are Halves, Solguards, Banished, and even Zeroes. Everyone is shouting. Everything is in chaos. The few children in the cave are running around with cans of water, making feeble attempts to put out the fire while trying not to be trod on by everyone who is yelling and shaking their fists.

I squint through the smoke to see swords and clubs being gripped.

A handful of Zeroes are in the cave, standing still as statues with their scythes in hand. I don't have time to wonder about how they got here when I never commanded them to leave their cave.

"All Halves should die!" a Northerner shouts.

That breaks me out of my paralysis.

"Stand down!" I yell, running forward to part the men and Halves who are on the verge of attacking each other. Ry, Wade, and Dayne are doing the same with other pairs of Halves and humans throughout the room. It takes all four of us to stop the fighting.

"Everyone relax and back up," I command.

There's grumbling, but the humans take their hands off the hilts of their swords and back away from the Halves.

"Now you," I tell the Halves in their language. "Stand down."

At a nod from Ekil, the Halves drop their clubs and move to cluster around their leader.

"I don't know how it started," Liglette says as she pushes her way through the crowd to us. She's panting, and her usually neatly braided hair is a mess. Valior, leaning on his cane, follows her.

"Why didn't you stop your people?" I demand. "I gave the Halves my word they'd be safe here."

"Perhaps we were a bit too free with the liquid sun," Valior admits.

I have to dig my nails into my palms to keep from screaming.

"We tried to separate them." My father, looking as composed as the rest of the cave is in shambles, threads his way through the crowd. "But I fear the Zeroes' presence riled up both sides more than it helped."

"And how, exactly, did you get the Zeroes over here?"

A rage I don't understand is building inside me. I feel a sudden urge to strangle him.

"I thought you summoned them," my father says, giving me a questioning look.

"Go back," I tell the Zeroes, making a violent gesture with my hand. "Now."

The crowd parts to give the Zeroes plenty of room as they file out of the cave. Once they're gone, I stride toward my father until there's hardly any space between us.

"Command my Zeroes ever again," I tell him in a deadly quiet, "and it'll be the last thing you ever do."

My father's eyes narrow, but he doesn't argue.

"Very well, Daughter."

With a single nod, he leaves the cave. The air is thick with tension as we all watch him go.

"Where's Wokee?" I ask, scanning the room. A cold sweat breaks out over me when I don't see him.

"With Vlaz on the Outside," Everlyn, breathless and covered in green dust, replies. "That hyenair came back all scared and snapped at me. Wokee's been calming him down."

I sigh with relief. But in a matter of moments, my relief turns to anxiety as I realize I'm going to have to tell Wokee about Jadem. He loved my aunt like family, and when he finds out what Jadem has done, it will break his heart the same way it broke mine.

Still, I owe Wokee the truth. Squaring my shoulders, I head back up the tunnel to the Outside.

❋ ❋ ❋

"Don't get too close," Wokee warns Dayne and me. "Vlaz has been acting strange lately."

There are still puddles of the sticky black muck shimmering in the sun's heat that we have to skirt around.

"It's okay, Vlaz," I say. "It's just us."

I hold out a hand to the hyenair, but instead of coming closer, his growl rumbles in his belly.

"Vlaz!" Wokee scolds.

Vlaz's growl turns to a whimper. He lowers his head and slinks away.

Wokee gives us an accusing look. "Where did you make him go?"

Dayne and I exchange a look. I give my brother a slight shake of my head. *Don't say anything*, I tell him with my eyes. I had planned to tell Wokee about Jadem, but now, seeing his face…I know it would crush him to learn the truth.

So, I tell him about the underground forest of black trees, instead. While I talk, Wokee takes a twig from the ground and prods it into one of the puddles of black goo. The stick immediately begins to disintegrate.

"Is this what killed all those Banished?" Wokee asks when I've finished.

My heart gives a painful jolt. I wish Wokee hadn't had to see those people being consumed by the black trees' residue. I wish I had protected him from witnessing something so gruesome.

"Yes." I swallow. "Did Jadem ever mention anything to you about trees that could grow underground?"

"Specifically, black trees with this black sap coming out of them?" Dayne adds.

Wokee thinks for a minute. "Jadem kept one cave in her fortress completely dark."

Dayne and I tense.

"There were plants growing down there that didn't like sunlight. Mostly medicinal fungus, but there were some bigger plants, too. Nothing as big as a tree, though." Wokee frowns. "Was there a water source nearby?"

"Flowing straight into the tunnel," I say.

"Mm." Wokee tugs on the sleeve of his cloak. "Trees need a lot of water."

"Could there could be any connection to Jadem's seed?" Dayne asks.

I start. I hadn't even been thinking about the seed.

"Why would you think that?" Wokee asks.

"Jadem gave us the seed, and she's involved with these trees," Dayne says. "I was wondering—"

"Jadem is—what?" Wokee demands.

Dayne goes still, realizing what he let slip out. He gives me an apologetic look.

"Screw the secret looks." Wokee stamps his foot on the ground. "What aren't you telling me?"

"Wokee," I say. "I don't want you to get hurt—"

"Stop it." He cuts me off. "Stop treating me like a little kid. I'm a Solguard. I don't need you to protect me. Now, tell me what's going on!"

His voice cracks, but it's not from emotion. His familiar high-pitched voice is changing. It's mostly scratchy, but a few words come out deep without him even trying.

I look at Wokee. His round face has elongated and his limbs are gangly. He's taller, too. It's like the changes happened over a single high day.

I feel simultaneous amazement at the change and guilt I hadn't noticed it sooner.

"Um, well," I say, stalling for time as I try to think of how best to break the news to Wokee. But there is no gentle way to say the truth.

"Jadem's alive," I say. "She's working with the Dusker Supreme."

Wokee's jaw goes slack.

"I know it's hard to understand—"

"She's *what?*"

"Alive," Dayne says.

"No." Wokee is shaking his head. "No, there has to be some mistake."

"We saw her ourselves," Dayne says. "And she's involved with these black trees."

"It can't be true."

Wokee's eyes are watering. His hurt fills me with an intense desire to send every one of my Zeroes after both Crowe and my aunt this second.

"It's true," I say, trying to keep my voice steady. "I'm so sorry."

"She taught me how to grow things," Wokee says in a small voice.

"We're all angry and confused," Dayne tells him, but Wokee doesn't seem to hear.

"She said I was the only one she could trust to tend her orchards."

"I'm so sorry, Wokee," I say again. I reach for him, but he steps back from me.

Wokee's chin gives only the hint of a wobble. He sniffs, wipes the sleeve of his cloak across his face, and clears his throat. When he looks up at me, his eyes are dry.

My heart aches for the pain he's feeling, as well as my own sense of betrayal.

*I'm sorry you've had to grow up so fast,* I want to tell him. But I know he wouldn't appreciate the sentiment. So, instead, I stay quiet and let Dayne explain our theory that the Duskers are planning to cart the trees' wood to Solis and use its poisonous residue to kill whoever is inside.

Wokee considers that. "Did you think of trying to burn one of the trees while you were down there?"

"No." I think about Hendrix and his guards. Something tells me he wouldn't have taken kindly to me lighting one of those trees on fire. I can't tell Dayne and Wokee about that, though, so I say, "I didn't exactly want to announce my presence."

"Well, how are we supposed to know whether burning the wood would actually be enough to destroy Solis?" Wokee asks. "The fortress is made out of stone, so it would have to be a *really* powerful fire."

"Well, we don't have access to any of the trees, and I'm not going back into Malarusk until the attack," I tell him. "We'll just have to assume our theory is right for now."

Wokee's gaze drops to the black substance at our feet. He raises an eyebrow.

"You want to try setting a puddle on fire?" I ask, not trying to mask my skepticism.

Wokee shrugs a shoulder. "It's sap from the trees. It could work."

"Only one way to find out," Dayne says, humoring him.

Wokee reaches into his cloak pocket and draws out a piece of flint. He crouches down next to the congealed black gunk on the ground, his tongue peeking out of the corner of his mouth in concentration. He strikes the flint.

I didn't really expect the black substance to catch fire; after all, there's no wood or any tinder. But the moment the spark touches the puddle, it's engulfed in flames. Except they're not like any flames I've seen before.

These flames are black as pitch.

# CHAPTER 19

What in the sun," Dayne breathes, "is that?"

"I've never seen…black flames," Wokee gasps.

We all stare, dumbstruck, as the black flames consume the puddle.

"I've never," Dayne whispers, his words trailing off as he stares at the flames.

In mere seconds, all that's left of the puddle are blackened, bubbling bits of earth.

Even though there's nothing left to burn, smoke still rises. We shield our faces, our eyes streaming as black smoke rises from the place where the puddle used to be. Dayne, who is closest, coughs until he doubles over.

All the while, smoke continues to billow around us. It's far more smoke than should ever have come from one small fire.

"Have you ever seen anything burn like that?" I ask no one in particular.

From the way no one answers, I can tell they're as disturbed as I am.

"The blue part of a normal flame is hottest," Wokee says. "So maybe the black color means it's an even hotter fire." He coughs into his sleeve.

I look up at the dense cloud of smoke hanging just over our heads. It sits like a mass, without dispersing, as it covers us in shadow.

"Let's all go back into the caves," Dayne says, his eyes bloodshot and still streaming tears. "Whatever we're breathing in, it can't be good."

"Well," Wokee says, his voice raspy from the smoke, "at least we know the fire doesn't last long, even if it burns hotter."

Dayne lets out a bark of laughter. "That isn't very comforting."

"Come on," I say. "We'd better go talk to the other Banished leaders. If the threat of burning the black logs at our doorstep doesn't motivate them to speed up our attack, nothing will."

I herd Wokee back toward the settlement.

"Dayne?" I ask, when he doesn't move to follow us.

He doesn't look at me. He's staring up at the black cloud of smoke still hovering overhead.

"I've never seen smoke do that." He looks back at Wokee and me. "Have you?"

When I look up at the smoke, I can't see anything through the haze. Not even the orange of the sun is visible through the dense black fog.

"Well, no," Wokee says, "but who cares about smoke? Fire is the dangerous part."

Shaking his head, Dayne follows Wokee and me until we're free of the smoke's shadow. I take a deep breath of hot, clean air.

"So, what do you think?" I ask Wokee as we make our way back to the settlement. "About Jadem's seed being connected to the black trees?"

"I don't think the seed grows the black trees." Wokee coughs again. "But we won't know for sure until it sprouts."

"You're growing it?"

"Well it's no good sitting around in a little box, now, is it?" he retorts.

"How long until it's grown?" I press.

"How should I know?" Wokee replies. "These things take time."

I bite back my response, that time is a luxury we don't have, and just nod.

"I'll know more in a few days," Wokee says. "By the time we leave for Malarusk, I might be able to tell you what it is I'm growing."

I don't hear anything else after the first part. *By the time* we *leave for Malarusk.*

"Wokee," I say, stopping to face him. "You know you can't come to Malarusk, right?"

Wokee stares up at me. There's an odd expression on his face.

"You'll be more use to all of us by staying here," I continue. "Who will take care of all the plants if you leave?"

It's the same argument I've used every time we need to leave Wokee behind, but it's the only one that has worked.

"Yeah, I know," Wokee says with a shrug.

I stare at him. I had expected more of a fight, or at least some anger that I'm treating him like a little kid instead of a Solguard.

"You understand that you need to stay here?" I ask.

"Sure," Wokee says. "I didn't really expect you to let me come, anyway. It's not a big deal."

I exchange a look with Dayne, who only shrugs his shoulders.

"Okay." I give Wokee a tentative smile. "Well, I'm glad you understand. I guess you really are growing up."

He returns my smile before running off. With a happy whimper, Vlaz bounds after him, his ears flopping with every step.

"Well, what now?" I ask my brother as we watch the small boy and the enormous hyenair chase each other.

"Why don't we get a little rest before convening the council," Dayne says, rubbing his eyes. "You go on and get some rest."

"That sounds good," I tell him, even though I have no plans to sleep.

*I'm going back to Malarusk.*

There's still a part of me that believes if I can just talk to my aunt, all of this will make sense.

*You were wrong about your own mother*, a voice in my head warns. *What makes you think you knew your aunt any better?*

Still, I have to at least try to understand, and I can't wait for the battle to do it. I'll just have to go back and wait until it's only Jadem and the Banished slaves before I approach her. Maybe I can leave a note telling her to meet me somewhere....

I don't tell Dayne what I'm planning, since he'd never let me return to Malarusk alone.

I check my shadow. Two hours until high day—plenty of time for me to get to Malarusk and back before anyone notices. I wait until Dayne has gone down into the tunnel. Then, I take off in the opposite direction.

# CHAPTER 20

I reach the stone wall bordering the far side of Malarusk and stop to catch my breath. It took me longer to get here than I expected. I'm still fast, faster than any human and most animals, but my muscles are tired.

Ever since I turned the Zeroes, I've felt their strength coursing through me. I still feel the tug of the bond between us, but I'm worn out in a way I can't remember feeling since I created the Zeroes. I still have more strength than any human should, but I can't shake the sense that something is missing.

My bond with the Zeroes also feels different. It doesn't hurt as much when there's distance between us. A few weeks ago, going this far away from them would have caused me actual physical pain. Now, there's only a dull ache to remind me of what is waiting back at the settlement.

I must have adjusted to the bond and my new strength, which is making both less intense than they were before. I know it's for the best—I can't take the Zeroes with me every time I need to go somewhere—but there's also a sense of loss that I can't place. I feel empty.

*I probably just need to sleep.*

I crouch so my head stays below the top of the stone wall.

Draping the cammamoss I brought with me over my head, I pull myself up onto the wall and peek over. I ignore the stones' heat as it sears into my palms.

Even though it's getting close to high day, the Banished slaves are still working feverishly. The hoods of their cloaks hide their faces in shadow, but I can see their exhaustion in the curve of their spines.

Carts come and go from inside the tunnel. I can't make out what they're carrying, and I don't want to risk getting any closer to find out.

I crouch just below the lip of the wall and wait for my aunt to appear.

As high day approaches, my patience wanes.

"Come on," I whisper. *I need to talk to you.*

The Banished slaves continue to work, but I see no sign of my aunt. I clench my jaw to keep from growling in frustration. If I go back to the settlement without talking to my aunt, I might not have another chance before we attack.

The higher the sun climbs, the more desperate I become. I can't leave here without talking to her. *I won't.*

I go back to the stream, the same place I entered the citadel the last time. Except unlike last time, there are still Dusker archers in all the lookouts.

I leave the cammamoss behind since it would disintegrate in the water. I step into the stream and let the current pull me under the stone wall and inside Malarusk.

I know how insane I am. The last time I was here, Hendrix found me. It was a miracle he let me go instead of killing me on the spot. This time, I might not be so lucky. But I don't turn back.

When I can't hold my breath for another second, I pop back up to the surface. It was so bright outside, and it's so dark in here. I blink the water out of my eyes and squint into the darkness. I'm in one of the underground tunnels that lead down into Malarusk.

When I tilt my head up and look over the muddy embankment, I can see the outline of Banished slaves on either side of the stream. Their hoods are up and they're so busy with their carts they don't notice me.

A feeling of defeat tightens my insides. Jadem could be anywhere in this underground labyrinth.

One last idea comes to me. Maybe one of the Banished knows where I could find her. If I can just get close without alerting the Duskers who are bound to be nearby, maybe I can convince one of them to deliver a message to Jadem. I'm not above resorting to threats and terrifying the Banished with my black eyes to ensure they don't betray me to the Duskers.

*Perfect*, I think, as one of the Banished slaves splits off from the rest and walks over to the stream.

The slave's gaze is fixed on some point above my head. When he reaches the stream, I can see the hollows of his eye sockets. The man's cheekbones are triangles of bone that look nearly sharp enough to cut through his flesh. His face is covered with soot, and his eyes are bloodshot. A shudder rolls through me.

"Hey," I whisper.

The man startles and looks down. When his eyes lock on me, his expression turns from confusion to alarm.

"Don't worry," I say as he recoils. "Please, I just need to talk to Jadem."

The slave's eyes dart all around. I can't see much past the area right beside the stream, but there must not be any Duskers in view because the man comes closer.

"I don't know anyone by that name," he whispers.

"She has one eye," I tell him.

Recognition dawns on the man's face. Hope surges in my chest.

"The Supreme's third." He lifts his pointed chin. "I know that bitch."

*The Supreme's third.*

"I need to talk to her," I say. "Do you think you could get her and bring her here?"

"Hah." The weak laugh costs him. The man starts to hack into the sleeve of his cloak. When he straightens again, I think I see blood on the fabric. "She isn't going to do *my* bidding."

"Tell her Hemera is here," I say, my heart beating a furious rhythm in my chest. "That's all you have to do. She'll want to talk to me, I swear."

The slave's eyes dart around again. "What's in it for me?"

"What do you want?" I ask.

He licks his soot-smudged lips. "Get me out of here."

"Fine, okay," I tell him. "Just bring the one-eyed woman here."

The slave gives me a short, jerky nod.

"Hemera," I remind him. "Don't forget."

The man disappears. I know I should stay hidden, but my nerves are strained to the breaking point. I pull myself out of the water just enough that I'll be able to see my aunt as she comes down the tunnel.

My heart flies into my throat when I catch sight of her, looking huge and imposing next to the shrunken man. Aunt Jadem is no more than twenty paces from me. The slave points right at me, murmuring something to my aunt between spasmodic coughs.

Aunt Jadem's eye finds me.

A thousand emotions flash through me before I settle on relief. She'll come over and tell me where to meet her so we can talk without the Duskers overhearing. She'll explain everything to me. And then, we'll go back to the settlement together.

She stares at me for another moment. She's wearing the Dusker cloak and mask that obscures most of her face, so I can't read her expression. But I can see her eye, and the look in it chills me. My aunt is staring right at me, after months of separation, and there isn't a trace of emotion in her gaze.

"Why do you lie to me, slave?"

Aunt Jadem keeps her voice neutral, but it carries across the tunnel. The other slaves stop what they're doing. They all keep their eyes downturned. Some of them even pull their hoods forward to hide their faces and hunch in on themselves.

"But, my lady," the slave stammers. "Hemer—"

A loud smack reverberates through the tunnel. There's the sound of squishing mud as the slave drops to his knees.

I watch in open-mouthed horror as my aunt lowers her hand.

"You dare to approach me?" she demands.

I want to climb up the muddy bank and go to her. I want to demand to know what the hell she's doing. But I can't move. Her voice and her gaze have me rooted to the spot. This isn't my aunt. And yet, it is. I'm overwhelmed and confused and have no idea what I'm supposed to do.

"And now, you're lying to me?"

My aunt's voice has risen in volume. I feel myself flinch, and I have to fight against the urge to sink back into the water and swim away as fast as I can.

"I ain't lying, M'lady. Look, she's right over—"

This time, there's no sound of a slap. There is no yelling rebuke. I cover my mouth with my hands to hold back my scream as Aunt Jadem drives her sword into the Banished slave's chest.

There's a sickening squelch as the slave's body collapses onto the muddy ground.

Aunt Jadem doesn't flinch as she pulls her sword free. She bends down to the stream and dips the blood-slicked blade into the water. She straightens back up and re-sheaths her sword.

"Get back to work," she snaps at the nearest Banished slaves.

Then, without another glance in my direction, she strides back in the direction from which she came.

As soon as Jadem is out of sight, the other Banished slaves in the tunnel seem to let out a breath. Then, they go back to work like they'd never been interrupted. They step over the prone body on the ground as they go about their business like it's nothing more than an inconvenience.

I stand in the stream, half in and half out of the water. Furious tears course down my cheeks. If I could make my throat work, I'd scream. If my legs hadn't turned to lead, I'd chase my aunt down.

A harsh horn sounds in the tunnel. The Banished slaves abandon their work and move in an orderly line deeper into the citadel.

I'm left alone with only the slave's corpse for company.

# CHAPTER 21

I return to the settlement, too spent to feel any of the emotions I should be feeling, which is a perverse kind of comfort. I keep stumbling on rocks because I'm not paying attention to where I'm walking. My mind keeps replaying the scene from the tunnel over and over again.

When I hear shouting and grunting coming from the settlement's main cave, fury flares deep inside me.

"What in the sun is wrong with all of you?" I demand, stomping forward.

When I step into the cave, my jaw drops. This isn't like the last time, when the humans and Halves were shouting insults the other side couldn't even understand. Before, the only casualties were some overturned food platters and a burnt tablecloth. This time is different.

I trip over something as I enter the cave and realize it's a body.

A Banished man limps toward me, leaving a trail of blood on the path as he clutches his leg. There's a piercing shriek as a Halve tackles him from behind and throws him to the ground. The Halve puts his foot on the man's back, completely oblivious to the way the man writhes and struggles beneath it.

Another Halve, her brown blood trickling from her mouth and pooling on the ground, is stretched out in front of the doorway. There's an Easterner who is pinned against the wall by a Halve's club. His face has turned as gray as a Dusker's cloak.

One of the Northerners draws her golden blade across a Halve's throat.

"Hemera, thank the sun." Ry, her hair a tangled, sweaty mess, has an arm wrapped around an Easterner who is cursing as he tries to lunge at a Halve.

"They've all gone crazy," she pants, squeezing until the man loses consciousness and slips to the ground.

Ry's words make my paralysis lift.

"Stop!" I yell.

No one drops their weapons. No one even looks my way.

"What do we do? They've all gone completely nuts!"

I turn at the sound of Wokee's voice. The sight of him here, in the midst of all this madness, sends panic jolting through my veins. I tackle a Halve that stumbles into his path, using my body to shield Wokee's.

"Get out of here," I tell him, practically throwing him out of the cave.

I spin in a circle, trying to make sense of the insanity unfolding all around me. There are dead Banished and Halves lying on the ground, their brown and red blood soaking into the earthen floor.

I need help. I need—

*Zeroes.*

I feel their presence through our bond. Concentrating all my energy into our connection, I will them to come to me.

I don't know if it will work since I've never summoned them this way before. But only a few seconds pass before they're bursting into the cave. Relief floods me at the sight of them.

The Zeroes' brutal posture and predatory stillness are in direct contrast to the chaos surrounding me. The sight of them makes everyone else, both humans and Halves, pause their fighting for a moment. It's enough for me to regain control of the situation.

"All of you drop your weapons. Now." The Banished are hesitant at first, but when I motion the Zeroes forward, the humans' weapons clatter to the ground.

"What in the sun are you all doing?" I demand. "Where are your leaders?"

"Useless, senseless beasts." Tut wipes his sword on his soiled cloak as he strides forward. "We don't need their help around here." His cheeks are red, and he's gasping for breath.

I want nothing more than to strangle this pathetic excuse for a man.

"I'll tell you what's going on." Jarosh, one arm wrapped around a Northerner's throat, gives the man another yank until his weapon falls out of his grip. "The filthy barbarians are trying to insult us. They're thieving ingrates and don't appreciate what we're sacrificing for them."

It takes me a moment to realize Jarosh is talking about the human soldiers, and the "us" are the Halves.

"Jarosh, he's turning blue." I put my hand on his arm, trying to extricate the other man as gently as possible.

"Rotten beasts," the Northerner chokes out when Jarosh releases him.

"And you're murderers!" Jarosh yells.

"If you think you're one of them, then they've melted your brain completely," the Northerner snarls back at Jarosh. "Why don't you go back to whatever hole in the ground you came from?"

"We were invited, you ignorant bastard!" Jarosh is shaking with rage.

"It's that lady-Halve you're always going around with," the Northerner spits back. "It muddled your thinking." He points an accusing finger at Camike.

It takes both Camike and Wade to restrain Jarosh as he lunges at the man.

"We won't fight with beasts," a Westerner says. She has an arrow nocked in her bow.

"You'd rather the Duskers slaughter us all?" Jarosh shoots back. "And you call *us* uncivilized?"

"You're not one of them!" the woman yells at Jarosh.

"I would have expected this kind of bigoted idiocy from the Northerners," Jarosh says, "but I expected *slightly* more from you people."

Voices rise again.

"Shut up." My voice isn't loud, but their attention turns on me.

"Humans started it." Ekil, his black eyes glittering with fury, strides up to me. He points a gnarled finger in my face. "You promised."

I round on Tut. "I gave the Halves my word that no one would harm them here. You let your people make me into a liar and put our entire mission at risk."

Feeling my energy, the Zeroes move closer.

"Devil creatures," an Easterner says as he shrinks away from the Zeroes. "They'll murder us in our sleep."

"They'll save your lives," I snap, but I can see the terror in people's eyes.

"Back up," I tell the Zeroes, motioning for them to line up against the wall of the cave. "Don't touch anyone."

"Humans kill," Brogut roars.

Ekil puts up a hand to calm him, but Brogut swats it away.

"Humans kill," he thunders again. He raises his tree trunk spear overhead, smashing it through the earth ceiling. "Halves fight back!"

"I don't know what that thing is saying, but I don't like it," Tut says, gripping his sword.

Two tall Northerners move forward, weapons in hand. Tut makes a feeble effort to push them back. But when Brogut roars again and stamps his massive feet until the whole cave shudders, the Northerners attack.

I push my way between them. Brogut, still enraged, pulls back his fist. I duck, but before the blow lands, one of my Zeroes throws Brogut clear across the cave.

"I told you to stand still and not to touch anyone," I say to the Zero, even though those words aren't ones the Zero can understand.

"They sensed a threat to you," my father says.

I hadn't even known he was here, although I guess I shouldn't be surprised he followed the Zeroes here.

"Their instincts are strong," he continues. "When their maker is threatened, they are driven to protect you. They will not break your command for any other reason."

"Look out!"

I'm so intent on what my father is saying, I don't register the warning until it's too late. By the time I look, Brogut's tree trunk spear is already hurtling toward the Zero that threw him. The Zero makes no move to defend itself.

I don't see the point of the tree trunk drive into the Zero's neck. I feel it.

# CHAPTER 22

I know there is no blood leaking out of my neck. They've told me so, again and again. They've pressed my own fingers to my neck, showing me I'm unhurt. It doesn't change the way I feel. It doesn't stop my brain from believing my life force is spilling onto the ground. It doesn't change the sensation of being surrounded by blood, choked by it, drowned in it.

My friends, Dayne, my father, and the Banished leaders are crowded around me. They're saying comforting things and pressing cool cloths to my forehead.

*I don't want any of you*, I want to scream. *Where is my Zero?*

If my throat wasn't too choked with imaginary blood, I would shout the words.

The lamplight is too bright, the voices too loud. I'm dying. My brain knows it, even if my body doesn't. An unfamiliar keening sound coming from my own throat.

Through the haze of my agony, I'm dimly aware of Jarosh and Camike, standing on Valior's podium, talking to both the humans and Halves.

"We can live together, even love each other," Camike's warm voice says. "Like my mate and me."

Hearing her talk about peace and love just makes me angry. If they hadn't all been so stupid, my Zero wouldn't be lying in a pool of its own blood.

*Shut up*, I want to scream at Camike.

My fury continues to boil and churn. The angrier I get, the more the pain in my neck eases. I sit up, ignoring the way my vision darkens. I push away the hands that reach out to steady me and the voices that are meant to comfort me.

*This isn't Camike's fault*, I tell myself. *It's Brogut's.*

Even thinking his name makes my rage flare so strong it feels like a living, breathing thing.

Brogut did this to one of my Zeroes before. I should have stopped him then. I should have killed him. My gaze narrows until all I see is Brogut. I won't let him take another of my soldiers.

I push my way through the Halves until I reach him. His tree trunk spear, the tip splattered with my Zero's blood, is still clutched in his hand. With a feral cry, I yank the weapon out of his grasp and beat it against the wall. I watch as it splinters and breaks into smaller and smaller pieces. I throw the stub away, hardly noticing when it hits a Halve in the stomach and makes him double over.

"Murderer!"

I feel my mouth form the word, but the shriek that comes out of my throat doesn't sound like my voice.

I pull my fist back and punch Brogut. There's so much force behind the blow that his body blasts a path through everyone and everything near him as he shoots back across the cave. There's a sickening *crack* as he hits the wall. Dirt rains down around him.

With a snarl, he's on his feet again.

"Come on," I make a violent gesture at him. "Let's finish this."

There's yelling and weak attempts to hold me back. I barely notice.

"You are Halve saver." Ekil moves in front of Brogut, blocking him from me.

"Get out of the way," I growl.

"No."

I pull the small dagger out of my belt. Faster than Ekil can blink, I have the blade pressed into the folds of his neck.

"Hemera!"

One voice in the chorus gives me a moment of pause. I feel Wade's hands on my shoulders.

"You don't want to do this."

"Yes, I do." I turn back to Ekil and dig the blade in a little more. "They won't get away with what they've done to me."

"He hasn't done anything to you," Wade says.

"He tried to kill me!" My shrill voice fills the now-silent cave.

"You aren't the Zeroes. Hemera," Wade pulls on me again, turning my black eyes away from Ekil. "You're not the same as them. You're you."

There's some emotion in his golden eyes I don't recognize.

"Hemera, you're better than this. Please."

My breath catches when I realize what it is. Wade is afraid…of me.

"Come on, little sis," Dayne says. "We'll meet with the Banished leaders. They'll—"

"I don't care about the Banished!" I scream. "My Zero is dead!"

"Come on, Mer." Ry quirks her lip in a nervous smile. "It was just a Zero."

Filled with a rage I don't recognize and can't begin to contain, I curl my hand into a fist and drive it into the solid mass of the wall. There is screaming from an adjoining cave as a gaping hole opens up and fills with dirt. My hand is sticky with blood, but I don't feel any pain.

No one speaks. They all stand motionless, identical looks of shock on each of their faces.

"Save that anger for the Duskers. You will need it soon enough." My father's voice comes from somewhere out of sight. I can't see anything except for the red of my fury.

*I have plenty of anger to spare.*

"Your Zero is not dead." My father ducks around Ekil so he's facing me.

I have to repeat those words in my head twice before I understand their meaning.

"Your Zero isn't dead," my father says again. "Daughter, the Zero is alive."

I didn't think there was anything that could stop me from what I meant to do. But these words make me lower my dagger.

"It's—alive?" My voice breaks, and my knees turn to mush.

The Captain nods.

"Liar," I snarl.

I saw the tree trunk spear piece its neck. I felt its blood drain. Nothing could survive such an injury.

"See for yourself."

I follow the direction of my father's gaze. The Zero is on its feet. The wound in its neck is still leaking brown blood, but it has slowed to a trickle. The gaping hole is smaller than the sharpened point of the tree trunk spear.

"How?" I ask, my voice cracking on the word.

"Have you forgotten your blood runs through its veins?" My father gives me an amused look. "The same healing properties you possess kept the Zero from succumbing to its injury."

I don't say anything. It's enough to just look at the Zero and know it's still here.

"Can they not be killed, then?" Valior, his rheumy eyes fixed on the Zero, hobbles closer.

Zeidan shrugs. "I've never encountered anything that doesn't die, eventually. But Hemera isn't like anything I've ever encountered."

Valior grins his missing-toothed grin. "It won't matter how many men the Duskers can throw at us. We've got an invincible army!"

There are shouts of *hooray for the invisible army* from the spectators.

*Like this is some kind of show meant for their entertainment.*

"There is nothing to celebrate here," Dayne says. "Let's not forget these Zeroes are weapons, and weapons are only as good as the ones who wield them."

I stare at my brother, stung by his insult. But he isn't looking at me. His attention is on my father.

"I control the Zeroes," I say, my tone almost violent. "I wield this weapon."

Dayne still doesn't look at me. He gives my father another glare before turning around and pushing through the gawking Banished, Halves, and Solguards.

"All the rest of you, get out of here," I snap. "Show's over."

The cave begins to empty. I hear snatches of whispered conversation about the "crazy Bisecter" and her invincible army. They talk about the inevitability of our victory with such a weapon on our side. They talk about plans for after the battle, when before, they were preparing to meet their doom.

"Not you." I grab Ekil's scaly forearm, keeping him from leaving with the others. "You and I need to talk."

The Zero is still alive, but that doesn't mean I can forget what Brogut tried to do…what he almost did. I made a mistake the first time Brogut attacked one of my Zeroes. I won't make the same error again.

"I want you to leave," I tell Ekil.

Ekil blinks at me.

"All of you."

"Battle is soon. You need Halves' help."

"No." I shake my head. "I don't need anything that is stupid enough to attack the very things that will save them."

With the Zeroes being what they are, I could probably take down the Duskers without the Banished, too. I file that thought away for later.

"Brogut gets angry sometimes," Ekil says. "He won't attack again."

"It's obvious you can't control him."

Ekil flinches back. I feel a little sorry, but not enough to change my mind.

"If you'd controlled him after the last time he attacked a Zero, this never would have happened," I continue.

"Where should Halves go?" Ekil asks.

A flash of anger passes through me. *A Zero almost died, and he's worried about where to go?*

"How should I know?" I reply. "Anywhere you want."

"Nowhere to go," Ekil says. "No water for Halves."

"In a few days, Malarusk will be destroyed and the Duskers overthrown," I tell him, heading toward the tunnel. "You'll have all your water back then." I laugh. "You can even move into Malarusk if you want."

I leave the cave with Ekil staring after me.

# CHAPTER 23

I finish checking on the injured Zero and close the door to their chamber. Even though its wound was barely bleeding anymore, I still made my father treat and bandage it.

My mind is full of everything that has happened in the last few hours as I force my tired legs to bring me back up the tunnel. More than anything, I wish I could fall asleep and wake up to discover what happened with Jadem was just a dream.

It's the wish of a child.

"Hemera Harkibel!" a voice thunders.

Jarosh, with Camike at his side, comes stomping down the tunnel. From the force of each stride, I'm surprised I can't feel the ground tremble underfoot.

He stops just inches from me.

"I know my Halve-speak isn't top notch," he says, stabbing a finger at my face, "so I'll just assume Ekil was trying to tell me about what's for dinner, and not that you *kicked us out* of the settlement."

"You did what?" Ry, coming from the opposite direction, stops to stare at me.

"What did you expect?" I ask, defensive. "After what Brogut did—"

"Mer, we need their help," Ry says, her eyes wide with astonishment. "The Zeroes—"

"Are all fine and good," Ry interrupts. "But we need the Halves. You can't just…dismiss a third of our army."

"Wade, Dayne, Banished leaders!" Jarosh thunders. "Someone get the hell over here and talk some sense into the Bisecter before I hurt her."

"Hah." I raise an eyebrow.

"Badly." Jarosh lowers his hand to the dagger at his belt.

Camike wraps her arms around Jarosh, crooning to him as she pulls him away from me. She gives me a dark look, which, coming from her, is as bad as anyone else drawing their weapon.

I feel sorry—sorry to have upset Camike, but not sorry enough to change my mind.

"What are you shouting about?" Wade asks Jarosh when he and the others have joined us.

"Just face facts," I tell Jarosh, ignoring the others. "We don't need you. It's not personal."

"Like hell it's not," he shouts. "You're just kicking us out because you're mad about that Zero."

I get the sense that if Camike wasn't holding him back, Jarosh would lunge at me.

"Hemera, you didn't really kick the Halves out, did you?" Wade gives me an incredulous look.

I feel my cheeks redden. "Of course I did. Brogut's a monster."

An insane laugh comes from Jarosh. "Brogut's the monster?! Have you seen your own reflection lately?"

His insult festers in my heart. I've been called monstrous—an abomination—all my life. But I never did anything to deserve that branding. *Unlike Brogut.*

"Why doesn't everyone just shake hands so we can move forward?" Dayne asks. "We're all friends here."

I stare uncomprehending at the people surrounding me. *Why do they all seem confused by the only logical decision I could make?*

"Little sis, you're not thinking clearly," Dayne says. "The Zeroes are poisoning your mind."

His tone is gentle, which somehow makes his words hurt more. I square my shoulders.

"I've never thought more clearly in my life," I reply. "The Zeroes are going to win this battle. Anything that's a threat to the Zeroes is a threat to the rest of us."

"The Halves aren't a threat to your precious Zeroes," Jarosh says, his chest heaving. "And you damn well know it."

"My Zeroes, my call," I reply.

"You sound like a child," Jarosh accuses.

"And you sound bitter," I retort.

"No, change that," Jarosh amends. "A child has *some* amount of good sense. You're a—"

"*Think* about this," Wade hisses to me. "Think about what you're doing."

"I have thought about it," I say, loud enough for everyone to hear me. "The Halves need to be gone by high day."

"We'll die. You know that, right?" Jarosh grinds out. "You know as well as any of us there isn't any water this side of the mountains. Our caves are probably overrun with hyenair, and I'm not talking about the tame variety."

"Like I told Ekil," I begin, but Jarosh cuts me off.

"Yeah, yeah, I know what you told Ekil." He makes a disgusted sound. "Whatever helps you sleep during the high day."

"I don't want to argue with you," I tell Jarosh, and I mean it.

Jarosh is one of my best friends. We fought together at Tanguro. But friendship isn't enough to hang the entire mission on. This battle is too important.

"Well, you did say one true thing," Valior says. "The Zeroes are yours, and thus, you have the power to keep or dismiss soldiers as you wish. We will not condone this choice, but we will not prevent it, either."

"I for one think this is the first intelligent decision she's ever made," Tut says.

I cringe at his gold-toothed smile, because it's genuine and directed at me.

"Well, if no one else will say it, I will." Jarosh extricates himself from Camike's grip so he can stand in front of me. "You're being a real bitch."

"My love," Camike says in the human language, but for once, Jarosh doesn't pay attention to her.

"These Zeroes have twisted your brain, making you think your friends are foes and foes are friends," he continues. "We aren't the ones you should be exiling."

"You're not one of them," I try to tell Jarosh, but he just laughs in my face.

"Oh, that's rich, coming from you."

"What's that supposed to mean?" I ask, knowing I would have been better off just walking away.

"You're not one of your precious Zeroes, either!"

I shake my head. "I'm sorry for the bad feelings," I tell him, "but my decision stands."

Jarosh glares at me for another moment. Ry, Wade, and Dayne won't look at me. Their apologetic gazes are fixed on Jarosh and Camike. Guilt gnaws at my insides, but there's nothing I can do.

*Leaders have the responsibility of taking action,* my father always says. I understand that now, more than ever.

"Jarosh, don't go." Ry puts out a hand to stop him, but Jarosh pushes past.

"I'm not welcome here," he replies. "I thought that was made clear enough."

"You're a Solguard," I say. "You don't have to leave. Just the Halves."

Jarosh turns on me and bares his teeth, like some kind of savage. "Where my mate goes, I go."

"Jarosh," Wade calls after him. He glares at me, and then hurries after our friend.

Dayne's disappointed look is almost enough to make me go chasing after them. *Almost.*

"Young lady, that is not a decision that would have brought your aunt pride," Valior says.

*My aunt.*

"Yeah, well, I'm not too concerned with her opinion right now," I reply.

✳ ✳ ✳

Later, I watch the Halves shoulder their small packs and depart—refugees of my own making.

When Brogut emerges from the tunnel, he turns my way. He doesn't carry any weapons. Instead, he has several packs wound around his waist and tied across his back. If I didn't know better, I would think he looked chastened, guilty even.

"Told you all humans were bad," he tells Ekil.

I'm gripped by an unexpected wave of regret. Ekil and I have saved each other too many times for him to be leaving like this. He wouldn't do anything to hurt me, even if he can't control his second-in-command. Ekil's my friend.

*What was I thinking, sending them away?*

Jarosh's words keep churning in mind. *We'll die. You know that, right?*

I want to tell Ekil to come back and tell Jarosh I'm sorry, but all of the Solguards and Banished are watching. If I take back my decision now, what kind of leader will that make me?

*A weak one,* my father's voice answers in my head.

If the Banished and Solguards think I'm indecisive and unstable, no one will want to follow me into battle. Besides, I reason, letting the Halves stay here would just give Brogut or any of the others a chance to attack someone else. I can't take that risk to the others in this settlement. I can't take that risk to the Zeroes.

I see Vlaz and Wokee standing together as they watch the Halves continue to file out of the tunnel. Craving their company, I make my way over to them, keeping my eyes on the ground so I don't have to look at the Halves' betrayed expressions.

As soon as I get close, though, Vlaz starts to growl. His upper lip quivers, exposing more of his fangs. There's a ridge of raised fur along his back.

"Vlaz?" Wokee backs away, alarmed.

Vlaz's yellow eyes are trained on me as he continues to snarl.

"Vlaz, it's Mer," Wokee tells him.

"Get away from him," I tell Wokee, my eyes fixed on the hyenair's exposed fangs.

"He never does this with me," Wokee says, distracted, as he puts out his hand for Vlaz to sniff.

The closer Wokee gets, the calmer Vlaz becomes. But the second I take a step toward them, Vlaz starts to growl and shrink away again.

"Maybe I still smell like the black fire," I say, more than a little unnerved.

"Maybe." Wokee looks unconvinced. "But I was as close to the fire as you were."

"Animals can sense what's inside, even when it cannot be seen." Camike has separated from the crowd of Halves and is walking toward me.

Jarosh is still with Ekil and the others, his eyes pinned on Camike. His mouth is set in a tight, angry line.

"What's that supposed to mean?" I ask her.

Instead of answering, Camike reaches up a hand and cups my cheek. "Your heart is being pulled in too many directions." She switches to the human language. "You will get better when they are gone." Her black eyes flick to the Zeroes, standing silently just outside the tunnel's entrance.

She lets her hand drop and, with a sad smile, returns to Jarosh and the Halves.

Tears burn the back of my throat. I hurry back down into the settlement without waiting to see the Halves leave.

The Zeroes follow me. I can feel their presence without needing to see or hear them. Having them at my back should calm my raging thoughts and emotions. Instead, it makes me feel energized, like I could run to the Wild Lands and back without breaking a sweat. The feeling I always get with the Zeroes, the sense that I need more—that I can have more—is less powerful than it was weeks ago, but the feeling is still there.

*What do the Halves matter when I have the Zeroes?*

My father is standing partway down the tunnel. There's an appraising look in his eyes as he studies me and the Zeroes in my wake.

"Are you going to question my decision to send the Halves away, too?" I ask, defensive.

"I have no idea whether it was a foolish or brilliant tactical decision," he replies with a shrug. "But I can tell you that, as a leader, it is unwise to succumb to regrets and doubt. You made a choice. Now live with it."

My father's blunt assessment is oddly comforting.

"What if the Zeroes aren't…enough?"

The Halves leaving did cut our army by a third, and we were already going to be outnumbered by the Duskers.

"What if the Zeroes get injured by the Dusker archers, and they can't take down the gate?"

I shiver at the thought.

"What if one of them gets hurt and it makes me…."

I can't finish the thought. The first time a Zero was injured, it was hours before I felt like myself enough to do anything besides curl into a ball and scream in agony. This latest time, it was minutes before I could react.

Even with as strong as the Zeroes are, there are bound to be injuries when we face the Duskers. What if I'm so incapacitated by feeling each of their wounds like they were my own that I can't lead them?

"I can come to Malarusk with you," my father offers. "I'll help heal any injuries the Zeroes sustain so they—and you—can get back to the fighting as quickly as possible."

"You'd do that?" Relief slackens my muscles, but the feeling is only temporary. I remember what Dayne said, about my father only doing things to benefit himself.

"I have nothing better to do," my father says with a shrug.

"Why are you helping me so much?" I ask. "What's in it for you?"

"You are my daughter. I see you in need of help, and I'm in a position to give it."

I narrow my gaze. "Why did you come here with us?"

He raises a white eyebrow. "If memory serves me correctly, you didn't give me much of a choice. Something about not trusting me to stay in the Lair."

"And you're fine with that?" I demand, suspicion growing inside me. "You've been stuck in this settlement for weeks, and you've done nothing except feed the Zeroes. For someone who's always scheming, that seems like it would be boring."

"Hardly." My father looks up at one of the Zeroes. "I wish only to be near the creatures that will one day rule this world."

The Zero standing next to my father inhales, the slits of its nostrils scenting the air for its master.

*I'm here*, I think, closing my eyes and feeling for my connection to it through the bond.

When I open my eyes and look at the Zero, I find it isn't staring back at me. I follow the direction of its gaze, but it seems to be looking only at the wall.

"Hey," I snap my fingers, concentrating on the Zero.

Its eyes swivel down. An involuntary shudder goes through me when its black eyes, mirrors of my own, come to rest on me.

"So, you're offering to come to Malarusk and help heal any Zeroes who are injured?" I ask my father. I don't take my eyes off the Zero.

"Now that your Halve healer is gone, I'm the only one who can help you."

*Yes, you are.*

"Strange how that keeps seeming to happen," I say.

"What can I say?" My father lifts a shoulder. "I make a point of being useful. And adapting. I find both are essential to staying alive."

"Climb aboard the wheel of change or be crushed beneath its weight?" I ask, repeating my father's old mantra.

He smiles. "Exactly."

# CHAPTER 24

I sit in the secluded cave behind the flour sacks.

Conflicting emotions pass through me too fast for me to examine any one of them closely. Camike's warning to me, that I wouldn't be whole again until the Zeroes were gone, disturbs me more than I want to admit.

But that's not all that's bothering me. In the past few days, I've felt a change in my bond with the Zeroes. I can't explain it, exactly, but it feels different than it did after I first made them. It's like the invisible strands holding us together have split—like every thread connecting me to every one of them has frayed into a thousand more, but far weaker ones.

I look to the tunnel just outside the cave, where the Zeroes are standing and awaiting my next order. I need to send them back to their own cave before the Banished and Solguards come back down from the Outside, but I'm reluctant to part with them.

Maybe I should have spent more time improving my communication with them instead of continually abandoning them. Now, everything else that had occupied my time just feels pointless.

"We need to talk."

I'm so wrapped up in my own thoughts the sound of a human voice makes me jump to my feet.

Wade is pushing past the Zeroes like they aren't the most lethal creatures in existence. My heart skips a beat, and my mouth goes dry. It takes me a moment to recognize the emotion making his eyes turn a hundred different shades of gold: anger. Maybe disappointment, too.

"Don't move," I tell the Zeroes, as their muscles flex and the metal links of their clothes begin to rustle.

"You're too close to them," I tell Wade. "Give them space."

Wade ignores me, ducking under a scythe's blade.

My fear rises. The Zeroes are instinctive creatures. If they think Wade is a threat to them or me, they'll attack him, no matter my orders.

"I said give them space," I tell Wade again.

"I'm not one of your Zeroes to command," Wade replies.

I gape at him, momentarily stunned.

Wade continues to push his way toward me. When he gets within reach of me, the Zeroes move closer until they make a living barrier between us.

One look at Wade's face, and I know what he's going to say to me. And I don't want to hear it.

"They think you're a threat," I try again. "Just let me send them back to their cave."

"If these Zeroes are as obedient and useful as you seem to think," Wade pulls two daggers from his belt and spins them around his hands, "I should be more than safe."

"Wade stop," I plead, starting to panic.

"I'm the leader of the Solguards now, and I need to know my soldiers aren't walking into a battle they can never win, especially since you dismissed a third of our army." His blades glint in the torchlight as he continues to spin them. "Show me choosing these creatures over the Halves was the right decision for all of us, and not just you."

The Zeroes could kill him in an instant, regardless of the daggers in Wade's hands. He knows it, too, but I can tell from the hardness in his eyes he won't back down.

I focus all of my attention on my bond with the Zeroes, pleading—demanding—that they leave Wade alone, no matter what happens.

"I won't let you or anyone else jeopardize this mission, or my soldiers' lives," Wade says. "It's up to me to keep the Solguards safe, and I won't let them follow you into battle unless I know your Zeroes will do what you've promised."

Wade shoves his way through my army until he's standing before me. I'm still not used to this harder, colder version of him. I have to force my hands to stay by my sides to keep from reaching up to touch the new, sharp lines of his jaw.

With him so close, everything else seems to matter less than it did a second ago.

"Wade," I begin, but stop. There's so much I want to say to him, but I can't find the words. I don't know how to undo what's happened between us. I have no idea if it's even possible, but I know there's nothing I want more than to try.

"Hemera." Wade's voice is husky as he closes the small gap between us. "This isn't you. I know you, down to your soul. And I know you're not yourself."

This time, instead of angering me, his words give me hope. *Is he saying what I think he's saying? That there's a path forward for us…together?*

"I love you, Wade," I tell him, getting the words out as fast as I can before I lose my nerve. "I love you so much."

There's a dull thump as Wade's daggers hit the ground. His hands reach up to hold my face, his touch rougher than the last time he held me. His eyes search mine, so intent I wonder what he's looking for.

"I've been so afraid," he whispers.

I reach up to trace the line of his jaw with my finger. "Afraid of what?"

"That I'd lost you."

My hand goes very still. Wade tightens his grip on me, like he's waiting for me to pull away.

"I love you, too," he says. "Whatever he's done to you, we can fix it. Together."

A flicker of anger cuts through my other emotions.

"You haven't lost me."

"Prove it." His body is flush against mine, and I can hardly think over the frantic beating of my heart. "The Hemera I love would never abandon her friends to starvation and sun-knows-what-else. Bring the Halves back."

I lean away from him, too surprised to say anything. It wasn't where I expected this conversation to go, and I'm unprepared to offer a response.

"The Halves are out there, with no allies and no place to go," Wade continues. "Find them. Bring them back. Make it right, the way I know deep down you want to."

I think of the way Ekil and Jarosh looked at me before they left.

"I don't know if they'd come back, even if I tried," I whisper.

"Try anyway," Wade replies, pressing his forehead to mine.

✳ ✳ ✳

I send the Zeroes back to their cave. With my nerves still on fire and my heart racing from being so near to Wade, I hurry back down the tunnel.

Wade was right. I have to find the Halves and set things right, especially with Ekil, Jarosh, and Camike. I was so wrapped up in my fury over Brogut, I made a decision that could hurt the rest of the army and jeopardize our attack on Malarusk. I can't let my personal feelings for a single Halve put every other soldier at greater risk.

As the leader of this army, I need to be better, stronger, than the others.

*We'll die. You know that, right?* Jarosh's words haunt me. These are some of my best friends I sent out to wander the desert.

*What in the sun was I thinking?*

It's not too late. The Halves will leave an easy trail to follow, and with my speed, I'll catch up to them in a matter of hours. Whether or not they'll even talk to me is a different issue, though.

From the way Jarosh looked at me, I doubt the Halves will accept my offer to return to the settlement. Ekil's trust won't be so easily regained. But there is something I can do, even if they won't agree to come back and fight with us.

Brice's map—really, my father's map—which led me to Tanguro for the first time, has all the travel caves marked. Some of them are big enough to provide shelter for the Halves. Some of them might even have old wells the Halves could use for water.

I don't know why I kept the map after I found out my father, and not Brice, had left it for me. But for whatever reason, I saved it and brought it

153

with me to the settlement. I had forgotten about it since I tucked it between the seams of my bedroll, along with the letter from my mother.

I can give the Halves the map. It might not be enough to repair the damage that's been done between us, but it's a start.

*You will save us all.* My aunt's words, which always felt like they were spoken in trust and confidence in me, now just seem like a taunt.

I stretch out my bedroll and find the open seam. I reach inside and search around until my fingers close on the map. I pull it out and stare at it. The edges are curled and the whole of it is water stained, but it's still legible. My fingers trace the path I traveled from Subterrane Harkibel to Tanguro in my search for Brice.

I was so hopeful and naïve back then. I was so foolish.

That was when I still thought Brice had been captured by chance, instead of being a lure to draw me on a path my father had predetermined. That was before I knew I had a brother and an aunt. Before I knew my mother made me in an experiment on herself in an effort to give the Solguards a weapon they could wield against the Duskers.

I lean back against the wall, the map still clutched in my hands. For the first time, it occurs to me that what I've done with the Zeroes isn't so different from what my mother did to me. I made the Zeroes because I wanted to defeat Crowe and get the Banished to agree to fight with us.

For the first time since I turned the Zeroes, I wonder if creating them was the right decision. I was so angry after Aunt Jadem's death, which, as it turns out, didn't even happen. At the time, all I could think about was revenge.

What was it my mother wrote in the letter…something about how some outcomes aren't worth their cost?

I reach back over to my bedroll. I find the slit in the material and dig my hand in, searching for the other piece of script tree bark I hid here.

My hand finds nothing.

I kneel, pushing my arm in farther, tearing a wider hole in the fabric. Still, I can't find the letter. A bead of sweat slides down my forehead. I ignore it. With both of my hands, I rip apart the seams all the way around the bedroll, until I'm left with two shredded pieces of thin fabric.

No letter appears between their folds.

I shake the material, waiting for the letter to flutter to the ground. It doesn't.

A wild, desperate panic I don't understand takes hold of me.

*Did I leave it somewhere else?* No, I remember cutting the slit in the bedroll and putting the letter inside. I felt it nestle between the two pieces of fabric. When I moved Brice's map from my pack to the same place, my fingers grazed the letter, right where I'd left it.

I search around, even getting up and walking slowly down the tunnel, like the letter might have just flown out of its hiding place and landed a short way away.

It hasn't. My mother's letter is gone.

# CHAPTER 25

Someone must have stolen the letter, because I know I didn't lose it. I wrack my brain for who might have taken it. Who else even knew I had it?

Dayne was the only person I told, and I already asked him if he had taken it. He hadn't.

Who would have known to open up my bedroll? And once they did, who would have wanted my mother's letter, anyway? Brice's map would have been a far more valuable prize. And yet, the map was left untouched.

I think back to the contents of my mother's letter. There were apologies, regrets, explanations. And on the back....

"No." I say the word out loud, even though I'm alone.

*No, it couldn't be that.*

On the back of her letter was a recipe for how she made me. Is it possible *that's* what the thief was looking for?

The reality of my situation hits me like the weight of an entire cave collapsing on my head.

If someone else has that letter, they'll know exactly what to do to make more Bisecters. That kind of power in any person's possession could have devastating consequences, the likes of which I couldn't dream up even if I tried.

*Think, Hemera.*

But there's nothing to be done. I can't very well interrogate everyone in the settlement to see if they've gained new knowledge about how to make more of me.

These thoughts are still churning in my mind when I find everyone—Solguards, Banished, and the leaders—in the main cave.

"What's happening?" I ask Wade.

"Tut's people finished the weapons," Wade says, "and Liglette's last herd of stags arrived."

A jolt of energy shoots down my spine. The last pieces we were waiting for are complete. It's time to attack Malarusk.

"I'll get the Zeroes," I say, already backtracking.

"Wait until we're moving out," Wade says. "We don't want them scaring anyone."

I bite back a retort. The humans should be kissing the ground beneath the Zeroes' feet. But Wade's only just begun to look me in the eye again. I don't want to risk starting a fight with him, especially when we're about to go into battle.

"The Halves," I say, holding up Brice's map like it's the explanation for why I haven't yet done what I promised.

Instead of spending the high day tracking them down, I used it to turn every pack I could find inside out and wrack my brain for who might have taken my mother's letter.

"Whatever you're looking so distressed about," Tut says, "forget about it. We're about ready to march out."

*No, it's too soon*, I want to say. *I have to find the Halves. I have to find my mother's letter. I have to—*

But I don't say any of these things, because at the mention of battle, the emptiness and anger I've felt since we got here lifts. It's replaced with a restless energy. I can't stand still. I keep going back and forth to the Outside, helping even when I'm not needed.

It looks like the settlement belched the whole of itself onto the Outside. Supply packs, weapons, and people are everywhere. The Westerners are trying to organize the pack animals, but the stags don't seem to be cooperating. They keep wandering off, and Liglette's people have to chase after them and find new ropes to tie them together. The Banished look already partially-defeated as they labor under the weight and heat of their heavy cloaks.

I groan inwardly. I imagine the Duskers right now, probably doing some kind of drill while they wait for the slaves to finish carting up their supplies. I imagine the only sounds coming from inside the iron gate to be the clink of practice swords and the crack of the slave masters' whips. It certainly wouldn't look or sound like the sheer bedlam going on around here.

*I never should have let the Halves leave,* I think. The weight of a hundred regrets presses down on my shoulders.

"Vlaz is all ready to go," Wokee announces.

I stay where I am, not wanting to upset the hyenair right before we're about to leave. I look at Wokee, supply packs strung around his bony shoulders.

"Wokee," I begin, but he stops me.

"I'm just holding these for Dayne." He rolls his eyes. "Sheesh, relax."

I crack a smile. Wokee has never been able to stand my over-protectiveness, but I can't help it. After everything we've been through together, he's as much family to me as Dayne.

I help Wokee disentangle himself from the supply packs.

"Do you have what I asked for?"

"'Course." Wokee pulls a crumpled package from the pocket of his cloak. As he does so, the ribbon Everlyn gave him so long ago comes out with it. Wokee blushes furiously before stuffing the ribbon back into his pocket.

I don't say anything about it as I accept the package and open it. Inside is a thin cord of woven blue threads.

"It's perfect," I tell Wokee. "Thank you."

I take Wade's Solguard pendant out of my pocket, where I've kept it since all efforts to clean it proved useless. The sun no longer gleams gold. Even though I washed the sticky black sap off the metal, the stain was impossible to scrub away. It's now a dull black color. I thread the cord through the pendant. When I knot it around my neck, the pendant feels heavier than I remember.

"You'll help Valior take care of all the children and old people?" I ask Wokee. "You'll keep them safe?"

*You'll keep* yourself *safe,* is what I really mean.

"Obviously," Wokee replies, offering me a weak smile. "I'm a Solguard. It's my job to keep people safe."

"Yes, it is," I say.

My relief at Wokee's acceptance of this decision, especially when I expected pleading and hysterics, is palpable. But as Wokee said himself, he isn't a little kid anymore.

"Thank you for understanding," I tell him.

"Mhm." Wokee's eyes dart to the side, where Liglette is trying to attach a large wooden crate to Vlaz's harness. "I better help." He makes a face. "They always put his harness on wrong."

"Not before you give me a hug," I tell him.

He takes a quick, furtive look around to make sure no one is watching, and then he throws his arms around my middle.

"I'll see you soon," I whisper into his curls, uttering a silent prayer it's the truth.

"Bye, Mer." He gives me his dimpled smile, the one that warms me to my very soul, before disappearing between Vlaz's enormous paws.

When Valior hobbles out of the tunnel, I pull him away from the dozens of Easterners who are vying for his attention.

"Will you have one of your scouts do something for me?" I ask.

He gives me a look that is keen and free from the liquid sun-induced wateriness I associate with him.

"What can I do for you, young lady?"

I give him the map. "Will you send one of your scouts to track down the Halves and give them this?"

Valior stares at me for a long moment, and then his gnarled hands close over the map. "I can do that."

"Tell your scout to tell them," I swallow. "That I'm sorry."

It's not enough, but for now, it's the best I can do.

Valior nods. He looks like he wants to say something else, but a group of Easterners absorbs him into their masses, and then he's swept out of my sight.

Ry, Dellin, and two other archers are striding toward Vlaz. They each carry two quivers stuffed with arrows. Their bows are slung across their backs.

Once Dellin has climbed onto Vlaz's back, I catch Ry's arms and pull her away before she can get on, too.

"Are you sure about bringing her?" I ask, nodding up at Dellin. "If she freaks out like she's done every other time we've gone near Malarusk—"

"She won't," Ry says. "She's ready now."

I bite my lip to keep my frustration in check. They are the ones who will be raining arrows down on the Dusker archers as my Zeroes break down the gate. If they fail because of Dellin, it will be my Zeroes who pay the price.

"Look," I try a different tack. "I know you trust her, but if there's even the smallest chance her loyalties are in question—"

"They aren't."

"The Duskers are still her people," I say, unwilling to give up. "She might not want to be one of them, but killing them is different."

"It won't be a problem," Ry says. "We can trust her."

She looks so calm and certain, so completely unconcerned. I want to shake her.

"Are you sure that's your head talking, and not your…emotions?" I ask.

Ry flushes. Her eyes dart to Dellin before coming back to rest on me. I know I'm the one with the gaze everyone's afraid of, but right now, I can't hold her stare.

"That's what I thought." Ry humphs before turning away from me, making it clear the conversation is over.

Restless, and with nothing to do until the Zeroes can be brought out, I pace on the outskirts of the activity.

Everlyn is overseeing the packing of her explosive powders. A minor scuffle breaks out when a thoughtless Northerner tries to pack her explosives next to the cookfire kindling. One of the Easterners has to restrain Everlyn, who is waving her small fists at the Northerner.

Valior marches between the Banished and Solguards, giving battle advice and offering sips from his flask, although he doesn't drink any himself. When he turns toward me, his old eyes are alight.

*The Duskers are the reason his brother is dead,* I remember. He must be as eager for this battle as I am.

Dayne, his lute slung around his neck, is moving back and forth between the Easterners and Northerners. Now that Jarosh isn't here, both groups have fallen to my brother to lead. I feel another wave of guilt for bringing this extra burden on him.

"Clarion," Tut's booming voice draws my attention as he strides toward my brother. "You see to it my people go into the fighting last."

*Fool,* I hear Liglette mutter under her breath. It's the most insulting word I've ever heard from her lips, and I'd be gratified if I wasn't so disgusted with Tut. His words have drawn the attention of others, who are watching to see what will happen.

"They'll enter the battle at the same time as everyone else," Dayne replies without looking up from the pile of weapons he's sorting.

"I'll be damned if my people are the ones thrown into the fray to get their heads chopped off," Tut says.

"First of all," Dayne puts down the weapons in his hands and gets up to face Tut, "it's more likely they'll fall from the crossbows than steel. So that should be one worry off your mind."

The bigger man towers over my brother, but Dayne isn't the least bit intimidated.

"Second of all," Dayne continues, "the glory of battle will belong to these fine men and women, and when they return, they'll have no use for a leader like you."

The Northerners surrounding Dayne look uncertain. Tut's face pales.

"Enjoy your holiday here at the settlement," Dayne tells him. "We'll let you know how your weapons fared against the Duskers."

# CHAPTER 26

The buzz of conversation and flurry of last-minute preparations stops when the Zeroes emerge from the tunnel. I'm at their head, but for once, no one's looking at me. All eyes are on my army.

The Zeroes' metal clothes and blades of their scythes gleam in the sunlight. Their mouths are rimmed with the blood of the last meal my father fed them. They look every bit the lethal weapons I promised they would be.

"Captain Harkibel's New Army," Valior pronounces with a sigh of appreciation. "I just thank the sun no one I care about will have to go up against them."

I feel an enormous sense of pride as everyone stares at the Zeroes.

I watch as the expressions on the Banished people—men and women who have never fought in a proper battle—shift from sick with anxiety to awestruck, and maybe even a little bit hopeful.

I hear the change in the snippets of conversation reaching my ears and see it in the way the soldiers regard the Zeroes. They believe my army will do what's never been done before.

I've told them the Zeroes will break down the iron gate and lead the rest of our army to the citadel's entrance. Until this moment, though, I'm not sure they really believed me. Now, with all one-hundred of the Zeroes on the Outside, there isn't a single person who doubts their strength.

They believe we have a chance. And it's because of me.

I'm torn between pride and the crushing weight of responsibility.

A Solguard puts his right hand, the one that has the Solguard tattoo underneath his glove, over his heart. Their faith in me heightens my own anxiety.

*What if I'm leading this entire army to their death? What if this battle is just like Tanguro?*

But it's not like Tanguro. We have the Zeroes now.

I feel for the bond connecting me to the Zeroes. My nerves must be keeping me from the overwhelming sense of relief I usually feel at our connection. I feel jittery, strung out. I've been waiting so long for this fight. Finally, after everything that's happened, it's here.

"All set to move out, Hemera," Dayne says, interrupting my thoughts. He skirts around the Zeroes to reach me, giving them a wide berth. "You might want to keep those creatures in back so they don't terrify the soldiers." He gives the Zeroes a sour look.

*Everyone else has accepted their presence*, I want to tell my brother. *Why can't you?*

"What's he doing here?" Dayne continues, before I can say any of what's on my mind.

I turn to see where he's looking. My father, mostly hidden behind the towering Zeroes, steps to the side.

"I asked him to come," I say.

"He's our enemy," Dayne hisses. "And you want to bring him into battle with us?"

"I need him with us in case any of the Zeroes get injured."

"Aren't you tired of giving him your trust, only to find he's betrayed you?" Dayne demands.

"It's not like that anymore." I shrink back a little. "He wants the Zeroes to stay healthy, and so do I. He hates the Duskers. He won't betray us, because he wants what we want."

There's a small part of me, a part I shove back into a place where I won't need to examine it too closely, that hopes my father might have another reason for helping us. That part of me wants his reason to have something to do with me and all the time we've spent together over the past several weeks. I want to see the approval on my father's face when my army overthrows the forces at Malarusk.

"Where's your sling?"

"What?" I had forgotten my brother was still standing next to me.

Dayne nods at my belt, which holds two daggers, but the loop where my sling usually rests is empty.

I shrug. "I don't need it."

Dayne frowns. "We're attacking the most formidable enemy we've ever faced, and you don't need your weapon?"

I let my gaze rest on the Zeroes.

"I already have my weapon."

✳ ✳ ✳

"I would like to say a few words before sending you all on your way." Valior, standing on a wooden crate, adjusts the hood of his cloak.

All the Easterners immediately fall silent and move to stand in front of him. The rest of us follow.

"You're all about to embark on a mission that none before us could have even dreamed of. The iron gate of Malarusk, impenetrable and a symbol of their unending authority over all the lands, will fall to us."

There is shouting and cheering from the crowd of Easterners, which is soon echoed by the rest of the Banished and Solguards.

Valior looks at his people, and then his eyes search the rest of the crowd. When they find me, his lips curve into a smile.

"The Zeroes have given us a chance to change the unending path we've been locked into for generations," Valior continues.

There are yells of "Captain Harkibel!" as soldiers thrust their weapons into the air. My face warms, but I don't feel a desire to melt into the crowd like I once would have. I made the Zeroes. I gave these people a chance against their oppressors. The Zeroes have given them hope.

"You all know about my brother, Velikor, may he rest in peace," Valior continues.

"May he rest in peace," the Easterners murmur in subdued tones.

"He died in the Malarusk dungeons, devoured by the wormkill."

Angry murmurs come from the crowd. Valior holds up a gloved hand to quiet everyone.

"Velikor was imprisoned for the crime of not being one of the Duskers' chosen, and then, for not conforming to their harsh laws. He was a Banished, as are we all."

A whoop comes from the Easterners, as well as some of the others.

"Velikor's death, his story, is not unique. So many of our loved ones have died by the Duskers' hands. We've all suffered because of them. Velikor's story is not mine; it's all of ours."

Valior waits for the crowd's reactions to die down.

"For too long, we've been weak and oppressed, living at the mercy of the Duskers. But now, for the first time, we have an opportunity to challenge their might."

Valior nods at me, and I signal for the Zeroes to step forward in unison. All eyes turn on them as the sunlight glints off one-hundred scythes.

"I wish I was young and strong enough to fight beside you," Valior says, "but since I am not, I'm going to ask you to take your vengeance—not just for Velikor, but for every sibling, parent, child, and lover the Duskers have taken from us—in my stead. Together, you will overthrow these tyrants. Together, we will build a better future for us all."

Boots stamp the ground. Oaths are shouted. Solguards fist the gloves of their right hand over their hearts.

"Woo!" Everlyn, who has found her way next to me, is shouting as loud as any of the soldiers.

When I look down at her, her face is alight. "It's really happening," she says, her voice breathless with excitement. "We're really fighting the Duskers!"

I give her an uncertain smile, hoping Valior made it clear to her she isn't coming with us to the battle. I would never let Wokee take such a risk, and I know Valior loves Everlyn the same way I love Wokee.

"Where is Wokee?" I ask her, searching the crowd for blonde curls peeking out from a blue hood.

"He went looking for some root or stem or something," Everlyn says, waving a hand as if to emphasize its unimportance. "He said he wouldn't be back for a while."

"Oh." I swallow my disappointment. It's probably for the best. If he were here, he'd probably be trying to change my mind about letting him come with us.

There's more chaos as the Banished leaders try to organize their groups into some semblance of marching formation.

Dayne, at the head of the Easterners, says something to them that makes them roar and thrust their swords into the air. The Northerners aren't with them, though. I look behind me for the gold thread sewn into their cloaks that makes them impossible to miss. They're between Dayne's company and Liglette's. There's no mistaking the man at their head. Tut is leading them, a gold sword strapped at his belt. I can't help the grin that comes to my lips.

I fall back until I'm near enough to talk to him.

"I thought you were staying behind," I say. "Something about not wanting to be the sacrificial lamb, if I remember correctly."

"I still don't." Tut lifts a shoulder, and I'm almost blinded by the reflection of sunlight on the gold coins sewn onto his cloak. "So, instead, I decided we'd be the hungry wolves."

A smile spreads across his face. Even with the hood of his cloak shadowing his face, I can see the flash of his gold teeth. I can't help but respond with a grin of my own.

Liglette's stags, burdened with supplies, labor at the back of the company.

"The Zeroes can help carry this stuff," I tell her, embarrassed I hadn't thought to offer before.

"The Zeroes are not beasts of burden," my father cuts in before Liglette can reply. To me, he says, "They are instruments of war. Don't degrade their importance by turning them into pack animals."

I don't know what he's talking about, but Liglette waves away my offer.

"Thank you kindly," she says, "but our stags are used to the burden. They will be fine."

I can't help but notice the way she purses her lips as she regards the Zeroes.

On my way back to the head of the column, I see Wade, surrounded by the Solguards. Unlike the Banished, the Solguards march in perfect formation. They aren't talking or milling around aimlessly like the Banished. There is a quiet focus about them. They may be fewer in number than any of the groups of Banished, but there's no doubt where the might of our human army lies.

Wade is wearing his normal blue cloak, but he's carrying a gold shield— a gift from Tut, no doubt—and has no fewer than a dozen weapons strapped to his cloak. He looks so much taller from where I'm standing. He looks almost regal.

A shyness I've never known around Wade comes over me. I don't know whether I should approach him. The last time we talked, it was almost like old times, but I didn't get the Halves to come back even though I'd promised to try. And there were all those things he said about me being different now.

As if he can feel the heat of my gaze, Wade looks over and finds me staring. I'm walking toward him before I even realize my feet are moving. He heads in my direction. Even though I can't see his expression under the hood of his cloak, I feel his golden eyes on me. We meet in the middle.

I'm conscious of every Solguard stopping to stare at us. Wade gives me an uncertain smile, and then his eyes drop from my face to something that's caught his attention.

"Hemera," he breathes.

I look down and see he's staring at the Solguard pendant around my neck.

"I'm sorry," I say, my hand reaching up to cover the tarnished metal. "I tried to tell you before." My words tumble out in my desperation to explain. "I tried to clean it, but I couldn't get the stain off."

"That doesn't matter," Wade says. He comes closer and brushes the pendant with his fingertips. "I'm glad you're wearing it."

I want to tell him I never would have taken it off if the cord hadn't broken. I need to tell him I didn't set things right with the Halves because I was searching for my mother's letter. But I don't get the chance to say anything at all.

Wade takes my face in both his hands and kisses me.

I'm aware of whooping and catcalls from the Solguards for a moment, and then I'm aware of nothing except for the feeling of Wade's mouth on mine.

He lets me go a moment later and grins at my dazed expression. "For luck." He winks, and then he's jogging back to his soldiers.

When we finally march out, with my Zeroes leading the way, it feels like nothing short of a miracle. The sight of our entire army amassed infuses us all with a new kind of strength.

As we begin to move out, the ones staying behind follow alongside us, shouting encouragement and tossing pathetic dried flowers and twigs—the last of what this desert has to offer—at our feet. Some of the children wave small flags with the rebel sun drawn on the cloth. Everlyn jogs beside me to give me last-minute instructions about how to use her powders to destroy the black trees.

I have a drawstring bag slung across my shoulders, which holds jars of green powder and sealed flasks containing purple liquid.

"Pour the liquid on the powder when you're in the underground forest," Everlyn tells me, "and then run like hell."

I scan the crowd of children and elderly once more, looking for Wokee, but he isn't among them.

I pick up my pace. I don't look back at the settlement as we march forward to Malarusk.

# CHAPTER 27

The closer we get to the hills separating the Banished territory from Malarusk, the quieter everyone becomes. By the time we've reached the path the Zeroes made through the rocks, a tense silence has fallen.

It's just after lowest day. It's later than we'd planned, which means we'll have less time to overpower the Duskers when we get to Malarusk. If high day comes and we haven't taken the first level of the underground citadel, our army will be stuck on the Outside during high day with no shelter. My Zeroes might be able to withstand the heat long enough to get back to the settlement, but the human soldiers won't. I'd be left to watch as they all succumbed to the Burn.

We pause at the end of the passage through the hills. As soon as we step onto the open stretch of land on the other side, Dusker scouts will see our party and report back to the citadel. We'll have to move fast.

We unload our supplies and distribute everything as quickly and quietly as we can manage. Liglette's people cover the archers in the last of the cammamoss Wokee brought all the way from Solis. It's dried out and the archers' cloaks flicker in and out of sight, but it's better than nothing.

The Zeroes and I make ready for our first, most important role. If anything goes wrong—if the Zeroes can't break down the gate—this battle will be over before it begins.

Ry, Dellin, and the other archers riding Vlaz lead the way as I, with my Zeroes in tow, prepare to leave the relative safety of the hills and cross the open land that separates us from Malarusk.

I try to catch Ry's eye, wanting some comfort or encouragement before we separate, but she's busy giving orders to Dellin and the others. She's speaking fast and using words only archers would understand. I stare at her, at the confident way she directs the others. There isn't a hint of fear on her face, only determination. A fierce pride for my friend warms my insides. Even though she'll be fighting from the sky and I'll be on the ground, it helps to know she'll be nearby, keeping the Zeroes safe while they do what they were made for.

I want to say goodbye to Wade, but I can't even see him among all the other soldiers in blue. A feeling of dread settles over me.

Dayne comes with me as I lead the Zeroes past the hills. Even though I know he'll be far behind me once the Zeroes and I start to run, I'm grateful for his presence now. My nerves are frayed and my stomach is a pit of snakes. When I came up with this plan, I hadn't really thought about what it would mean for the fate of the entire army to rest on my shoulders.

The true enormity of what I'm trying to do hits me for the first time.

"I can't do this," I gasp.

The iron gate looms before me in my mind, sturdy and surrounded by Duskers armed with crossbows.

"Look at me."

Dayne puts a hand on each of my shoulders. He smiles at me, his warm, blue eyes creasing at the edges in the way that reminds me so much of our mother. But even the thought of our mother fills me with anxiety and betrayal, when before there was only love.

*If only she had never left me that stupid letter. If only Aunt Jadem hadn't betrayed us. If only—*

"Aunt Jadem was right about one thing," Dayne says into my ear. "You are going to save us all."

I gulp, feeling the burden of everything we're risking somehow even more intensely than I had before.

"Ready, Mer?" Ry, her face set in grim concentration, grips Vlaz's reins in one hand and her bow in the other.

She looks tiny sitting on Vlaz's back.

"Ready," I reply, trying to will the feeling to come true just by saying the word.

Ry turns to the archers sitting behind her. They exchange a few words, and then Ry gives me a nod.

I take a deep breath, readying myself. This first part needs to happen fast. We have to take down the iron gate before the Duskers can reinforce it…or kill all of us. If my Zeroes can't take down the gate, we'll all be done for.

My brother pulls me into a quick embrace. "The rest of us will be right behind you, little sis."

I nod, hating how this feels like goodbye.

At a command from Ry, Vlaz beats his wings. We all watch the hyenair rise. I imagine the Duskers in the lookouts, shielding their eyes and shouting to the others below. If they don't already know they're under attack, they will soon enough.

I turn all my attention on the Zeroes.

"Come."

Without waiting to see if they'll follow, I step out onto the open land.

# CHAPTER 28

My feet fly over the ground. There's the pounding of a hundred Zeroes' footsteps as they follow at my heels. The thought of their strength gives me courage.

We're running so fast that I imagine the Duskers in the lookouts must see only a great, metallic blur headed by a speck of blue. With any luck, they'll have no idea what they're dealing with until we've broken down the gate.

The closer we come, though, the more my confidence ebbs.

The gate looms more massive with every step. The closer I get, the more the already-thick iron seems to swell and grow taller.

Arrows begin to strike the ground no more than a dozen paces in front of us. In seconds, we'll be within range of the Dusker archers.

*What was I thinking?*

There's a reason no one has ever attempted to attack the citadel before. The iron gate is too tall, the Duskers too many. This mission is suicide. I've led all of the Banished into a fight they can't possibly hope to walk away from. Panic begins to overtake me.

I feel a change in my bond with the Zeroes. It's slight, barely there, but I recognize it for what it is. My fear is making them hesitate, to sense a danger to their master they hadn't before perceived.

A shadow passes overhead, and I look up. Vlaz is flying straight toward the gate. He dips lower, and arrows whiz toward the Duskers in the lookouts.

The Duskers return fire. Their black arrows search the sky for their target, but the sun's brightness makes it impossible for them to sight Vlaz.

There's so many of them shooting, though, it's only a matter of time before they start hitting their mark.

*Move, Hemera.*

I put on a burst of speed to cross the last bit of distance to the iron gate. I don't have time to consider whether all of this was a huge mistake. Right now, all my thoughts are on the task ahead.

The Duskers are preoccupied with Ry and the others, and so we reach the gate unchallenged. None of my Zeroes have been injured or shot.

*So far, so good.*

The thought has barely passed through my mind when a sharp horn cry sounds from inside the gate.

Dayne said we'd have one minute between the alarm and full-on attack from every Dusker with a crossbow. If we don't get the gate down before they're assembled, they'll shoot every one of us, and we'll be powerless to stop them.

*Hurry.*

"Break it down!" I use the hand gesture my father and I discussed back at the settlement, the one my Zeroes recognize as the cue to destroy. The one-hundred line up across the length of the iron gate.

They don't hesitate. Their muscles bulge as they brace their feet. I position myself at the far end where the gate's hinges are melded to the mountainside.

Some of the Zeroes use the long, curved blades of their scythes to hack at the iron gate. Others have abandoned their scythes altogether, using their bare hands to beat at the iron barrier.

The bond flares up inside my chest. I've never felt so strong.

A primal shout rips from my throat as I hurl my body at the towering gate.

There was a time when I would have questioned whether my strength was enough for the task before me. But now, with the Zeroes by my side, an unyielding power pumps through my veins right along with the blood I share with them. A sense of surety washes over me, calming and focusing me.

*Now*, I think, channeling all my energy and force into this single purpose.

The impact of my shoulder hitting the barrier shudders down the length of the iron gate—iron that's gone unchallenged since it was first built.

I strike again. And again.

Arrows pierce the ground all around us, but I don't pay any attention to them. I don't try to look for Vlaz in the sky or Liglette's hunters crowding behind the Zeroes. I pummel the gate, urging the Zeroes on with every strike.

My entire body shakes with the vibration of the metal as it groans and bends against me. I grit my teeth against the sear of skin melting away from my hands as I press them against the sun-scorched metal.

And then, with a groan of protest, the gate's hinges snap away from the mountainside. The gate tilts inward. With a last, collective shove, the Zeroes push on the leaning gate until it breaks away from the mountain entirely. With a thud that makes the ground tremble, the gate falls flat on the ground.

I let out a roar of satisfaction as cries of disbelief and dismay come from inside the compound. For the first time in history, the gate to Malarusk is broken. The entrance to the great citadel is wide open.

There's no time to celebrate or marvel at what we've accomplished. There's no time to gloat that such a feat has never before been attempted, let alone carried out successfully.

Frantic horns sound from below ground inside the citadel, louder somehow, now that the iron gate has fallen. Without anything to block my view, I can see Dusker soldiers pouring out of the ground like smoke.

Terror fills me at the sight of the soldiers in gray, with their loaded crossbows. They converge on the ground above their citadel.

There's no panic or confusion among our enemy. Even as their own archers fall from the lookouts with Solguard arrows sticking out of their throats, the Duskers maintain their orderly lines. They take aim at us....And my Zeroes and I are directly in their path.

I hear the trampling of hooves behind me. Liglette, riding a stag, lets out a war cry. She has both hands on her bow, but the stag seems to know where it's going without any direction from its rider.

I'm worried the stag will get its hooves caught up in the stray pieces of metal lying on the ground. But the stag gathers itself and leaps right over the gate's tangled remains.

The rest of Liglette's people follow. Arrows sail from their bows. They're dressed more for a hunt than battle, but the Duskers fall to their arrows all the same.

Stags and their riders drop as the Duskers retaliate. Someone screams, and I turn in time to see two stags go down. Green powder arcs through the air before it's carried away by the wind.

*No.*

More of Everlyn's powders…the explosives we're depending on to disrupt our enemy's orderly lines, are lost with every volley of the Duskers' arrows.

I yell and motion frantically to the Zeroes, ordering them to spread out and give the Westerners cover while we wait for the rest of our foot soldiers to catch up.

It must have taken longer for us to get the gate down than I realized. There are more Duskers than I imagined, and they're still emerging from the caves below. They'll overwhelm our little army with their sheer numbers.

Even though there are only four riders atop Vlaz, they're managing to kill more Duskers than all of the Westerners combined. They're targeted in their attack, taking out the Duskers closest to the Zeroes first. Together, we're able to keep the Duskers at bay long enough for the rest of our army to come charging through the opening.

Wade and the Solguards are first, closely followed by Dayne and the Easterners.

The Duskers don't scatter as our army converges. They don't stare in disbelief at their destroyed gate or at the Zeroes with their scythes. They don't scream and plead with the Dark God. They form lines with impossible precision, an exercise that took our army over an hour. Their hoods hide whatever emotions might lie beneath.

Their remaining archers kneel and take aim. The rest of the Duskers draw their swords. And then, as one, they attack.

I draw my daggers.

"Forward!"

I keep low to the ground as the Zeroes and I lead the charge. I scream as the tip of an arrow grazes my ear. Dull roars tell me the Zeroes are not immune to the arrows' biting pain, but none of them slow for even an instant.

The Duskers' front lines march forward, their movements calculated and synchronized.

I can sense the moment the Duskers realize the Zeroes are not Halves…are not anything they've ever seen before. In spite of all of their training, the Duskers take one look at these towering creatures, with the curved blades of their scythes gripped in their inhumanly strong arms, and hesitate. We do not.

Screams fill the air as bodies begin to fall.

# CHAPTER 29

Raw, unbridled rage fills me. My blood pumps fast and hard. The Zeroes must sense my emotion, because they're frenzied in their killing. From where I'm fighting, I glimpse one Zero raise a Dusker over its head and pitch the man's body at least fifty paces. Another throws aside its scythe and sinks its teeth into a Dusker's neck.

The Zeroes clear a path to the nearest tunnel, where Duskers are still emerging. I direct a handful of the Zeroes to surround the Westerners, who are carrying what's left of Everlyn's explosives. They move out to the left, carving a path to the second citadel entrance. I command dozens more of the Zeroes to flank Dayne and the rest of the Easterners. I stay beside my brother as we fight our way to the first tunnel.

When we reach the opening, and I see the sheer number of soldiers in gray ascending onto the Outside, I lose my nerve. Even with the gate destroyed, this mission is still insane. Back in the settlement when we mapped everything out on rolls of script tree bark, there was none of the blood and gore there is now. We had discussed the way the Duskers would outnumber us, but numbers on a page are not flesh and swords and crossbows.

The Duskers are too numerous and too strong. They form rings around each of the tunnel entrances, making it impossible for us to get near.

"We have to thin them out," I yell as Dayne and I fight side by side.

"Liglette!" Dayne roars over the din of fighting.

"Here!" Her stag plows through our enemies to reach us. She shoves a bag of Everlyn's powder in my hand before her stag wheels around and darts off again.

I reach into the bag and pull out one of the pre-mixed jars of powder and flasks filled with purple fluid. Dayne and the Zeroes carve a path for me to the tunnel. Gritting my teeth against the bite of an arrow in my thigh, I pause long enough to unscrew the caps on each jar.

My hands are shaking and slippery with blood, and by the time I open the flask and dump it over the powder, three Easterners are killed.

I throw the concoction into the hole in the ground.

"Run!" I shout.

We all do.

I'm thrown to the ground as an explosion rocks the earth. There are screams from below. I can't help but grimace at the thought of mud sliding down into the tunnels and drowning anyone down there.

But the underground citadel was well-built, and the tunnel doesn't collapse. In only a matter of seconds, the Duskers are emerging into the sunlight, stumbling as they hold their gloved hands over bloody wounds. They're soon followed by soldiers who weren't injured in the blast and are prepared to fight.

"More explosives," I hear someone call.

"There aren't any more," Liglette shouts back.

I grasp the bag still slung over my shoulders. I want to use it to help the people fighting around me now, but this powder has to be saved for the underground orchard of black trees. No matter what happens here today, I have to make sure I destroy the trees. The Duskers can't be allowed to keep their most dangerous weapon.

The thought of the Duskers setting the black logs on fire outside of the Eastern settlement while Wokee and Everlyn are still inside makes me wrap my hands even tighter around the bag.

We'll just have to fight our way down into the citadel.

I direct my Zeroes to spread out between the other tunnel entrances to help the knots of Banished and Solguards fighting for access to the tunnels below.

Tut, who wields his sword as well as any Solguard I've ever seen, cuts down one Dusker after another as they come up from inside the tunnel. He looks nothing like the cowardly Banished leader I thought I knew.

His soldiers follow behind, far less proficient with a blade but just as enthusiastic, as they shriek and slash at anything in gray.

"Well done, Captain Harkibel," Tut calls to me. He stabs his sword down again. "I'll admit I didn't think you'd pull this off."

I give him a weary smile. "For an old coward, you've proven quite useful, yourself."

Tut gives me a gold-toothed grin.

The Westerners, led by Liglette on her stag, are fighting at one of the other tunnel entrances. Liglette keeps her people organized, steering them in a body as they drive the Duskers back down into the tunnel. The ones who get past Liglette's people face a handful of my Zeroes. The blades of the Zeroes' scythes move so fast they look like nothing more than a blur.

I direct twenty more of my Zeroes to help Wade and the Solguards fighting for entrance to the third tunnel. With the Zeroes I have left, I skirt the edge of the fighting masses to get to the other side of the compound. Our progress is slow, and I keep directing groups of five and ten of the Zeroes to break off and help pockets of Banished who are surrounded by Duskers.

With every passing moment, my impatience grows. I need to get into that underground forest of black trees before the Duskers gain control of the battle.

But there's something else driving me, something I didn't mention to the other leaders.

I need to get inside the citadel because I have business with Crowe.

We didn't discuss the Supreme much, since everyone assumed she would be too well-guarded for us to even set eyes on her. But I have different ideas.

I used to think Crowe was the one responsible for murdering my aunt. Now, I know Jadem is still alive, but I'm convinced that whatever is going on with my aunt is Crowe's fault. No matter what else happens, I've promised myself I'm going to find Crowe and kill her. And if Hendrix is with her, so much the better.

I still haven't forgotten how he let me go, even when I was in his grasp. I haven't forgotten his ominous threats. Instinct tells me I'll find him before

I encounter Crowe. If there's anything I know with certainty, it's that only one of us will see the battle's end.

Some of the Banished have already made it to the far side of the compound, and I'm dismayed to see the Duskers aren't the only ones battling against them. The Banished slaves are fighting alongside the Duskers, wielding wooden poles and blunt swords. The free Banished are reluctant to attack their former friends. The slaves, compelled by their Dusker masters, don't share the same hesitation.

I drag my attention away from the gruesome scene to stare at something that hadn't been here the last time I came to Malarusk. There's a mammoth, lumpy mass hidden by an enormous burlap covering. There is enough of whatever is stockpiled under the covering that the stack easily reaches the height and girth of a small mountain.

Rows and rows of Duskers surround the stockpile, their bodies serving as a living barrier against my army coming any closer. Whatever is beneath the burlap, the Duskers are guarding it with their lives.

A tremendous roar comes from just overhead. Vlaz, with Ry and the other archers still on his back, swoops low.

"Hemera," Ry shouts. "The Easterners need help. They're—"

I don't hear the rest of what she says as Vlaz soars back up again, but it's enough. I send all but a handful of my remaining Zeroes back to help Dayne and his soldiers.

Panic flutters in my chest, and I have to keep myself from racing back there myself to fight by my brother's side. If my own errand wasn't so urgent, I would.

Ry steers Vlaz back again, this time pointing him right at the Duskers amassed around me.

The soldiers in gray scream, scattering as Vlaz plows through them. Mud and bodies fly through the air. Vlaz's claws rake a man in two, and in spite of my hatred for the Duskers, I can't watch as the hyenair continues to ravish their forces.

Many of the Duskers have retreated back inside the citadel, so for the first time since the battle began, I have a moment to breathe.

I stare at the carnage. Soldiers on both sides lay dead, their bodies stretched out on the muddy ground. I'm about to make use of the opening Vlaz has created to descend into the citadel when a flash of blue catches my attention.

At first, I assume it's one of the Solguards, but he looks too small to be a Solguard. There's something about his movements, too…something familiar. When I look again, the soldier is gone.

*Strange.* He'd almost looked like—

A scream tears from my throat as an arrow slices through my calf. When I stare down at my leg, there's no hint of a wound. I look around for the Zero that's been injured, but I don't see it.

*Where's my father?* He should be here, helping my Zeroes.

No sooner has the thought crossed my mind, I see him. He's surrounded by Zeroes over by the mountainous, covered mass. An overwhelming feeling of jealousy grips me. Their attention is fixed on *him*.

To my inexplicable irritation, my father found the Zero with the leg injury before me, and he's already bandaging the wound.

"There are too many of them," a Solguard I don't recognize shouts. "And the slaves are fighting against us. We have to retreat."

"Go," I say, forcing my gaze away from my father. "I have to get into the tunnel."

"You can't—"

"Zeroes," I call them. Their reaction is sluggish, our bond weakened by everything else going on around us.

"Protect the Solguards," I command them.

As if waking from a stupor, the Zeroes spring to action. The small party moves off, spreading out to cut down slaves and Duskers.

"Captain Harkibel," a Northerner begins, but I'm not listening. There's a group of Duskers just inside the mouth of the tunnel surrounding one of their captains. They're waging a furious battle against a group of Solguards who are pushing the Duskers back into the tunnel.

When another one of the Duskers falls, a gap is left in the circle, and I can see straight through to the man at its center. He's wearing his hood and mask, but it doesn't keep the sunlight from illuminating his emerald green irises.

*Hendrix.*

He bends his head to listen to something one of his guards says. Then, two of the guards usher him back down into the citadel.

I run, shoving my way through Duskers and my own soldiers to get into the tunnel. I don't stop to fight any of the Duskers for fear of losing sight of Hendrix.

In a matter of seconds, I'm surrounded by Duskers, cut off from my Zeroes and the rest of my army. A few of the Duskers aim their weapons at me, but as soon as they come close enough to see my face, they fall back. I sense a ripple of conversation among them, and then all the Duskers nearby start to part ranks. It's like they're trying to give me a clear path forward. Surprise mingles with alarm.

The hairs on the back of my neck prickle. *This is wrong.* The Duskers would never let any harm come to one of their leaders. I should turn around right now and stay with the rest of my army. I should stick to the plan.

But already, there is a swarm of Duskers separating me from Wade and the Zeroes. It's like they're granting me—and only me—entrance into the tunnel.

I shouldn't go down into the citadel alone. I know it. And yet, the urge to follow Hendrix and see what he's up to is irresistible.

I slosh through the muddy stream and into the dark tunnel. Ahead, I see a lantern bobbing along. Hendrix stops walking and turns around. I press myself against the wall, willing him not to see me. His green eyes focus on something just past me. And then he turns and continues down the tunnel.

My heart races at the close call.

I squint into the darkness ahead. There could be a hundred Dusker archers waiting around the next corner to take me out. Hendrix might have seen me, after all. He could be hiding behind the first bend in the tunnel, his sword poised for the killing strike.

And yet, something tells me he wouldn't have let me live this long just to give me an easy death in the citadel's tunnels.

*You're going to give the Duskers exactly what they want if you keep going.* I imagine my friends' warnings in my head. *Don't be stupid. Stick to the plan.*

I only have a few seconds to decide what to do. Hendrix could be leading me into a trap. *Or he could lead me to Crowe.*

With that thought, I descend into the darkness of the citadel.

# CHAPTER 30

My sense of foreboding only grows as my eyes adjust to the darkness. I had expected the tunnel to be full of Duskers and Banished locked in combat, but it isn't. The tunnel is empty.

A cold feeling of dread creeps over me.

I slink down the path like a prey animal walking into a hyenair's den.

The last time I was deep inside the citadel itself, when Jadem brought Dayne and me in as her prisoners, there were guards positioned at every branch of the tunnels. Now, there are no guards, no soldiers…no one.

Still, I can't shake the feeling I'm being watched. A shiver runs down my spine.

I see Hendrix's lantern bob for the space of a moment before it disappears around a corner. I hurry to catch up.

Now that the sounds of battle are gone, my ears begin to adjust to the far subtler noises within the tunnel. There's the steady drip of water along the wall, probably from the over-saturated ground above. And there's the steady pound of footsteps moving away from me. They're keeping a good pace, but they're unhurried.

I reach down to my belt, before remembering I didn't bring my sling. I feel a flash of anger at myself, at my own arrogance, for thinking I didn't need my trusted weapon.

I shouldn't have left all the Zeroes on the Outside. I should have taken at least a few of them down with me.

*Stupid. What was I thinking?*

I reach for my bond with the Zeroes, calling for them.

A cold sweat breaks out across my forehead. I feel…nothing.

When I turn my attention inward, I realize I don't feel the tension that comes every time there's more than a short distance between the Zeroes and me.

Instead of the feeling of cords being pulled too tight, I just feel a dull ache in the place where the bond usually rests within me.

*Maybe it's an above ground-below ground thing,* I tell myself in an effort to ease my growing panic. The Zeroes can't be dead. If they were, I would know it. I would be writhing on the ground along with them.

Whatever the reason I can't sense them, it doesn't matter now. The Zeroes can't help me, and if I have any hope of finding Crowe, I need to keep moving.

I try to silence my footsteps as much as possible as Hendrix leads me deeper and deeper into the citadel. After more than a dozen turns, I've lost track of the way back to the Outside.

Maybe he knows I'm following him and this was his plan all along—to lead me into the depths of Malarusk and then disappear, leaving me to wander around until I finally succumb to exhaustion and dehydration.

*Wouldn't that be ironic,* I think. *The leader of the most powerful army in the world dies from getting lost....*

There's nothing for me to do except keep going forward.

When Hendrix turns back again, I flatten myself against the tunnel wall. He stares down the tunnel, but he isn't looking in my direction. I clap a hand over my mouth to stifle the sound of my breathing.

As Hendrix continues to peer into the dark, empty tunnel behind me, I stare at him. His hood is thrown back and he has pulled down the mask covering his face. His green eyes are luminous in the dark, and his pure Dusker skin glows white in the dim light of the tunnel. He's like no one I've ever seen before.

Now that I know what Hendrix looks like, I can't stop thinking how Fake Hendrix—the man whose skin they painted and eyes they dyed— didn't even come close to looking like the real Hendrix. If I had known this Hendrix before, I never would have been fooled by the imposter.

Jadem knew the real Hendrix. She had worked by his side for eight years. She probably knew him better than any Dusker save Crowe herself.

There's no way my aunt saw Fake Hendrix and mistook him for the real one, which means she was deceiving us even then.

Anger so powerful it overwhelms every other emotion takes hold of me. It shortens my breathing until I'm dizzy.

Why in the sun would Jadem lead Dayne and me into Malarusk on false pretenses, take a hostage who she knew wasn't the man we were after, and then pretend to barter with Crowe when they were working together the whole time?

*Because,* a voice replies in my head, *it was the only way she could get back to Malarusk without raising suspicions.*

Jadem was willing to put both Dayne and me at risk—first in the dungeons, and then in the wormkill tunnel—just to return to the citadel without any of us being the wiser.

If anything had happened to Dayne….

I clench my fists by my sides, forcing back the tide of dark thoughts about my aunt. If I'm going to live through whatever is lying ahead, I can't have my mind going in a thousand different directions.

The deeper I follow Hendrix into the citadel, the more I notice the earthen walls are gleaming with moisture. There are puddles along the path, and when no underground lake appears, I realize Hendrix must be heading toward the underground forest of black trees. It's a more circuitous route than floating directly there via the stream, but Hendrix doesn't strike me as a man willing to get wet to save himself time.

I take hold of the bag secured to my back to reassure myself everything is still intact. The powders inside are still dry, and the last remaining flask of fluid is sealed.

I remember the way the black flames devoured a single puddle in a matter of seconds. I remember the way those Banished slaves looked, covered in the trees' black residue, as they disintegrated before my eyes.

I won't leave here until I've destroyed the underground forest.

Hendrix turns onto another tunnel. I hang back, wariness taking hold of me once again. My hand goes to the dagger at my belt. If Hendrix wasn't my only hope of finding Crowe, I'd kill him right now.

I'm not sure if Hendrix has figured out I'm trailing him or not. It's possible he knows and is leading me into a trap, but it's also just as likely he is so intent on wherever he's going he hasn't noticed me at all. He's probably on his way to deliver a report to Crowe right now. The thought sends a jolt of nervous anticipation through me.

The lantern bobbing in Hendrix's hand is the only source of light in the otherwise black tunnel. The path declines so steeply I need to keep one hand on the wall to keep from losing my footing in the mud and rolling all the way to Hendrix.

*You're a fool for following him*, I tell myself.

If I cut my losses now and turn back, I could keep following the tunnels that lead up. I'd find the Outside eventually. I might even come out of the citadel right where Wade and the Solguards are fighting.

If I turn back now, I might get out of this alive. If I don't, it's more likely I'll be slaughtered by an army of Duskers waiting down here just for me. They'll leave my body in some cave where none of my people will ever find it….

But even as these thoughts cross my mind, I know my need for answers is too strong. My desire to confront Crowe is irresistible. I take a deep breath of stale air and keep going.

# CHAPTER 31

A powerful, noxious smell fills the tunnel. It takes only another step for me to recognize it as the scent of the black trees. Already, my eyes are watering and my nose is stinging.

My boots slush through mud as I creep forward. I'm so on edge that I almost jump out of my own skin at every splash of water. I keep waiting for Duskers to leap out of the darkness and surround me.

Hendrix's lantern moves farther ahead. As I hurry to catch up, my foot catches on an uneven part of the tunnel and twists painfully. I look down to see what I've tripped on. It's then that I notice the two deep, parallel grooves running down the center of the tunnel.

I remember the wooden carts I saw the slaves pushing up onto the Outside. I couldn't see what they were carrying, but there were dozens of them, and my memory of the carts seems to fit with the spacing of these grooves. It's then that my mind turns to the mountainous, covered stockpile on the Outside that hadn't been there just days before.

I had assumed the slaves were carting up weapons and supplies for the Duskers' journey to Solis. But what if that wasn't what was inside the carts? A sick feeling of foreboding takes hold of me.

I release a shuddering breath. The air in here is too close. It should be cooler in here than on the Outside, but it's stifling. Refusing to be caught off guard by the attack I know could be coming at any moment, I squint through the sweat that rolls off my face and stings my eyes. There's a queasy feeling in my stomach that has nothing to do with the smell of the black trees.

I grip my dagger. It gives me some small comfort, not because I think it would be of any use against a Dusker's crossbow, but because it gives me something to do with my hands. I curse myself again for thinking I didn't need my sling.

A part of me keeps hoping the Zeroes will feel my growing terror through the bond, and that they'll come down here to face whatever is waiting at the bottom of this tunnel with me.

They don't appear.

The water is up to my ankles now. It runs down the sides of the walls and catches in the carts' grooves as it gathers and flows steadily downward. The tunnel curves, and I blink in surprise at the bright illumination of this part of the tunnel.

Lanterns hanging from the wall throw light and shadows over everything. There are empty carts lined up along the side of the tunnel, confirming my suspicion that their wheels are responsible for the grooves in the path. With every flicker of the lanterns' flames, figures seem to move from behind the carts.

I'm so focused on the shadows, which turn out to be nothing, that I barely notice when the path finally levels off and the tunnel opens up. I approach a wide arch, with two more lanterns hanging from either side. The archway marks the end of the tunnel.

*Trap,* my instincts scream.

My body starts to shake. I hate that I'm afraid. I hate that, once again, the Duskers have bested me.

*Keep going,* I order myself. *If Hendrix is ahead, that means there must be a way out. Find it. Escape.*

I step up to the archway. It's then that I realize that what looked to be the end of the tunnel are really two large, wooden doors. Relief floods me.

The doors have no obvious handles. Reaching up, I wrench one of the lanterns off the wall and use it to illuminate the doors.

I suck in a breath. Images are painted over every surface of the rough wood. The pictures themselves are abstract, as though intentionally blurred by the artist, but the gist is clear. Painted black flames lick the bottom and sides of the doors.

Swirls of dark paint stretch upward from the fires across the doors, like the rising smoke is swallowing up everything else, even the physical doors themselves. There are images of people running away from the smoke, their mouths open in screams. I can feel their terror growing inside me, but then I feel ridiculous because it's only a painting.

At the place where the dark swirls touch the bodies, the people turn into wisps themselves, becoming part of the growing darkness.

My hands start to shake, and my breathing grows ragged. *It's just a painting*, I tell myself. Still, I linger far longer than I should, staring at the disturbing images.

A tingling sensation crawls up the back of my neck. I know, without question, that Crowe is somewhere behind these doors.

Shaking myself out of my stupor, I find the heavy iron handle, which had blended into the swirls of black paint, and pull. The door opens.

I find myself in the forest of black trees. At least, I'm in the cave that used to hold the forest of black trees.

My senses are assailed with the acrid stench of the black sap I've become so familiar with. And yet, the black trees are gone. Just…gone. There's no trace of them.

I step farther into the huge cave. I stop just before walking into a solid mass in front of me. I stare down, blinking at the dark shape.

I realize I'm staring at the stump of one of the black trees. A trickle of sap oozes from the stump's innards like black blood. The stench makes my throat burn and my eyes tear up.

I walk a little deeper into the cave. The path takes me from one black stump to another. There isn't a single tree still standing in this cave.

There's a tightness in my chest that has nothing to do with the horrible smell.

I look around, like I might see the rest of the trees stacked up against the wall or something. I grip the bag of explosives in my hands, but there's nothing to use it on.

The trees are gone.

I stand gawking as I wrack my brain for what to do next. The trees didn't just disappear. They have to be somewhere….

With a sinking realization, I know exactly where they've gone. The huge covered pile on the Outside…the one that hadn't been there a few days ago. *That's where they are.*

The slaves weren't carting supplies from the citadel to the Outside like I'd assumed. They were carting the logs.

*Why didn't I realize it sooner?*

I turn around and run back the way I came. I need to get to the Outside. I have to get my people away from that the massive store of black logs, and then I need to set the explosives.

I don't know how the Duskers will set fire to the black logs without killing their own soldiers alongside ours, but I'm not going to wait around to find out. I shove my way through the doors. I don't remember which way I came from, so I take the first tunnel that leads upward at a dead run.

I barely think about where I'm going. My mind is filled with everything that needs to happen next.

As soon as I'm on the Outside, I'll get the Zeroes to surround any of the Banished who are still fighting near the covered pile. If I'm right, and I'm sure I am, the logs from the black trees are under that covering. As soon as my people are far enough away, I'll explode the stockpile.

The path I'm following leads me to another archway, this one much smaller. I race through the opening and come to a dead stop. Instead of finding myself in another tunnel, I'm standing in a large cave.

There's a person standing on the other side holding a candle. I don't even have a chance to take a breath before the person speaks.

"Hello, Hemera Harkibel."

# CHAPTER 32

The voice is unfamiliar…feminine—soft and musical. It doesn't sound like the voice of the Dusker Supreme. And yet, I know beyond any doubt it belongs to her.

I step into the cave even though every instinct screams for me to turn and run back the other way.

"At last we meet," she says in that disarming voice. "I've heard so much about you."

"Crowe." Her name comes out of me as a growl.

The Supreme pushes back her hood and lifts the candle to illuminate her face in an eerie glow.

The last time I saw her, it was through the gap between the iron gate's hinges as she pretended to first bargain with, and then kill, my aunt. I was struck then by how small and fragile she had seemed compared to Jadem.

Up close, I can see Crowe's delicate features. Her tiny nose, perfectly-shaped lips, and rosy cheeks are more doll-like than Dusker. Crowe's white skin and gray eyes seem to be the only remotely Dusker parts about her.

My instincts know better than to trust this illusion.

I look around, trying to get my bearings in case I need to run. From what I can tell, we're in a rectangular cave. It's narrow, but long, almost like a tunnel that's closed off at either end. We're standing somewhere in the middle, with either side of the cave ending beyond the candle's light.

The dimensions are odd for a cave. But as I direct my attention back to Crowe, I wonder why I'm wasting my time looking at my surroundings when Crowe has been using all this time to study me.

Sweat trickles down my back.

The single candle seems a bit dramatic," I say, disconcerted by my own nervousness. Crowe peers at me over the flame of her candle, which she holds in one hand. There's something else in her other hand, but I can't see what it is. *Probably a dagger.*

"Dramatic is my middle name." Her lips curve upward in a false smile.

A second later, two Dusker guards holding crossbows step into the light.

"If you think two guards with crossbows are enough to keep you safe from me," I say, "you need to get some new spies."

Crowe laughs. It's a tinkling, delighted sound. "I heard you were a brave little thing. Or maybe," Crowe taps her chin with a delicate, bone-white finger, "I heard you were very foolish." She tilts her head, still smiling, to consider me. "I have heard so much about you, it's difficult to remember it all."

There's nothing soft or delicate about Crowe's gray eyes as she stares at me. There's an undercurrent of something unyielding in their depths.

*Like cold steel*, I think.

There's something else nagging at the edge of my mind…something about her face that disturbs me beyond reason, beyond even the fact that I'm looking at the Dusker Supreme.

With a start, I realize I've forgotten everything I planned to say to Crowe. I had almost forgotten why I came here in the first place.

"What did you do to my aunt?" I demand before I lose control of this conversation.

Crowe lets out another high-pitched laugh that sets my teeth on edge.

"*Do* to her? I didn't do anything to her."

"You're compelling her…you threatened her. You did something. I know it."

"Jadem?" Crowe calls.

My breath catches as my aunt's familiar figure appears from the shadows.

"Yes, Supreme?"

The sound of my aunt's voice makes me go as still as stone. It isn't filled with love and warmth the way it always used to be, but it's her voice. My aunt steps into the light of Crowe's candle.

I want to go to her, but she stays beside Crowe.

"Tell me what's going on," I say to Jadem. "What happened to you?"

"I did what I had to do." My aunt's words are remote, distant. "I don't ask for forgiveness."

"Don't be so modest, Jadem," Crowe says. "You are the Dark God's messenger. You're the bringer of his greatest prophecy."

"The darkness," I say.

"It's coming, and there's nothing the Solguards can do to stop it," Jadem replies.

She speaks the words mechanically, like they belong to someone else, even though they're coming out of her mouth.

"You're the Solguard leader." My voice comes out as a croak. "Why? Why would you betray us?"

*Why would you betray* me?

"Don't take it personally," Crowe says before my aunt can speak. "Our arrangement goes back to a time before she'd ever laid eyes on you."

I ignore Crowe, focusing all my attention on my aunt. "Tell me," I say, hating the way it sounds like begging. "Tell me why."

Jadem's one eye seems like it might be starting to gleam with unshed tears, but that could just be a trick of the candlelight.

"After your brother and I escaped from the Malarusk dungeons years ago, I bargained with Crowe to spare the Solguards," Jadem explains, still in that faraway voice. "Crowe agreed not to destroy Solis, so long as the Solguards never attacked the Duskers."

My mind is spinning. I remember something Wade told me when I first met him. He said that since she had gotten out of the dungeons, all Jadem wanted to do was hide in the fortress and keep everyone safe.

But it wasn't because she was afraid. She had made an agreement with Crowe not to attack the Duskers.

I want to scream. I want to grab my aunt's cloak and shake her until her head wobbles like a ragdoll.

"But I broke the agreement when I brought the Solguards to Tanguro."

We'd won that battle because of my aunt's help, but it hadn't prevented us from losing Tanguro to the Duskers only a few month later. This realization sends a shockwave of guilt through me, which is followed by anger for my guilt.

"The Supreme would have killed every Solguard in retribution if I didn't do something," Jadem says.

For no reason I can understand, tears prick at the corners of my vision. "What did you do?"

"I lied to you about kidnapping Hendrix. It was the only way I could think of to return to Malarusk without telling you the truth. If I could have done so without you and Dayne, I would have."

I remember our elation at getting Hendrix out of the citadel, and then my horror when I realized Aunt Jadem wasn't with us. I remember watching the iron gate close while my aunt was on the wrong side. I remember the darkening of our captive's eyes and skin as the feeble disguise wore off. I remember watching my aunt kneeling in the mud at Crowe's feet.

"We renegotiated," Crowe says. "I'm a forgiving person, most of the time." Her gray eyes seem to harden even more when she says this last part. "And I have a soft spot for creative solutions."

"What does that mean?"

"It means that my position among the Duskers had grown less stable. As I'm sure you've heard, I didn't inherit my position in a strictly legitimate manner."

I remember Dellin saying that Crowe, with Jadem's help, killed the rightful Supreme and took his place. According to Dellin, Crowe was the only Dusker to take the position by force rather than inherit it.

Crowe continues, "With the growing power of the Solguards and threat from the Halves, there was unrest among the Duskers. I needed a way to quash that uncertainty and forevermore solidify my position among them."

"What do you have to do with any of that?" I ask Jadem.

"Killing the leader of the Solguards is something my predecessor never succeeded in doing," Crowe says, answering for her. "By pledging herself to my service, Jadem affirmed my authority as the true Dusker Supreme to all those who might try to challenge me."

"Why bother with the whole charade of faking her death, then?" I ask.

I hate myself for engaging in this twisted conversation, but I have to understand.

Crowe replies, "Your aunt believed a death, witnessed by you, would be the only means of keeping you away. And I agreed."

"Why not just kill her?" I ask, my anger reaching a boiling point.

My aunt flinches. I give her a hard stare, willing her to understand she's the one who betrayed me, and I won't spare her another bit of my guilt.

"Like I said…creative solutions. Your aunt could give me more than just dominion over my own people."

"I grew the darkness trees in exchange for your life," Aunt Jadem says. "No Dusker can kill you."

"You did all of this, just to save me?" I ask, horrified.

I want to clamp my hands over my ears. *Don't tell me this,* I want to yell. *Don't put this on me.*

"There's nothing more powerful than a willing sacrifice," Jadem replies.

I've heard these words from her before, but when she said them the last time, I hadn't realized what kind of sacrifice she meant.

"I didn't need you to save me!"

"Well, that at least, is up for debate," Crowe says. She's been following every word of our conversation. I didn't think it was possible, but somehow, my hatred for her deepens.

All fear has left me. In its place is a bitterness that seeps through to my bones, just like the black sap that ate through the Banished people's flesh.

"Your soldiers up there are losing this fight," I snarl at Crowe. "They'll all die, and then it will be like the Duskers never existed."

If my words make her afraid, Crowe doesn't show it. She just smiles. But it's an ugly, twisted smile that contorts her features.

"I don't care about killing Solguards," she says. "I don't even care about the Halves anymore. Once the darkness comes, none of you will matter."

"Oh really?" I let sarcasm draw out my words.

"Really," Crowe replies.

There is a long pause during which we regard each other. Crowe is the first to speak.

"Now, you will want to think very carefully about every decision—every move—you make from here on out." She makes a delicate gesture with the candle. "For I can assure you the consequences will be dire."

Before I can reply, one of the guards flanking her takes Crowe's candle from her hand. He reaches up and lights a wick on the wall. A burning flame erupts overhead. As I watch, the flames spread along the top of the wall, illuminating the cave as they track to both the left and right.

I follow the direction of Crowe's gaze, which is fixed on the far-left side of the cave. The flame has almost reached that still-dark corner. She's quivering with anticipation, like she can't wait to see what the fire will reveal.

Dread takes hold of me.

As the fire reaches the left end of the cave, I can just make out two figures standing against the far wall. I have to blink several times for my eyes to adjust to the brightness.

A strangled gasp comes from somewhere deep inside me. At the same time, Jadem lets out a low, keening cry.

# CHAPTER 33

emera," Wokee cries. Even from here, I can see the terror in his enormous, round eyes.

"No," I choke. "You're not supposed to be here."

*It's a trick*, some hopeful part of my brain says. *They disguised someone to look like Wokee, just like they did with Hendrix.*

"I'm sorry." Tears stream down his cheeks. "I just wanted to help."

"Wokee's back in the Eastern settlement," I say, trying to ignore how much this imposter looks *and* sounds like my friend.

*It's not Wokee. It's not Wokee. It's not—*

The guard prods the boy.

"It's me." Wokee hiccups. "I hid inside one of the supply crates when no one was looking. I'm sorry. I just wanted to be a good Solguard."

Wokee is shaking with the force of his sobs.

All my hope drains out of me. I know my friend well enough to know beyond any doubt this is no imposter.

The guard standing beside him holds the blade of a dagger against Wokee's neck.

"My guard has orders to slit the child's throat if you take even a single step in his direction," Crowe says.

"What are you doing?" I cry. "Let him go!"

"Wait." She puts up her finger.

Almost against my will, I tear my eyes away from Wokee just as the fire overhead reaches the opposite end of the cave.

"I'm so sorry, Hemera," Jadem says in a near-whisper.

A sick feeling twists my stomach as my brain processes what my eyes are telling me. Two guards, each with a sword in one hand and a dagger in the other, stand on either side of a man in a blue cloak.

I lock eyes with my brother.

*No.*

"What are you doing?" I scream at Crowe. "What do you want from me?"

I can't stop the tears from spilling down my cheeks as my thoughts splinter into a thousand different directions. All that's clear to me is that Wokee is on one side of the cave, and Dayne is on the other…and there is no way for me to reach them before their guards kill them.

My breathing turns to short, ragged gasps.

"Now I expect you understand the situation." Crowe's voice is light and airy, but her eyes are merciless. "But do you know why?"

The horror of what I'm seeing makes it impossible for me to speak. I can't even move.

"The two people you care about most, at opposite ends of the tunnel." Crowe smiles, making my blood run cold. "Even if you're as fast as my scouts say, you'll never be able to reach them in time."

"Jadem." I choke on the tears burning my throat. "Do something. Please."

Jadem keeps her eye fixed on the ground.

"Don't ask your dear aunt for mercy. She's the one who told me about your love for these two."

"She didn't—she wouldn't—"

"I'm sorry, Hemera," Jadem says again. "It was the only way to keep you safe."

"I'll never forgive you for this," I tell her on a sob. "Never."

Jadem covers her face with her hands, refusing to look at me or the prisoners.

"You can't do this," I say, not even trying to mask my hysteria.

"It really is a kindness you don't deserve," Crowe says. "I'm giving you a choice you never gave me."

My fear is a hard knot inside my stomach, weighing me down, making me feel like I'm drowning.

"One of them is going to die. It is up to you which you wish to save."

I look from one end of the tunnel to the other, panic making it impossible to think. Even from here, I can see the guards' muscles flexing in anticipation. They know I might try to rescue their hostages, and they're ready for me. The two guards standing beside Crowe have moved closer to her. Their eyes and weapons are trained on me.

"After I learned of what you'd done," Crowe says, "I wanted to kill you. But then, I realized death would be too small a punishment. I could torture you, but even that would come to an end eventually. I wanted to cause you eternal pain.

"I realized if I took away someone you loved, that pain would last for the rest of your miserable life." Crowe stares at me. "I happen to be an expert on that sort of pain."

I don't understand, but I can't get my mouth to form words. My feet stay planted on the ground, my mind a whirl of incoherent thoughts.

"Time will not stand still," Crowe says. "Make your choice."

"No." My knees tremble and my teeth chatter, even though it's a million degrees down here.

I look at my aunt, pleading with my eyes, but she still won't meet my gaze.

"What do you want from me?" My voice is filled with desperation.

"I want you," Crowe says each word deliberately, like she doesn't want me to miss a single one, "to experience the agony you have caused me."

My brother's voice comes from the other side of the cave.

"Kill her, Mer! Don't worry about—"

One of the guards cracks the hilt of his sword across Dayne's temple.

I scream as Dayne slumps to the ground. The guards' blades are poised over him as Dayne struggles to sit up.

I look at Crowe—this tiny, insignificant person. If it wasn't for the two people she holds captive, she'd be nothing to me. And yet, here I am—a Bisecter who commands an army of the strongest beings ever to exist—and I'm as helpless as I've ever been.

Crowe looks at me with unadorned loathing. It's more than the hatred of an opposing leader, though. It's something much greater.

Back in Subterrane Harkibel, I thought my father was paranoid for keeping me so hidden from the Duskers. But now, I understand. The Duskers always hated the Halves for being different. The Duskers saw them as an offense to the Dark God. More than that, though, they must have feared the Halves' strength.

I represent the opposite of darkness in every way. Crowe must be willing to do anything to destroy me and remove the threat I pose to her dominion.

"Kill me," I say, my knees so weak I'm afraid I won't be able to stand. "I won't try to resist. Just let them go."

"If you had given me that option, I might have afforded you the same courtesy. But alas, you made your choice, and now I'm making mine. You will not leave this cave with your family intact." All the mirth is gone from Crowe's face. In its place is something cold and unrelenting.

"You can tell all your soldiers you killed the Bisecter," I plead. "If making Jadem your servant gave you more power, then killing me    "

"I'll have all the power I can manage soon enough," she says, the corner of her mouth lifting. "This is not about what you are. It's about what you've done."

"What I've done?" I echo. My brain is sluggish from terror as my eyes shift from Wokee, to Dayne, to Crowe.

A sob—Wokee's—fills the otherwise soundless cave.

"What kind of a monster are you," I choke out, "to hold a *child* hostage?"

"Ha!" Crowe's face is screwed up in bitterness. "She says *I'm* the monster."

Crowe raises her hand—the one holding something I couldn't see before. For the first time, I get a good look at what she's been clutching against her side. It's a child's doll.

I squint at the ragged thing, temporarily stunned into silence. The doll's clothes are tattered and one of its sewn eyes is dangling off.

Horror fills me before I even understand why. When I look at Crowe, I'm stunned to find her gray eyes are fixed on the doll and brimming with tears. Her knuckles are white from the force of her grip.

"*You* are the monster," she says in a strangled voice that is nothing like the composed way she spoke before.

I realize where I've seen this doll before. My heart stills in my chest. This doll belonged to the little Dusker girl, the one my Zeroes killed when I first took them out of the Lair to test their strength.

Dark spots flash across my vision at the memory of the band of Duskers in the distance…my father telling me it was time to see the Zeroes' in combat…my sense of triumph at the easy way the Zeroes destroyed the Duskers….

And then, after, panic when I realized there had been a child with them. Deep, bone-rattling shudders wrack my body at the memory of the small corpse stretched on the dusty ground.

It's an image that has plagued my dreams every high day since then.

But from everything I know about Crowe, she wouldn't mourn the loss of one child so much, unless….

I look at Crowe again, but this time, I see her features on those of a little girl. Glassy gray eyes staring up into nothing. Marble-white skin streaked with blood and dust.

"My daughter," Crowe says in a voice almost unrecognizable compared to the silky tone she'd used before. "You killed my daughter." She looks down at the doll, a raw, broken expression on her face. "My Laurel."

"Your daughter," I whisper.

My chest feels like it's being crushed by an invisible weight.

"My daughter," Crowe repeats. "You killed the whole company, so it was two days before I found out." She presses her lips together. When she speaks again, her voice wavers. "My scouts found her doll next to a pile of bones. The Burn vultures left nothing else."

I can't catch my breath.

Crowe hugs the doll to her chest. "My fearless little angel of darkness, reduced to a pile of bones." Her eyes swim with unshed tears.

"I didn't mean to." My voice is a whisper. And then, because it's easier than guilt and grief, I let anger swell inside me. "What in the sun were you thinking, sending a child up to Darkness Peak?"

I hear Jadem suck in a breath, but I don't even glance at her. Whatever she's thinking, I don't want to know it.

"It was a routine pilgrimage. She was carrying food for the scouts," Crowe says in a snakelike hiss. "It was her first mission, and she begged for it. She wanted a chance to prove her worth. She wanted to be like her mother."

I have nothing to say to that. I never imagined I might understand the Supreme, let alone feel sorry for her. But I do. If I could go back in time and take back every one of those Duskers' deaths to save the little girl, I would.

No one else in the cave dares to speak. No one even moves.

Crowe hugs the doll to her chest for a moment longer, and then she drops her arms. The doll falls onto the ground. Crowe doesn't move to pick it up. She takes a long, shuddering breath.

When Crowe raises her eyes back to me, her vision is clear. There are no remnants of tears or any of the emotions that were written across her face only moments ago.

"You took my family," she says. "And now, I'm going to take yours."

# CHAPTER 34

Cold, invisible hands wrap around my chest and squeeze. I can't speak.

"You might have been able to break through my gate and kill my guards with your bare hands," Crowe says, "but you're powerless now."

*She's right*, a voice in my head whispers. My Zeroes killed Crowe's daughter, and now the people I care about most are going to pay the price for something I caused.

Dayne warned me about the harm the Zeroes would bring. Now, he and Wokee are here, their lives at risk because of my choices.

"I'm so sorry."

"No, you're not. But you will be." Crowe's lips curve into a sneer.

"I tried to stop them—"

My voice sounds so weak, even to my own ears.

"Most people would have crumbled over the death of their most beloved, but it made me stronger." Crowe gives me a steady look. "Let's see if you're as strong as everyone says. Let's see how you hold up when you lose what you love."

"Please, it was an accident," I beg, but Crowe speaks over me.

"Choose now. Which of your loved ones can you bear to live without?"

My mind has gone entirely blank. Panic edges out every coherent thought.

*Zeroes.* The thought comes to me with a last burst of hope. I send every ounce of my dread and desperation down the bond. *Come to me.*

I wait for the familiar tug of their comprehension, their reaction to my order, the loosening of the cord stretched between us as they close the distance. But I feel nothing.

"Hemera." Dayne's voice is clear, even though I can see the blood oozing from the gash on his head from here. "Save Wokee, and then get the hell out of here."

"Please," I beg Crowe. "I'll do anything."

My breathing is too fast, and the dark spots racing across my vision make it difficult to stay on my feet. It's the same feeling I used to get in the tunnels of Subterrane Harkibel, when I thought the ceiling was going to crush me beneath its impossible weight. I feel as helpless now as I did before I had any idea what being a Bisecter really meant.

I know now, and still, it won't help me with this impossible decision.

Dayne. My brother. The brother I didn't know I had and now can't imagine my life without. He's been with me since I left Subterrane Harkibel. He's saved my life more times than I can count. He's always given me his support without ever asking for anything in return.

Even with what I am, I've always known Dayne is the stronger one. Losing him would be the same as losing myself.

My eyes flick back to the left side of the tunnel. It seems like forever ago when I pulled Wokee from the dirt and rubble on that hilltop. He's become the little brother I never had. There were so many times when I might have given up if it hadn't been for Wokee's sense of humor and unfailing loyalty. How could I get through even a day without him?

Images flash through my mind, of Wokee carefully tending Jadem's plants after she could no longer do so herself…following Evelyn around the fortress even as he pretended he wasn't…riding Vlaz, whooping with the sheer joy of flying on the back of a monstrous creature….

I remember standing with both of them in Solis next to the quilt made out of living flowers that Wokee grew to memorialize Jadem. I remember the three of us saying we were a family, and that we would always protect each other.

A sob rips free from my throat.

I look from Wokee, paralyzed by fear, to my brother. His blue eyes, the eyes of our mother, beg me to do what he says.

*I can't.* I can't choose. *I have to choose.*

"Guards," Crowe calls. "Give her until the count of five." Her eyes bore into mine. "If she hasn't made up her mind, kill them both."

"One," Wokee's guard calls out.

"Two," shouts Dayne's.

"Hemera, do it," Dayne says. "I couldn't live with myself if you didn't save the boy. You know that."

"Three."

"I can't do this without you," I gasp.

"I'm ready," Dayne says. "Let me make this sacrifice and find peace. Please."

"Four."

My body is wracked with grief and despair.

"Wokee," I gasp. "I choose to save Wokee."

"No!" Wokee wails.

Crowe nods her head. By the time my gaze has swiveled to Dayne, one of the guards has run him through with his sword.

"No!" Wokee and I scream.

A horrible gurgling sound comes from my brother.

The guard stabbed him in the stomach. It will be a cruel, slow death. But the guard beside Wokee hasn't lowered his blade. I know if I take even a single step toward my brother, Wokee will die, too.

"My love, we're ready for you," a deep, male voice says.

Some part of me registers that Hendrix has entered the cave, taken one look at my face, and smiled. The rest of me is still rooted in place as my brother's blood drains from his body.

"Good." Crowe motions to Jadem, and the three of them move toward the adjoining tunnel with the two guards flanking them.

"Has she begged for death yet?" Hendrix asks Crowe. The hatred in his green eyes turns on me.

Crowe looks up at Hendrix. "I don't think she's begged enough." She turns back to the remaining guards. "Kill the boy."

Before the scream of rage and desperation can even leave my throat, a new voice speaks.

"Unhand the boy. All Duskers, drop your weapons."

Crowe's face first registers shock before darkening into something ugly as the newcomer steps into the cave.

Dellin, her hood thrown back and her ever-filthy face wiped clean, stands before us. She pins the Supreme with her gaze. For someone who was terrified of coming within viewing distance of the iron gate, there's a fearless challenge in Dellin's eyes as she stares the Supreme down.

"You have no authority here," Crowe says in a high-pitched voice that belies her words.

Dellin steps fully into the cave. She walks past me and stops directly in front of Crowe. "Look at my face," she tells the guards standing on either side of Crowe. "Do you recognize me?"

Dellin's voice is commanding. There's no sign of the cowardly, untrustworthy girl I've come to know.

The guards look at Dellin, and then at each other. Slowly, they both nod their heads. Their eyes are round with fear and something else I can't decipher. I have no idea what's going on, and I don't care.

*Dayne is dying.*

"Good," Dellin says, her voice commanding and unhurried. "Unhand the prisoners."

"I am your Supreme!" Crowe yells. "You answer to me!"

I don't wait to wonder why the Dusker guards stay where they are, their weapons held slack at their sides. I don't wait to see what will happen next. I run to Wokee. His Dusker guard wears a stunned expression, and his weapon lies forgotten on the ground. I pull Wokee along with me as I sprint down the length of the cave. Even though I pass right by Crowe, Dellin, and the guards, no one moves to stop me.

Dayne is unconscious now. The Duskers stay where they are as I kneel beside him.

I yank off my cloak and press it to his wound. I know the blood is coming too fast for me to keep him alive for long, but if I can just get him to the Outside, there has to be someone who can help him....

Supporting Dayne's weight with one arm, and holding Wokee's hand with the other, I pull them both to the tunnel's entrance.

There are more Dusker guards standing in the cave's opening, blocking me from the tunnel. I refuse to let go of Wokee or Dayne, and so I can't fight the Duskers. I stand still, not knowing what to do.

Dellin's back is to me and her voice is low, so I can just make out what she's saying. She lifts her chin as she tells Crowe, "For a long time, I didn't want to remember."

"So, are you returning, then, after all these years of hiding?" Crowe demands. Her voice sounds strained and more than a little crazed.

"Not today," Dellin replies. And then, she raises her voice. "Let my friends pass."

She says it in such a commanding way the guards blocking the tunnel don't hesitate to step aside, even as Crowe shrieks for them to stay where they are.

"I—" I begin, wondering if this is some kind of trap.

The question *who are you?* hovers at the edge of my lips.

"The tunnel is empty," Dellin tells me. "Go."

I don't dare stay here for another second to see if the guards will come to their senses. I let go of Wokee's hand and lift my brother into my arms. I get a last glimpse of an open-mouthed Crowe, who is now so enraged her face is turning purple.

I pause in front of my aunt, who is standing off to the side, seeming not to know what to do or where to stand.

"Come with us," I say.

Even as the words leave my lips, I'm filled with revulsion at my offer. I should leave Jadem down here to rot. The fact that I still want her to come with us, still want to find some logical reason for why she did all of this, makes me even angrier.

Jadem is the reason my brother is dying in my arms. She's the reason why Wokee was almost killed. And yet, I can't help but try.

"My place is here," Jadem says. She turns her back on me.

There's no room inside me for any more grief. If I don't get Dayne to someone who can save him, and fast, he'll die.

"Aren't you coming?" I ask Dellin as soon as I'm in the tunnel.

She shakes her head. "You go."

"You dare—" Crowe begins, but Dellin cuts her off.

"You've tarnished the office of Supreme long enough. Your days of being a thief and imposter are coming to an end."

I don't know what they're talking about, but I don't care.

Whatever secret Dellin's kept all this time, and whatever is going on between her and the Duskers now, I'll never question her loyalties again. If it weren't for Dellin, both Dayne and Wokee would be dead. That's a debt I'll never be able to repay.

Dellin takes her eyes off Crowe for a fraction of a second to look back at me. There's so much meaning in the look she gives me I don't know how to begin to decipher it all. I stare back at her, willing her to understand what my mouth can't seem to say.

*Thank you. I'll never forget this.*

But Crowe isn't finished with me.

"I wonder, *Bisecter*, what your little army of rebels will think of you when your imperviousness to the sun no longer matters." She gives me that twisted smile. "Will you still be the one they follow?"

"Your Dark God has abandoned you," I reply, pushing Wokee ahead of me, "so I guess we'll never find out."

"I wouldn't be so sure of that."

"Go," Dellin commands.

I do.

"I'll have my vengeance!" Crowe screams after me.

I keep expecting to hear the sound of footsteps pounding the ground behind me.

"Hurry," I tell Wokee, even though I know he's running as fast as he can.

"Hemera." Wokee's voice trembles. "I didn't mean—"

"Save your strength," I tell him. "There'll be time for apologies later."

We race back through what used to be the darkness tree forest and is now just a cave full of stumps, and up another tunnel.

I don't have time to process the hatred pumping through my veins. The only thought on my mind is Dayne, and how I'm going to save him.

I choose the tunnels that incline the most steeply, pushing Wokee to keep going as we make our way up to the Outside.

As we reach the muddy streams funneling down into the main tunnel, Wokee's pace slows. He keeps falling, but with Dayne in my arms, there isn't much I can do besides encourage him to keep moving.

I want to scream in frustration. Wokee is moving too slowly, even though I know he's going as fast as he can. His legs are getting bogged down in the mud and he keeps losing his footing. I can't leave him, but all my thoughts are on my dying brother.

"Climb on my back," I tell Wokee.

After a brief scramble, he does. With Dayne in my arms and Wokee clinging to my back, I stumble onto the Outside.

# CHAPTER 35

We emerge on the far side of the citadel, where the Banished and Solguards are still battling the Duskers. It's like no time has passed.

It's strange to see the battle still going on up here after everything that happened underground. The only difference between when I left and now is that the tide of the battle seems to have shifted. Instead of the Duskers overwhelming us, it looks like there are more Banished and Solguards.

I notice all of this on the periphery. My only real concern is Dayne.

"Hang on," I tell my brother, even though I know he's past hearing me.

Wokee jumps from my back, blinking in the brilliant sunlight.

The first observation that cuts through the clamor of my panicked thoughts is that the Zeroes aren't with the Solguards, even though that's where I had ordered them to be.

My second observation is that the bag of exploding powder is no longer around my back. I have no idea where or when I lost it. I'm standing close enough to the gargantuan, lumpy pile to touch the burlap covering, but I have nothing with which to destroy it.

I don't even care. Nothing matters except for Dayne.

Now that we're on the Outside, I don't know what to do next. Dayne's eyelids flutter once, and then he goes still again. I carefully lower his body to the ground to check his wound.

A gasp shudders out of my lungs.

Blood still leaks from the congealed mess of fabric and skin on my brother's stomach. The smell of iron and the heat of his blood coating my hands make me retch. I ignore Wokee, who is tugging on the bloodied sleeve of my cloak and whimpering. I can't see through the tears clouding my vision.

"Camike!" I yell to no one in particular. "Get Camike!"

She brought Jarosh back from the brink of death. She can heal my brother, too.

"She's not here," Wokee says in a small voice. "The Halves didn't come, remember?"

It all comes rushing back to me. I sent the Halves away.

*Think, Hemera,* I command myself before my crushing despair can swallow me whole. There will be time for regrets later.

*My father.* The thought is like a beacon of light in the darkest of caves. My father used to be a healer. If there's anyone who can help my brother, it's him.

I reach for the tether connecting me to the Zeroes. If I can find them, I'll find my father. But when I turn my attention inward, there's nothing. I had thought the emptiness I felt when I tried to call them before was because of the distance separating us. And yet, even on the Outside, I can't feel them.

*Where are you? Why won't you answer me?*

This time, when I reach for the bond, I feel something. It's weak, barely there, but it's something. It's not enough for me to call them, though, or even for me to feel where they are.

I stop a Solguard who has just pulled his sword free from a Dusker's corpse.

"Where are the Zeroes?" I demand.

"They were fighting with us," the Solguard says, his eyes bulging when he sees Dayne in my arms, "and then they left. I don't know where they went."

"Hemera! What's—"

Wade, his cloak covered in mud and blood, his sword slicked with both, sloshes through the stream to me.

"Zeidan," I yell to him. "Get Zeidan."

Nodding, Wade says something to a Solguard beside him. The other soldier takes off running, five other Solguards surrounding him.

I barely notice as Wade commands a handful of Solguards to surround Dayne, Wokee, and me. Dimly, I'm aware that there are too many Duskers on this side of the citadel compared to the side by the iron gate.

*It doesn't make sense*, a voice in my head warns. The bulk of the Dusker force should be on the other side, fighting the Banished and defending the main tunnel. Instead, they're over here, where they seem to be converging near the covered pile.

All other thoughts flee from my mind when I see my father appear, flanked by Solguards and Zeroes. I don't wonder or care about why the Zeroes are staying by him when I had called for their presence moments before. All that matter now is Dayne, and getting my father to help me save him.

"Have you seen Dellin?" Ry, her quiver empty, sprints through the mud and shoves past the Solguards to get to me.

"Yes," I say, distracted, my eyes tracking my father's progress across the space separating us. His escort leads him around the far side of the covered stockpile to avoid the worst of the fighting, and I lose sight of him as they all disappear behind the towering heap.

*Hurry up*, I want to scream.

"Well, is she alright?" Ry demands. Even though I'm not looking at her, I can hear the frustration bordering on panic. I hear it without really processing any of it.

"I think so," I reply, taking a wad of bandages Wade offers me and pressing them to Dayne's stomach.

"You think so?! And what in the sun is Wokee doing here?"

"Ry." Wade takes her elbow and says something I don't hear.

She looks down, sees Dayne stretched out on the ground, and covers her mouth with her gloved hands.

Wokee cries, "This is all my fault. I didn't mean to. I didn't know."

"Where is my father?" I yell.

"I'm here, Hemera."

"You have to help him. He's wounded, but he's breathing." Words trip and stumble over themselves in my haste to get them out.

*Save him.*

My father kneels in the mud beside Dayne, Wokee, and me. The Zeroes make a protective ring around us without me even giving them the command.

*Strange.*

I don't give the Zeroes another thought as my father leans over Dayne's prostrate form. He peels away the sticky remains of the bandages and what used to be my cloak, using the dangling sleeve of his own cloak to keep Dayne's stomach covered in shadow. Dayne doesn't scream or even flinch. He doesn't move at all. If it wasn't for the slight rise and fall of his chest, I'd think….

We all suck in a collective breath at the sight of the carnage that lies beneath. Wokee begins to wail.

"Hemera," my father says.

"No." I shake my head, knowing what he's going to say and refusing to hear it.

"Look at him, Daughter."

I go on like I haven't heard him. "I know you hate each other, but you said you wanted to build a world where I fit in. I don't belong in a world without Dayne."

"He's lost too much blood," my father says. "The wound is too deep. Even if I could stitch it shut, he'd keep bleeding on the inside."

When Jadem first proposed going to kidnap Hendrix, Dayne had said no one escapes Malarusk without a sacrifice. After our mission failed, we thought the sacrifice had been Jadem's life. This time, it's Dayne's.

There's a hole in my heart the likes of which I've never felt before…not when Brice sacrificed himself for me…not even when I watched my mother die.

I can't let him go.

"I'll give you anything you want," I say, wracking my brain for the right words. I'm sure if I can make the right offer, my father will fix this. "Just save him."

"Hemera." Wade's voice is soft in a way that makes my heart shatter into a thousand pieces. "You better say goodbye."

Ry and Wokee are sobbing.

"Never," I choke out.

"Please," I say to my father. "Please, try."

There is no smug satisfaction on his face, no *I told you he was weak and no good* look about him. My father just inspects the wound one more time and shakes his head.

"I know what Dayne means to you, but your friend is right. It's time to let him go."

Something inside me breaks. I grasp the collar of my father's cloak before he can even blink. "You have to do something. You have to save him!"

My father knows better than to try to pull free from my iron grip. Instead, he gives me a pitying look at whatever crazed expression is on my face.

"His body is too weak," my father says. "But—" He trails off. His gaze is fixed on my brother's prone body.

"But?"

My heart hammers in my throat.

"There might be something," he says, gesturing for me to release him.

"Tell me," I beg.

My father gives me a hard look. "We could turn him into a Zero."

A choked sound comes from someone—I'm not sure who.

"He'd hate that," I say. "And he wouldn't even be him anymore."

"There's a new experiment I've been wanting to try," my father says. "I haven't tested it yet, but if it works, I believe it will allow the human subject to retain much of his former consciousness after the transition."

A mixture of hope and despair muddles my thoughts. "So, he'd still be himself? He'd remember who he was?"

"Theoretically." My father shrugs. "But like I said, I haven't tested it."

I can't look away from my brother, where fresh blood is oozing from his stomach.

"How?" I ask. "How would it work?"

"Hemera, no," Wade gasps.

"How would it work?" I ask again, louder this time.

"I believe if we inject your blood into the femoral artery in his leg, rather than his neck, it will convert the rest of his body before reaching his brain. That should allow him to retain much of his human mind while only receiving the Zeroes' physical enhancements."

"You can't be considering this," Wade says, appalled.

I ignore him. All of my focus is on my brother's bleeding stomach and my father's words.

"And his memories?" I ask. "Do you think he'd lose all of them?"

"It's possible that since you and he share some elements of your blood already, he might retain more of himself." My father shrugs again. "We'll have no way of knowing until he has changed."

I swallow. If Dayne remembers who he was before the transformation, he'll hate me for this. If he doesn't remember, that will be even worse.

"You think it might really work?"

My father inclines his head, considering. I hold my breath, hardly daring to hope, but breathless with the possibility.

"He's weak," my father says. "He might not survive the transformation."

"He'll die anyway if we do nothing," I snap, no longer trying to contain my impatience. I pull out my dagger and yank up my shirtsleeve, ready to pour my life force into Dayne. But at the last moment, I remember my blood isn't the first step.

*Halve blood.*

My father bled Ekil into the Dusker prisoners as the first part of their transformation. And, because of me, there are no Halves here. A wail of defeat escapes my lips.

"That shouldn't be a problem," Zeidan says, understanding the source of my hopelessness. "Dayne was already exposed to Halve blood."

"You mean when you tortured and almost killed him in the catacombs?" Ry chokes out through her tears.

"Shut up, Ry," I snarl in a tone I don't even recognize.

"There should still be trace amounts left," my father continues. "It might be enough."

"Might?" I ask.

"You know as well as I do this isn't an exact science."

"Hemera, *think* about this," Wade begs.

There's a pressure on my sleeve, and for a fraction of a moment, I turn my attention to where Wokee is tugging on me. His eyes are brimming, and there are tear tracks cutting through the grime on his face.

"Dayne hates the Zeroes," Wokee says, his lower lip trembling. "He wouldn't want to become one of them."

A part of me knows Wokee is right, even though the rest of me fights against such an admission.

My aunt's words return to me, even though I try to shut them out.

*You will save us all.*

Dayne had said he believed in those words, even though he no longer believed in Jadem. Yet all I've done is leave a trail of pain and death in my wake. I look down at my brother's bloody, broken body. A feeling like I've been here, in this exact same position I'm in now, sweeps through me.

Brice—the first man I loved—appears on the ground before me, as real as if I were looking down at him instead of my brother. He tried to protect me the only way he knew how, and he died for it.

I see the dead soldiers at Tanguro, an entire army I failed to protect. Even Crowe's daughter, her small body in a tangled heap, her gray eyes open and staring at the sky....

"I won't let him die," I say. "I can't."

"Think about what your brother would want," Wade grinds out through clenched teeth. "It isn't this."

"And if you had a chance to save Sal?" I ask him. I know I'm being cruel, but I don't care.

Wade doesn't say anything.

"He's my brother," I say savagely. "It's my decision."

"Then what is your choice?" my father asks. "You have little time left to decide. He won't last much longer."

I look at my friends. All of them are shaking their heads. *No,* they're silently begging me. *Don't do this.*

I lift my gaze to my father.

"Tell me what to do."

# CHAPTER 36

There are gasps around me, but I ignore them.

"Make a slit here." My father gestures to a place along Dayne's thigh.

I use my own shadow to shield Dayne's leg from the sun while I pick up my dagger from the ground. My arms are trembling so badly I have to grip the dagger with both hands. I blow out a steadying breath, and then I make a small slit in Dayne's leg.

He doesn't flinch.

Without waiting for my father's instructions, I slice the dagger across my wrist. Brown blood springs to the surface.

"Just a drop to start," my father warns.

As I raise my wrist, the beads of blood balanced on my forearm, I look at my brother's face. My breath catches when I see his eyes—the beautiful blue he inherited from our mother—flutter open.

His mouth moves like he's trying to say something, but before any sound comes out, his eyes close again.

I look at my father, who nods once at me. I let a drop of blood fall from my wrist to Dayne's open vein.

The moment my blood touches him, Dayne's skin begins to steam. An audible hiss rises from the spot. My brother writhes.

I had forgotten what it was like to watch this transformation. The memory of turning the hundred Duskers into Zeroes comes back to me in a rush.

An inhuman scream—the first sound he's made since he was stabbed—rips from my brother's throat.

"Hold him down," my father commands.

The world shrinks to the three of us.

I brace Dayne's shoulders as my father peels open his eyelids, examining Dayne's pupils.

"Another two drops," he orders.

Dayne's body convulses. A horrible choking sound comes from his throat, and then a white foam tinged with blood gurgles from between his lips.

"I'm sorry," I tell my brother, willing him to understand even as he gasps and chokes.

My father motions for more of my blood.

My hands slip away from Dayne as his body starts to jerk and buck.

"Hold him down," my father growls.

It should be easy for me to do, but I'm shaking and my hands are slick with sweat and blood.

Wade moves to my side and places his hands over mine, steadying me. Gratitude fills me at his silent show of support. The expression on his face is grim as we hold Dayne still together.

The awful screams coming from Dayne drown out every other sound in the battle.

I gnash my teeth together, wishing I could clap my hands over my ears to block out the sound of my brother's agony.

I didn't think it could get worse, but then, Dayne's screams turn into words.

"Kill me," he shrieks. "Kill me."

He continues to repeat this refrain until I think I'll go mad. I beg him, try to explain, but he's far away in a place where my voice can't reach him. Somewhere nearby, I hear Wokee sobbing.

It goes on like this for what feels like forever.

When Dayne goes still, my first thought is that in spite of everything, I've just killed him anyway. His head falls back on the ground. The muscles in his ashen face stop twitching. The skin all around the place where my blood touched him is black.

"Is he—" Ry's voice breaks from somewhere nearby, but I don't take my eyes off my brother.

"He's alive," I say. I know it from the feeling that's nestled inside me. A new tether, in the place where I can no longer feel the hundred others, pulses. It isn't as strong as the memory of my bond with the other Zeroes when I first changed them, but it's there.

My father moves closer. He presses his fingers to Dayne's neck and forces his eyelids open. Finally, he sighs and steps back.

"He still has a pulse. It might take time—"

Before my father can finish his sentence, Dayne's eyes fly open. At the same moment, his hand shoots up. His fingers find a hold around my throat before I can even react. Out of the corner of my eye, I see Wade and my father struggling against Dayne.

The strength in my brother's grip is unlike anything I've felt before. But that isn't what keeps me motionless even as he squeezes the life out of me.

Our gazes lock. I know it's Dayne whose sinuous arm is squeezing my throat, but it's no longer his eyes. His blue irises, the blue that always made me feel like my mother hadn't left me, no longer exist.

Dayne's eyes are black.

# CHAPTER 37

With some effort, I separate my neck from Dayne's grip. My fingers graze over my raw skin, feeling as it heals beneath my touch.

Dayne sits up and looks at his hand, the one that grabbed me, like he doesn't recognize it as his own.

Then, he collapses back onto the ground. His eyes stay open, but they're not looking at me anymore. He watches—we all do—as his limbs stretch and fill out before our eyes. New muscles bulge through the tattered remains of his cloak.

My brother blinks, shakes his head, and looks at me. His unfamiliar black eyes meet mine. A shudder passes through me.

"What have you done?" Ry breathes.

"I couldn't lose him," I manage to choke out.

Dayne gives no indication of hearing the exchange, or caring even if he did. I'm desperate for him to speak, to prove he remembers who I am…that he remembers who he is. Instead of the recognition I'm hoping for, he closes his eyes. I'd be afraid he was dead, but his chest is rising and falling. It almost looks like he's sleeping.

Panic replaces my temporary relief. If Dayne has lost all his memories…if he's become just a hulking, instinctive creature with no loyalties to me aside from the blood I gave him, is he still my brother?

Screams cut through the battle, temporarily taking my attention from Dayne. I can't expect the Duskers to leave us alone as I try to begin to understand what I've done to my brother.

"Zeroes," I say, my eyes still on Dayne. "Attack the soldiers in gray. Kill them all."

Out of the corner of my eye, I see the Zeroes standing nearest to me shift on their feet.

"What are you waiting for?" I snap. "Get moving."

They don't move.

I stand and walk over to one of them. I expect it to sniff the air in that disturbing way it does, for its black eyes to swivel on me, and for our connection to flare.

But none of these things happen. The Zero is staring at something past me. When I turn to follow the direction of its gaze, I startle to see the Zero is looking at my father.

"It seems the transformation is finally complete," my father says, wiping his bloody hands on his cloak. "It took longer than expected, and mid-battle is hardly an opportune time. But at least it's finally done."

*What?*

My throat has gone very dry.

"Zeroes," my father says in a powerful, commanding voice. "Assemble."

I stare, hardly believing what I'm seeing, as the Zeroes begin to converge from all sides of the compound. Even the ones that had been fighting alongside the Northerners near the ruined gate are coming.

They scent the air as they arrive, but this time, they aren't searching for me. They gather around my father. Their black eyes are trained on him, awaiting his command.

"Hemera?" Wade asks, looking from the Zeroes congregating around my father to me.

"Tell me they aren't under his control now," Ry adds.

"They're not. They couldn't be."

I reach inside myself for the tethers that link me to each of the one-hundred. Some tiny fragment of the bond remains, but it's like sensing a shadow in place of something that used to be three-dimensional and alive.

"I made the Zeroes," I say, not understanding. "My blood runs through their veins. How could anyone else besides me control them?" I stare at my father, too bewildered to feel any anger. "How could you command them?"

A smug expression is plastered on my father's face. It's the same one he always wore as Captain Harkibel when he discovered something new and was just waiting to share it with the Dwellers. It's the look he wore when I awoke in the catacombs, bound in chains and surrounded by his servants, and realized he was the one in control of Tanguro.

"What have you done?" I ask.

"You are correct, Daughter," my father says. "The Zeroes do respond to blood, but their loyalty belongs to whichever maker's blood runs strongest in their veins."

*Right. So why—*

"Your blood is no longer the most prominent," he says. "For months now, I've been slowly introducing my own blood to them. It took time—their bodies would have rejected it otherwise—but today proves the influence of my blood is now greater, and that I am their master."

My heart is racing. "The meat," I say, remembering the disgusting, bloody meat my father insisted on feeding the Zeroes himself.

"That's right." A slow smile spreads over his face.

And then, like a punch to the gut, I remember the wound on my father's arm. It wasn't deep, and yet it was always leaking fresh blood. I couldn't understand why he didn't stitch it up.

"You fed them…your blood."

"Right, again." My father's eyes gleam. "Of course, it was a much longer and slower process than injecting their veins with my blood outright, but I'm a patient man."

"I knew it," Ry says. "I knew you were just a—"

I don't hear whatever else she says. I stand, dumbfounded, as everything I thought I knew crumbles into dust.

The black anger that's been a part of me ever since I created the Zeroes, that's lent me strength beyond my wildest imaginings, is gone. In its place is a gaping emptiness. I see the Zeroes crowded around my father, and it's like the best part of myself has abandoned me. It's like everything that ever mattered to me is gone…except it's not gone, it just belongs to someone else.

"Dayne warned me," I choke out. "He said you'd betray me."

He said my father wouldn't do anything for me unless it served his greater purpose. I hadn't wanted to believe him. I'd even gotten angry with him.

My father shrugs. "That all depends on your definition of betrayal, I suppose."

"I trusted you." My breathing is coming in short, painful gasps. "I did everything you told me to do."

"You did that because you had desires of your own," my father replies. "We're all doing what we feel we must."

"And what *must* you do?" Wade asks. He keeps one eye on my father and the other on the battle still raging all around us.

"I am making a world in which my daughter belongs."

"You didn't need to steal the Zeroes for that!" I shout.

"I know you, Daughter," Zeidan says. "You don't have the stomach for much of what will need doing in the coming months. I intend to take on that burden for you."

"You thieving, murderous monster," Ry accuses. "Mer isn't going to let you get away with this."

But we all know her bluff for what it is. What could I do? My father is in control of my Zeroes. I can't fight all of them, nor would I want to. Whatever ghost of a connection still remains between us, I couldn't stand to hurt them.

With a jolt, I realize the emptiness I've felt in my heart for days now, the weakening of my connection with the Zeroes, is because of what my father has done.

"I won't let you get away with this," I say. "No matter where you try to hide, I'll hunt you down."

"I thought you might take that perspective," my father replies. "I wish you could see my actions for what they are—true concern for your well-being. But, as you know, I don't take chances."

"Meaning?"

"Meaning that when you find me next, you will find me changed."

"Changed, how?" I ask through gritted teeth.

My father reaches into the pocket of his cloak. For a moment, I think he is going to pull out a dagger and try to kill me. Instead, he pulls out a folded piece of script tree bark. I recognize it the moment he unfolds it and I can see the writing.

All the breath leaves my lungs in a whoosh.

"You stole my mother's letter."

"Yes."

"What—what are you going to do?" A cold fear, as powerful as the feeling when Crowe told me to decide between Dayne and Wokee, floods my insides.

My father cocks his head, as if to say *you already know what I'm going to do.*

When he says the words out loud, it's so much worse.

"I'm going to turn myself into a Bisecter."

# CHAPTER 38

I lunge for my father.

"I should have killed you the first chance I had," I scream.

Before my hands can wrap around his throat, a dozen—two dozen—iron grips are forcing me back. A group of Zeroes hauls me away. The rest encircle my father, the blades of their scythes glinting in a silent threat.

Until a little while ago, the Zeroes had been bound to protect me. Now, they stand by my father like he was their master from the first. A brokenness fills me, the likes of which I've never known. I feel hollowed out.

"In time, I hope you'll come to understand I'm doing what is necessary. I'll build a world that celebrates the strength you've had to bear alone for so long." My father speaks from behind his protective screen of Zeroes. "You won't be feared anymore, because you won't be the only one of your kind."

"You're just as sick and twisted as you ever were," I say, but there's no venom in my words. They hang there, empty and meaningless, just like I feel.

"You'll see, Daughter. Everyone will bow down to you and me, as they do to the Dark God now. Instead of worshipping phantoms, though, they'll be worshipping flesh and blood."

I shake my head. "No one will look at us and see gods. They'll just see monsters."

"Some will, at first," my father agrees. "But there will always be those who see beyond their current existence. Any who are willing can take the leap and become Zeroes themselves. They can realize for themselves the strength they've observed in others." He looks at me, his eyes shining. "You know firsthand how intoxicating it is to feel their raw power."

*I did know. And now, that feeling is gone, stolen by the person who helped give it to me.*

"There will always be those in power and those who are subservient," my father continues. "We may as well build a society that makes sense— one that is based on power that is real rather than imagined."

"If that's true," I say, my tone full of acid, "then since I'm the most powerful person alive, I should have control over the Zeroes."

"That won't be true once I am changed," my father muses.

I have an uncontrollable desire to rip his face off, but there are one-hundred Zeroes separating us.

"You don't have the mind for ruling an entire world. You think small." Zeidan turns a meaningful look on the battle around us. "You seek to overthrow the Duskers. Even if you succeed, they'll be replaced by others who are no different. The world under my reign will be glorious to behold."

He snaps his fingers. The Zeroes grip their scythes and form into organized lines. With a flash of anger, I realize they've practiced this move before. While I was helping to plan the Malarusk attack and discover what in the sun was going on with Jadem, my father was stealing my army.

"Those Zeroes are mine!"

I leap in the air, fingers grasping like claws, wanting nothing more than to squeeze the life out of him with my bare hands. I swipe at the first Zero that comes between us.

Before, the force of my blow would have sent the Zero flying through the air. I could have killed it with just that single strike if I'd wanted. Now, the opposite is true. The Zero sidesteps my blow, which is clumsy and slow, and slams me to the ground.

I get to my feet. All of my movements feel sluggish, like there are giant weights attached to my arms and legs. I can't understand what this feeling is until, out of nowhere, the word comes to me.

*Weak.*

I remember the surge of power I felt with every Dusker prisoner I transformed into a Zero. I remember how I felt their strength burrow into me. It was like their strength combined with my own, making us stronger than we would have been without each other.

I've never felt so…ordinary.

Even though I know I'm still stronger than any human or Halve, my abilities feel like wooden stakes that have been filed down to blunt nubs.

My father, his eyes bright as he gives the Zeroes orders, spares me a glance.

"When you're ready, Daughter, we will rule this new world together. We'll be the same."

"You'll never be like me," I say, but even those words feel weightless.

"Let me through!" a familiar, feminine voice shouts at the Zeroes. Dellin, her gray eyes wild with fear, shoves her way through the creatures.

"There you are," Ry begins, but Dellin cuts her off.

"No time," she gasps. "Duskers are…." She clutches at her chest as she tries to catch her breath. "Just come on!"

I hesitate.

"Let him go," Wade snarls. "We'll deal with him later."

I want to argue, but there's no point. The Zeroes won't let me anywhere near my father.

"I'll kill you for this," I promise.

He doesn't respond. He motions to the Zeroes, and then they're all leaving. None of them look back at me.

I watch my father, memorizing the way he looks in this moment, surrounded by my Zeroes.

*I will kill you.*

✳ ✳ ✳

My limbs still feel heavy as I kneel onto the ground and lift my unconscious brother—or the Zero that was my brother—into my arms. He's so heavy I can barely manage.

A muffled sob comes from Wokee. I try to tell him everything will be alright, but I can't make the words come.

I'm desperate for Dayne to wake up. I need to know how much he remembers about his former self. At the same time, I don't want him to wake up. As long as he stays passed out, I won't have to face the truth of what I've done to him.

Now that the Zeroes are gone, no longer blocking my view to the battle, it's like a screen has been lifted. Bodies are littered across the muddy ground. There's the clang of swords and the click of crossbows as the fighting continues.

Dellin leads us straight toward the mountain of black logs, which I've just noticed aren't hidden anymore. The burlap covering, its underbelly coated in the black, sticky goo, has been tossed in a heap off to the side.

Shouts of agony are coming from nearby, where Banished and Solguards are beating at their own clothes and writhing on the ground. They're covered in the black sap.

"What the—"

I turn just in time to see a tide of black sap rolling out from beneath the log pile. The viscous fluid separates into thousands of tiny streams, filling the ground with a spiderweb of poison that is impossible for the Banished and Solguards standing nearest to avoid.

"It's getting everywhere," Dellin shouts. "They're using it to cut our army off from theirs."

Sure enough, I see the Duskers have gathered on a wide swath of ground, which is the only area of the battlefield that isn't being contaminated by the black sap now trickling out from beneath the pile of black logs.

"We need to get our people away from here," Wade says, already on the move.

Ry puts her index fingers in her mouth and lets out a piercing whistle. Vlaz's shadow appears a few seconds later. He lands outside of the path of the black sap, keeping away from the poison-saturated battlefield.

Ry leaps onto his back, pulling Dellin up behind her. Vlaz takes off again.

"Retreat!" I hear Ry yell as Vlaz flies over the Solguards and Banished still locked in battle with the Duskers.

We all move back until there's a matrix of poisonous, black rivulets separating our army from the Duskers. Still carrying Dayne, I follow a group of Solguards to where the rest of our army is huddled on a strip of land that hasn't been overrun with the poisonous sap.

Now that it's uncovered, I realize just how impressive this mountain of black logs really is. It's as tall as any one of the mountains separating the Banished lands from Tanguro. I can't even see its summit, which is lost in the blinding orange haze of the sun.

Even at this distance, my throat burns and my eyes sting from the reek of the black sap that has poisoned the air and water around us. I feel ill from the stench and a sense of foreboding.

My mind fills with visions of Tanguro, of the wasteland it became after every one of my soldiers was killed.

My breathing turns to sharp gasps as I imagine the same thing happening here. This attack was my idea. If our people are slaughtered here, there will be no one left to oppose the Duskers. There will be no one to protect the old people and children still in the Eastern settlement.

*What have I done?*

The two armies face each other, still separated by a section of black ground now poisoned from the sap.

My gaze is fixed on the Dusker archers. Unlike our archers, whose arrows have long-since been spent, their crossbows are still loaded. We're within range, and yet, they make no move to shoot.

If they wanted, they could destroy our front lines and we would have no way of stopping them.

*Especially now that the Zeroes are gone....*

The sharp pang of fury is quickly overcome by helplessness. With all of the battleground now poisoned, there is nothing we can do except wait and see what the Duskers are planning.

Once again, Crowe has bested me, and there is nothing I can do. I want to scream. I can't just stand here and do nothing. But even as the thought crosses my mind, exhaustion like I've never before experienced weighs me down. I almost collapse under its weight.

I put Dayne's unconscious form down, far away from the edges of the contaminated ground, and gently arrange his limbs so he'll be more comfortable. I'm too weak to hold his new, unnatural weight any longer.

Vlaz, with Ry and Dellin on his back, lands nearby. Dellin's face is shadowed by her hood, but I can still see her bone-white skin gleaming beneath. If I had any room left for questions, I would ask her about what happened down in the citadel. She and I have time to exchange only a brief glance before her attention is back on Ry.

Out of habit, I back away from Vlaz before he starts snarling and baring his fangs at me. Vlaz sees Wokee standing beside me, though, and trots over. All of my muscles stiffen as I wait for the same reaction he's had to me ever since I returned from my father's Lair.

Vlaz gives Wokee a nudge that's powerful enough to knock him over. Wokee doesn't laugh the way he usually does. He doesn't even smile when Vlaz starts to bathe his face with his enormous purple tongue.

After another moment of being ignored by Wokee, Vlaz comes to me. He sniffs me once, and then he lowers his forepaws to the ground and lifts his giant flopped ear for me to scratch.

I can't even remember the last time he reacted to me this way. It makes tears spring to my eyes.

Vlaz, noticing Dayne beside me, takes a step toward him. His black nose works back and forth, and then, just like I had expected when he caught sight of me, Vlaz's upper lip begins to quiver. A low, rumbling snarl comes from deep in his belly.

"Vlaz," I say, my voice cracking.

My next words die on my tongue as my brother opens his eyes. Their black depths stare straight into mine.

"Dayne?" My heart throbs against my ribcage. I can hardly breathe.

He doesn't speak.

Vlaz takes another step toward Dayne. Before I can react, the hyenair whimpers and scoots away, like my brother had just struck him. Dayne, for his part, seems completely oblivious to Vlaz's terror. His black gaze stays fixed on mine. It's an effort not to shudder and look away.

"Here," Ry says when she reaches us. She's cradling something in her arms, which she offers to Dayne.

My heart twists when I see what it is: Dayne's lute. I have no idea where Ry got it from, but it's here now. If there's anything that can remind Dayne of who he is, it's his most treasured possession.

Dayne doesn't look at Ry or the lute. His black eyes are staring, unfocused, straight ahead. Ry puts the instrument onto the muddy ground at Dayne's feet and backs away, like he's some kind of wild beast.

"Come on," Wade's voice is filled with impatience as he pushes his way through the small crowd to us. "You have to see this."

"We better go with him," I mutter to no one in particular.

Dayne, his movements jerky like he's a puppet on strings, follows Wade.

There's a loud crack. Wade, Ry, and I all suck in a breath.

Dayne's lute lies on the ground, smashed beyond repair. Dayne stands still, with his bare foot still wedged in the instrument's splintered remains, as his black eyes stare straight ahead.

I search my brother's face for disappointment, anger, anything at all. He turns his head to me, the new slits of his nose flaring as he scents my blood. I don't see even the slightest hint of emotion on his face. I don't feel any distress through the bond. All I feel is his strength and need to obey.

"Let's go," Wade mutters. "We'll sort through this mess later."

*This mess...the one I've created.* My brother.

*He* is *still my brother,* I assure myself. But even as the thought crosses my mind, I can't look into his black eyes.

"What are they doing?" Ry asks, her attention now fixed on the Duskers.

I tear my gaze away from Dayne. The Duskers have dropped their weapons on the ground and are turning their attention on something just out of sight.

"This can't be right," I murmur.

If nothing else, the Duskers should at least still be firing their crossbows at us.

Now that we're closer, I can see that the Duskers nearly triple the number of our soldiers. They look like they could battle for another week without tiring, while our soldiers are bloody and swaying on their feet from exhaustion. Especially with the Zeroes gone, there is nothing keeping the Duskers from destroying us.

And yet, the Duskers stay on their side of the black ground separating us. The whole of their attention is focused on something else. It's like they've forgotten we're even here.

I remember Crowe saying *I don't care about killing Solguards anymore.*

"Look at their faces," Wokee manages between sniffles.

Even though their hoods are up and their masks are in place, we're close enough now that I can see the expression in the Duskers' eyes. When I look, I realize they don't appear defeated. Instead, they all wear an expression I've never seen on a Dusker's face before. They look happy.

# CHAPTER 39

I follow the direction of the Duskers' spellbound gazes. Either it was recently constructed or I hadn't noticed it before, but there's a crude scaffold made from normal script tree wood beside the mountain of logs. It was obviously built with haste in mind. Even from here, I can see the ill-fitting planks and precarious anchoring beams. The top of the scaffold is only partway up the log mountain, but it's still so high that I have to crane my neck all the way back to see it. The top of the scaffold is as close as it could be to the black wood without coming in direct contact with the logs.

Two figures stand on the top of the scaffold. Their hoods and the blinding sun make it difficult to see their faces. Still, I don't need more than a glance to recognize the diminutive Supreme, looking as doll-like as ever, and Hendrix standing at her side. Even with his hood up, there are flashes of green as his gaze scans the crowd. He looks more godlike than any Dark God statue I've ever seen.

Dayne shifts on his feet beside me. I turn to look at him, barely managing to repress the shudder that wants to take hold of my body.

Dayne's black eyes stare straight ahead at nothing in particular. There's no hint of emotion on his face, which I hardly recognize. His gray-and-honey hair is gone, replaced by a few white strands. He's tall and filled out in a way that is so different from my slight brother who inherited all of my mother's grace.

When he senses my gaze, Dayne turns his eyes on me. The two slits that have replaced his nose open and close as he searches for the blood of his master.

I swallow. I can't bring myself to speak to him, because I'm too afraid of what I'll discover when I do. *Will he talk back? Will he remember who I am? Will he remember anything at all?*

After what happened with the lute, I'm too much of a coward to find out.

I turn my eyes back up at the platform, where Crowe and Hendrix are standing.

*If it wasn't for Crowe, my brother wouldn't be like this.*

I understand her grief at her daughter's death, but that was an accident. Hasn't she taken so much more from me? Jadem left us to be by her side. She tried to kill the two people I love as my family.

I don't even think about what I'm doing as I pull Wade's sword from his grip. The ground on the other side of the log pile is dryer and free of the poisonous sap. If I can skirt around the Duskers and come at the scaffold from behind….

"Hemera, you can't," Wade says.

"I can, and I will."

*I'm going to kill her for what she's taken from me…for what I've lost.*

My father is gone, but at least someone can pay for their crimes against me.

"They'll kill you before you even get close." Wade grabs my arm and pulls me back. "The Duskers are planning something."

I go to shrug off his touch, using enough force that no normal person could keep their hold on me. Wade's grip doesn't budge. I stare in confusion at his hand, which is still wrapped around my forearm.

Whatever happened to me when my father stole the Zeroes robbed me of my strength. I'm exhausted in a way I can't remember ever feeling. The sun is too hot, my heart too heavy.

A dark kind of despair steals over me. Without the Zeroes' strength, what do I have? Without them, I don't know who I am anymore.

My legs give out, and I would have sunk to the ground if it weren't for Wade's hold keeping me on my feet.

I'm useless. I'm a leader without her army.

I forgot what it felt like to just be me, without my Zeroes. I hadn't realized how much I'd been relying on their borrowed strength. Now, without them, I feel…empty.

I'm a pair of black eyes without anything of use to go with them.

It's only because of Wade's hand still on my arm, and Wokee and Dayne beside me, that I know I haven't lost everything. Still, without the Zeroes, it doesn't feel like enough.

"Look!" One of the Duskers standing on the other side of the poisoned ground points up at the scaffolding. "It's time."

A hush falls over the crowd as everyone directs their attention up to the platform. The Duskers' masks protect their faces from the Burn, but the Solguards and Banished need to shield their faces with their gloved hands as we all squint up at the platform. Whatever the Duskers have been up to, we're about to find out what it is.

Without the Zeroes, and with everything that has happened, I can't bring myself to care.

I get one glance of my aunt in the crowd. She's dressed in gray like the others, and if I wasn't so familiar with the shape of her and the way she moves, I wouldn't have even known it was her. Jadem fits in with the Duskers so completely that not even the Solguards standing across from her recognize her.

Bitterness curdles my insides.

At that moment, Crowe looks down at Jadem from her perch on the platform. I can't read either of their expressions, but it seems like one of understanding. It makes me hate them both even more.

I turn my attention back on the scaffold as Crowe raises something to her lips. At first, I think it's a horn, but then she starts to speak into it. The cone-shaped contraption amplifies her every word so those of us on the ground can hear. In her other hand is a torch.

"My fellow Duskers and subjugates," Crowe says.

"Subjugates?" a Solguard mutters.

Wade holds up a hand, silently telling everyone to wait. Something hangs in the balance…we can all feel it…but only the Duskers know what's going on.

"The Dark God spoke to me of a world where we could live without fear of the sun, where there is only darkness," Crowe says.

I exchange a look with Wade. This is the same prophecy the Duskers have been promising for generations.

"The sun will set, and the darkness will come."

*More Dusker propaganda. What is Crowe's game?*

"The Dark God gave me the dream that would bring His most treasured promise to fruition."

More laughter comes from the Solguards and Banished. The Duskers are still staring at their leader in rapt attention.

I wish I hadn't lost Everlyn's bag of explosives. If I had it, I could end all of this right now. But I know all too well that wishes and regrets can't change what's already done.

Crowe sweeps her hand holding the torch toward the mountain of black logs. "These trees will bring the Dark God's prophecy to fruition."

Beside me, Wokee clenches and unclenches his fists. I know, without even having to look at him, the hurt and betrayal written all over his features. Wokee has always shared Jadem's love of all things that grow, and he learned most of what he knows from following her around the orchards in Solis. I can only imagine what it's doing to him to see how Jadem used that same knowledge to help the Duskers.

I think about the living Solguard symbol, the wall of flowers, that Wokee grew in my aunt's honor. My blood boils on Wokee's behalf.

"We are the Duskers. And when the darkness comes, we will rule the world."

The Duskers' chorus of *Go in darkness* fills my ears.

"The darkness is no longer coming. It's here."

Crowe stares directly at someone in the crowd when she says these words. I follow the line of her gaze to Dellin, who is standing between Ry and Vlaz. Dellin stares straight back at her.

Once again, I wonder who Dellin really is. I don't have time to consider it further as Crowe lifts the torch in the air.

"Go in darkness!"

As the Duskers answer her cry, she throws her torch onto the mountain of logs.

The Solguards and Banished stare, uncomprehending, as a black fire erupts. It begins to devour the nearest logs at an impossible rate.

Even though they're between the burning logs and the sap-poisoned ground, the Duskers don't panic. Their movements are precise and unhurried as they move away from the flames, keeping to the dry and unpolluted ground on their side of the battlefield.

I motion for everyone around me to back up, even though the Duskers are closer to the fire than we are.

*What is Crowe thinking?* If the flames spread outward from the mountain of logs, they'll kill her army before they even reach ours.

"Get back!" Wade and Ry are yelling as they herd our people away from the raging inferno.

Cheers and shouts come from the Duskers all around the pile, even as they choke and wheeze from the gray-black smoke. They don't even seem to notice the danger.

I stare up at the platform as chaos rages around me.

Crowe is climbing down the scaffolding. The beams shift under her slight weight, but she scales the wooden planks like she's some kind of tree nymph. Hendrix isn't far behind her, but unlike Crowe, his every move is jerky and uncoordinated. Even though I can't hear it from this distance, I can see the way his body convulses as he coughs on the black smoke swirling around him.

My hands itch for my sling. If only I had it, I'd be able to take down both of them before they reached the ground. Anger and regret pulse through me in equal measures.

I bend to the ground and find a stone the size of my fist.

I squint into the harsh sunlight and take aim. I wind my arm back and hurl the stone with all of my strength.

My aim with my sling was precise. I always hit my mark. But with just my arm, my throw goes wide. The missile misses Crowe. Instead, it hits Hendrix square in the chest.

I hold my breath as I wait to see what will happen.

Already unsteady on the wobbling boards, the unexpected force of the stone makes Hendrix's precarious balance falter. He teeters for an instant, clinging to the side of the scaffold. His left arm and leg do a wild dance as he tries to regain his purchase. When the scaffolding shifts again, he's pitched off the side.

I feel a momentary sense of victory before it transforms into horror.

Hendrix's body is airborne for only a second before he's thrown onto the roaring black inferno.

Hendrix screams. It's an inhuman sound, full of suffering beyond comprehension. It makes the hairs on my arms stand on end. Even as much as I hate Hendrix, I can't stand to see any person suffer like this. And yet, it's impossible to look away.

His green eyes, the only bit of color in a sea of black flame, search around wildly.

A burst of flame leaps from his boots up to his legs. The black flames crackle as they take hold of his cloak.

Acid churns in my stomach at the sight of Hendrix's agony. I wanted him dead, but not like this....

Out of the corner of my eye, I see Crowe reach the bottom of the still-wobbling scaffold. She backs away from the raging fire, doubles over to cough, and then looks back for Hendrix.

She searches the lower part of the scaffold for him. I see panic overtake her when she realizes her second-in-command wasn't right behind her. And then I see her gaze travel up to the burning mountain of logs.

Crowe lets out an inhuman shriek when she catches sight of her lover being consumed by the black fire. Their eyes connect, and for a moment, I forget who they are and what they've done. I'm overcome with pity for them both.

Crowe races back to the scaffolding, where black flames have spread from the log pile and are now licking at the top beams. The flames are eating away the wood as they track a swift passage down to the ground. Crowe doesn't seem to notice. She climbs, completely oblivious to the way the boards tremble and sway beneath her.

Everyone's attention is fixed on Hendrix, but my gaze is drawn to the scaffold where someone else is climbing up behind Crowe.

Jadem.

The scaffolding was unsteady enough under Crowe's slight weight, but with the addition of Jadem's, it pitches to the side. I watch, my heart in my throat, as Jadem wraps her arms around the smaller woman.

Crowe screams. I see her lash out with her fists and elbows. Jadem tries to pin her arms to her sides, but the scaffolding lurches. It takes all of Jadem's strength to keep her and Crowe from being pitched into the fire, too. Crowe's attention is fixed on Hendrix as she strains toward him.

All the while, the black flames continue to track a path down the normal wood of the scaffold.

I see, rather than hear, one of the scaffold's beams crack. The whole structure starts to collapse.

Jadem leaps, pulling Crowe with her.

They land on the ground out of the range of the scaffold's boards, which are toppling to the ground and shooting off black sparks. Crowe gets to her feet and runs toward the burning mountain of logs, but Jadem yanks her back.

*No!* Crowe's mouth forms the word. She stretches both hands in the direction of the blaze as Jadem hauls her backward.

My aunt's mouth is moving, but I can't hear whatever she's saying. Crowe doesn't seem to hear her, either. All of her focus is on the flames devouring Hendrix.

Even with all of the bedlam, Hendrix's agonizing shrieks fill my ears. He's surrounded by the all-consuming black fire. Black sparks erupt from his arms and legs. Every part of him is burning.

In spite of everything the Duskers are responsible for, I'm sick with horror at the sight before me. The black flames have engulfed him, but he isn't dying fast enough. Every piercing shriek is a reminder of his agony.

Hendrix opens his mouth one final time, but no sound comes out.

The last thing I see before there's nothing human left of him are two green pinpricks amid the black flames. Then, even those are gone. Hendrix is gone.

It is a sight I know I will see again and again in my dreams.

Crowe sobs out his name once. Then, she turns away from the fire. Her gaze cuts straight to me, where my arm is still extended from throwing the stone. I haven't moved…haven't been able to do anything except watch the terrible scene unfold.

Crowe raises her arm. It wavers as she points a gloved finger at me. "Hemera Harkibel!" she screams.

Her expression is hidden beneath her hood, but Crowe's voice is both a threat and a promise.

It shouldn't unnerve me as much as it does.

When I look back at the fire, I startle. The mountainous stack of black logs has disappeared. The flames consumed every bit of the wood, leaving only a giant swath of land covered in the sticky black sap.

Still, as long as no one gets too close to the logs' molten remains, we'll all be fine. The fire didn't kill anyone except Hendrix. For what feels like the first time since the battle began, I take a deep breath.

My lungs are immediately filled with the acrid tang of the polluted air. I swallow my cough as I feel Crowe's hate-filled gaze fix on me.

Eyes still watering, I meet her stare, trying to communicate her failure in my glance.

*Whatever you were hoping to accomplish, you've failed,* I want to say. *All this work and planning was for nothing.*

But my vision is clouded by the billowing, black smoke that is rising from the place where the logs used to be.

A great black cloud, more like a solid mass, begins to rise. It's condensed at first, hanging just over the logs' smoldering remains. But as I watch, it begins to move upward and expand.

A black haze fills the air. Unlike the smoke from any normal fire, this mass continues to rise and spread, but it doesn't dissipate. It's like someone is pulling a giant black sheet across the sky. Wherever the smoke goes, the land below is drenched in a shadow so profound it's like we're underground.

My mind goes blank until a raw terror I don't understand begins to fill me.

*This is wrong!* I want to shout.

One by one, the Duskers' cheers die off. Solguards and Banished who were backing away from the oozing black sap are no longer concerned with what's on the ground. Faces tip up, trying to make sense of what is happening in the sky above.

The smoke continues to rise, higher and higher.

# CHAPTER 40

I crane my neck and look up. Even that small motion feels unnatural; my eyes should immediately be filled with blinding light. Now, the sun is just a faint gray blob beyond the ever-expanding haze of the black smoke. Burn vultures circling just overhead become invisible as the black smog envelops them.

It seems impossible, but within minutes, the smoke has blotted out the sun's brightness for as far as the eye can see.

Wade looks at me through the dense haze. We're standing right next to each other, but with the dark shadow stretching over the ground, it's like I'm looking at him underground with only a fogged-up lantern.

A strange look crosses his face as he tips it back to look up at the spreading black mass. And then he does something that makes me forget about what's going on overhead. He pushes back his hood.

I gasp.

"What are you doing?" I rush forward to stop him, but my movements are sluggish. By the time I reach him, it's too late.

There's nothing to protect Wade's face from the Burn. I search his bare throat, waiting for the red, oozing blisters to break out over his bronze skin.

Nothing happens. His skin doesn't begin to melt off. There is no scent of burning flesh.

The Duskers around us have begun a steady chant.

"Go in darkness. Go in darkness. Go in darkness."

When nothing happens to Wade, the others around him begin to push back their own hoods to better watch the smoke rise and expand above us. First Ry and Dellin, and then Wokee. Next comes Tut, Liglette, and the rest of the Banished soldiers. Vlaz lets out a low growl as he snaps at a passing wisp of black smoke. All around us, soldiers are pushing back their hoods and staring uneasily at the ever-darkening sky.

The Duskers stop chanting. As if they're one, they do something I never thought I'd see. They strip off their cloaks, gloves, and masks. All they have on are their shirts and pants, which won't shelter them from the Burn.

They stand on the Outside, without protection.

I wait for the blisters that should appear on their skin. I wait to hear the sound of screaming and sizzle of burning flesh. But the Duskers' expressions are serene, reverent, as they stare up at the sky.

There is no Burn…because the sun is gone.

# THE END

＊　＊　＊

Because reviews are so important for a book to be successful, please consider leaving a brief review on your favorite retailer if you enjoyed *Dusker Dark*. Many thanks!

* * *

Sign up for Stephanie Fazio's e-Newsletter to learn about upcoming books at:
https://StephanieFazio.com/subscribe/

# Acknowledgements

Once again, I find myself at another stop in the amazing journey that is this series. I have many people to thank for completing this novel.

To Ellen Schaeffer, my editor. Thank you for your help with everything from grammar to plot. This book wouldn't be the same without you.

To my team: Whitney Dorr, Teodora Chinde, Sebastian Lacle, and Ellen Schaeffer. I couldn't have done it without all of you. Special thanks also to Bob Brodsky and the rest of my ARC team. You guys are the best!

To Rachel Fazio and Julie Gibbons for just generally being fantastic.

To my parents, for their unwavering encouragement. Thank you, Mom, for all the phone calls and chocolate.

As always, to my fantastic readers who have supported and encouraged me, and taken this journey along with me.

To my wonderful husband, Andrew Brodsky. You are my muse, my inspiration, and my soul mate. I love you.

# About the Author:

Stephanie Fazio is a fantasy author. She grew up in Syracuse, New York, and prior to writing full time, she worked in the fields of journalism, secondary education, and higher education. She has an undergraduate degree in English from Colgate University and a Master's degree in Reading, Writing, and Literacy from the University of Pennsylvania. Stephanie lives in Austin with her husband and crazy rescue dog. When she isn't writing, she's getting lost in parks, hosting taco nights, or ironically and miserably losing at word games, but having fun while she does it.

**Connect with Stephanie Fazio:**

**Visit her Website:** https://www.StephanieFazio.com
**Sign up for her newsletter:** https://StephanieFazio.com/subscribe/

# Discover other books by Stephanie Fazio

Conclude the Bisecter series with Book 4, *Captain Harkibel.*

## AVAILABLE JANUARY 2020!

StephanieFazio.com